MW01171677

Sunshine

&

Roses

This book is dedicated to the Lord because it's my first. He alone gets that honor.

ACKNOWLEDGEMENTS

The King of my Heart gets first place. I can't do life without Him and I am so thankful He gives me beauty for ashes. All glory and honor belongs to Jesus.

I want to give a shoutout to the hubs and my babies. Without Steven, Lily and Bennett, my life wouldn't be what it is—they bring joy, peace, happiness and wonder to my life every single day. I'm so blessed.

A big thank you to my parents for being the calm in my sea of craziness. They are like a haven in a storm, and even though I'm all grown up, they offer support and love and rest like no one else.

And I've got to mention Granny Harville because she read the first really, really, really rough draft (Britt did, too!) and always talks "books" with me.

Brittany, my dear sister, thank you for pushing and insisting I finish this thing like at least 20 times. You are PRETTY POWERFUL boss babe! Thanks for being the very first person to ever read this in the midst of your very busy life.

To all my family and friends that have impacted me and shown love, shined a light for Jesus in this world. . . or have given me some great material to use for a character—I'm glad you were a part of this journey.

Um, also…Rachel Hollis. *Girl, Wash Your Face* changed my life. I probably would have archived this story and given up completely on getting it published if I hadn't read her book, so she deserves a mention!

Sunshine & Roses

CHAPTER ONE

This wasn't Evie Michaelson's first rodeo, but her knee still bounced with nervous energy as she mentally traced the patterns of the commercial carpet in the dinky airport terminal. Flying would never be on a list of her favorite things to do.

"Are you sure you don't want me to go with you?" Her mother asked her for the one thousandth time since Evie's agent, Moira Newell, called the house last Thursday.

Clutching the handles of her bright turquoise purse, her mother's knuckles turned white. Sending her one and only baby off to LA for the second time in less than a year was throwing her traditional Southern mama for a loop.

"Yes, Mama. I promise, I'm sure. We've been through this. Besides, last time I checked, I spent three years at Auburn on my own before any of this started. Please quit worrying about me—I'll be fine," Evie assured. If her mother needed to hear her say it a few more times before she believed it, Evie would put the phrase on repeat.

Her mother didn't understand Evie's need to do this by herself, but it was vital that she did this solo. She needed the independence—and it wouldn't hurt to be seen as such among her peers and other industry professionals. The last thing she wanted was to give off the impression that she was a young girl, fresh from the sticks, who had to have her mother in tow as a chaperone. She was 22 years old for crying out loud!

Seriously, about a third of the girls from her senior class were already married and pregnant and even more of them were getting ready to settle down. Why was it seen as perfectly normal in the rural South for young women to be getting married and popping out kids before they were legally able to drink or rent a hotel room on their own, but flying solo and traveling to other cities and new opportunities was met with total judgy disdain?

"Yes, I know, sweetie," her mother replied. "You've got a good head on your shoulders, but I can't help worrying. I'm your mother and it's my job." She sighed. "You'll remember what I told you, right?"

Evie rolled her eyes. "Yes, Mama. I'll mind my manners, and I'll make sure my costumes aren't too skimpy, and I'll act like a lady at all times day *and* night." Evie repeated the mantra her mother had drilled into her nonstop over and over—ever since the request came in last week for her to compete on the upcoming season of *Song & Dance*. Evie remembered the life-changing moment from last week in detail:

The brown paper sack started to slip from Evie's fingers as she struggled to get the back door open. She made an unintelligible growl-like noise while clinging to the doorknob and yanking hard. Why on earth did she make it a personal challenge to bring all the groceries into the house in one trip every single time? She stood desperate and panicky on the back porch— arms overflowing as a gallon of milk cut off circulation in two of her fingers. Beads of sweat broke out on her forehead as she attempted to shift the heavy haul, her wool pea coat turning into a stifling enemy as she kicked frantically at the door to get her mother's attention. She waited, all the while playing a dangerous game of Russian roulette with that milk and three other slippery sacks.

"Evie, that agent lady called while you were out," her mother said in greeting when she finally opened the door in response to Evie's desperate kicks. Her signature Southern drawl floated across the kitchen as Evie whooshed past her, dropping the armful of groceries onto the tile counter top in blissful release. Her heart was already pounding from the exertion, but finding out Moira was trying to get in touch with her revved up her adrenaline level even more. If her agent, Moira Newell, actually took the time to call her family's ancient house phone, then she must have something pretty darn important to tell her.

"Did she leave a message? I'm surprised she didn't call my cell phone," Evie mused as she helped her mother sort through the contents of the grocery bags. Her talent agent only and always called her cell phone. Moira referred to Evie's mother as being a little too "Old South" for her taste and avoided conversations with her at all costs. Whatevs. She got it. Moira was of the fast-paced, Los Angeles agent tribe— no nonsense ever, concise, never wasted words,

11

sometimes a bit rude, and all business, all the time. Evie's genteel mother, Sue Anne Michaelson, on the other hand, could and would talk the ears off a billy goat in a lilting, rhythmic tone that meandered through conversations at her own precious and leisurely pace.

"She said she tried, but it kept going straight to voicemail. That's why she called the house. You probably didn't have service." Mrs. Michaelson's muffled voice floated from somewhere within the packed refrigerator as she finagled more space for the yogurt, milk and green grapes Evie had picked up at the Piggly Wiggly.

"Good Lord, Mama, no one ever has cell service in that crusty old pile of bricks this town calls a supermarket," she said under her breath, referring to the one and only ancient grocery store in Thompson, Alabama. Born and raised in teensy tiny Thompson, naturally, its population of less than seven hundred citizens felt like one big, extended family to Evie. That, however, didn't mean she would ever be okay with Thompson's lack of modern amenities—like a Target and cute coffee shops with free Wi-Fi.

"There's no need to get all sassy about the grocery store." Her mother stopped her task to stand straight and put Evie in her place. A few of her blonde curls hung askew and with her hands on her hips, she looked a little on the crazy side, which was in complete opposition to her typical, perfectly polished appearance. "Let's just be thankful we don't have to drive all the way to Dothan to pick up milk or bread," she emphasized while staring down Evie.

"Yes, ma'am." Evie sighed and turned back to the groceries. Geez. She'd just made a truthful observation. There'd been no need for her mother to go all Southern etiquette police on her.

The epitome of a true, Southern woman, Sue Anne Michaelson might have used a little too much hairspray and totally went overboard on the Lilly Pulitzer, but everyone in Thompson found her charming, with a heart always wanting to bless someone else's. Telling Evie to be thankful instead of complaining was a prime example of her life's goal to remind her daughter, and anyone else that came across her path for that matter, that there was a bright side to every situation and they had best mind not to forget it.

Her mother's character was displayed vividly as of late, thanks to Evie's recently acquired "celebrity" status. A few months ago, their lives had turned upside down when Evie had placed second on the hit reality show, *America Sings*. Mrs. Michaelson switched gears from the PTA chairwoman and Awana leader accustomed to sleepy, small town life in Thompson to a cross-country jet-setter constantly spending days at a time in Los Angeles, attending meet and greets, and helping Evie manage a mind-boggling rise to fame. But still, her mother tended to get a touch bossy and overbearing when it came to Evie making her own life and career decisions. She also shared her opinions on the matter in the most passive-aggressive, mother-of-all-guilt-trip ways known to mankind, and lately Evie was feeling the need to put some distance between them again.

In Evie's mind, as far as her new "career" was concerned, she tended to roll her eyes and use a lot of quotations when referring to it. It was still the most awkward thing ever to be called a celebrity. She wasn't like a member of the Hollywood elite or anything—*maybe* she'd pass as a high "D" or a low "C" on the categorized list. Most definitely not an A-lister.

Sure, *America Sings* was one of the hottest shows on television, but she didn't win the thing—she'd came in second place. So, when she stopped by a store or went out for dinner, it didn't make the evening news, and that was perfectly fine with her. For the most part, her life wasn't all that disrupted. However, when she found herself in bigger cities where tourists were on the lookout for recognizable faces, people would approach her for autographs and pictures and stuff. It freaked her out that people wanted her autograph, but she appreciated their support even if it was still so new and weird to her.

Also, since competing on *America Sings*, she'd been given plenty of opportunities to perform at, or at least attend, a lot of cool events and benefits. That was the part of the whole experience with having "celebrity" status that she loved the most—getting to sing and share with others her love for music. She found it both scary and fascinating that four other reality shows had shown interest in casting her in just the past couple of months since *America Sings'* fall season wrapped.

So far, none of the offers had piqued her interest enough to pursue them. In all honesty, she was holding out for a solid recording contract with one of the bigger labels, but in the meantime, she was content with performing as many live shows as she could—even if her strict contract with *America Sings* did make the live show opportunities few and far between.

But when summer rolled around, that was another story. *America Sings* was promoting the heck out of the upcoming 57 city tour featuring the winner, Wes Young, herself and the rest of the show's top ten finalists. When the tour kicked off in 102 days at Madison Square Garden, her life would take off at breakneck speed and the exposure was going to be over the top when June 28th finally arrived. Every time she thought about touring, she pinched herself—unable to believe she would be performing on so many different stages across the entire country. In the meantime, each day sure ticked by awfully slow.

"Anyway, Ms. Moira wants you to call her back as quick as you can. She said something about an offer you wouldn't want to pass up," her mother continued as she opened one of the kitchen's ornately-carved, highly-glossed oak cabinet doors and placed a box of instant oatmeal on the shelf, the moments earlier reprimand already forgotten.

Evie pulled the remaining groceries out of the bags with lightning speed as her mother continued to put everything in its proper place. Funny how her mom delivered potentially life changing news with such casualness. If anyone else walked into their kitchen that afternoon, they would assume it was an average Tuesday and Evie and Mrs. Michaelson were shooting the breeze about a neighborhood garage sale or potluck supper at church rather than a huge opportunity for Evie's career.

"Okay, thanks, Mom. I'm going upstairs to call her back right now." They'd finished with the groceries, and Evie tossed the information over her shoulder as she hustled from the country blue kitchen and flew up the back staircase to her room as fast as her red canvas shoes would take her. Sure, she made enough money between the royalties, paid appearances and live performances that had come along with being the runner up on *America Sings* to afford a place on her own, but so many areas of her life were in the midst of change, and her family's rambling, clapboard farmhouse on Wandering Springs Road was the one constant in the whirlwind that was her life. Weird that the one place she'd been desperate to escape as a restless preteen was dearer to her now than anywhere else on the planet.

She reached her room at the end of the hallway wallpapered in tiny rosebuds and kicked off her shoes before pacing anxiously in front of the iron bed, the fluffy cream rug soft beneath her freshly bared feet. She needed a minute to gather her thoughts and compose herself. After taking a few calming breaths, Evie pulled her phone from the pocket of her faded jeans and dialed her agent's number. To put an end to the anxious pacing, she took a seat on the bench beneath one of her windows. She perched pensively on the aqua cushion and chewed at her bottom lip as she waited for Moira to answer.

"Moira Newell's office" the clipped voice of Moira's assistant greeted just after the third ring.

"Hey Claire, it's Evie Michaelson returning Moira's call," she blurted out.

"Hello, Ms. Michaelson. Just one moment," she said with polite brevity before putting Evie on hold.

"Evie, It's Moira," her agent said in greeting seconds later.

"Hey, I was returning your call?" The statement came out like a question as Evie stumbled over the words, cringing at the way she sounded like a scared, little 12-year-old.

"Thanks for calling me back so quickly." No nonsense Moira always got right to the matter at hand, "I received an offer for you earlier today, and I don't think you should turn this one down."

"Great, let's hear it," Evie responded eagerly, even though Moira's insistent tone made her wary.

"The producers for *Song & Dance* are tapping you as a contestant for their upcoming sixth season. Rehearsals start next week, and the show's premiere is the following week," Moira explained with enthusiasm as the words flew from her mouth. She'd never heard Moira this animated before about anything. Not even when she'd told Evie that her boyfriend of four years had proposed.

Despite Moira's excitement, Evie sighed like a deflated balloon. Was this really her agent's idea of a great offer for her? Another reality show? Did she even know her client? After she'd turned down four other shows, she'd assumed Moira had caught the hint, but

Evie gave her the benefit of a doubt. Maybe this pitch had promise—especially since Moira was presenting this offer with such gusto.

"I'm not all that familiar with the show," Evie started out cautiously, trying her hardest to sound neutral and not utterly disappointed.

What Evie did know was that each season, a fresh bunch of moderately famous musical artists were paired off with one of the show's professional dancers, and the duos prepared two performances for each week of the competition—a song and a dance. Then, the pairs were voted off or judged or something like that, based on their performances each week.

There were lots of dance shows and singing shows on television, but none, save *Song & Dance,* combined the two into one competition. It placed a lot of pressure on both professionals to work extra hard and coach their prospective partner. The show was one of the most popular reality competitions on television, and Evie didn't want to admit straight out to Moira that she'd never actually watched an entire episode.

"We can fill you in on all of the details and contract negotiations, but as your agent, Evie, I have to tell you that this is a fabulous opportunity for your career. You'll get tons of exposure, and with your Southern charm and fresh, youthful look, I can't imagine you not making it all the way through the competition to the finals."

"But I can't dance," Evie replied flatly, despite Moira's smooth attempt to sell her on the pitch. To Evie, her lack of dancing skills seemed like reason enough that doing a show featuring a dance competition wasn't a good idea. However, the possibility of being exposed to a whole new audience intrigued her a little.

"That's the whole point—you learn how to dance from a professional, and you get the chance to showcase your musical skills in the meantime. And by the way, that isn't entirely true—I've seen you perform—you've got rhythm. But anyway, that's neither here nor there."

Moira continued her suave spiel, "Just so you're aware, I'm really pushing for the producers to pair you with either Grant Merritt or Adam Salko. They're both well known, they've both won before, and they're really good at building relationships with their partners. I think pairing your *America Sings* momentum with one of their fan bases would almost guarantee a win. But with either pro, I'm sure you will become America's next sweetheart."

While the opportunity now sounded much more exciting than when Moira initially presented it, there was no way Evie was about to make an immediate commitment to do the show at that exact moment over the phone. Moira acted as if there was nothing to think about when deciding, but that was so not the case. Evie was already wary about doing another reality competition, especially when it required her to work so closely with someone else to determine the outcome. Plus, that whole "reality star" stigma worried her, as well. And frankly, her stomach turned at the thought of dancing live on network television while judges and millions of viewers picked apart her every step.

"Can I mull it over tonight and get back to you with an answer first thing in the morning?" Evie ventured diplomatically, bracing herself for the guaranteed bristly reply.

A long pause ensued before a loud exhale of frustration resonated over the line. "Alright, Evie, but I need to know your decision as early as possible tomorrow. The producers really want you, but they need to know ASAP, or they'll move onto someone else. We're lucky another contestant backed out and this spot is even open. Please think long and hard about doing this. *Song & Dance* could catapult your career much further than you could even begin to imagine— I've seen it happen before. And don't worry about any engagements you have lined up—your publicist and I can either work them into your rehearsal schedule or move them to a later date," Moira added before saying a curt goodbye and hanging up abruptly.

With the conversation over, Evie tossed her phone on the little side table by the bench and curled up among the brightly patterned pillows scattered on the window seat. Staring out at the grassy pastures fringed with pine and oak trees just beyond the backyard, she settled in with a notebook and a pen, jotting down a list of pros and cons about joining the cast of *Song & Dance* as they came to her, before proceeding to re-read and re-hash them over and over as the sun made its descent below the treetops. Every time she pictured herself dancing in front of the cameras and a live audience, nervous shivers raced down her spine. She wasn't at all certain that the show was something she really wanted to do, but not doing it seemed to be an even less appealing option.

She'd have to uproot again—by her calculations, she would be in LA up until time for the *America Sings* tour to begin if she made it through the competition all the way to the finals. That meant she'd be lucky to be at home for a total of a week or two throughout the next seven months. She threw a pillow across her face and squeezed her eyes closed as the possibilities overwhelmed her. Could she handle being on the road and away from everything familiar and comfortable for that long of a time? Not likely.

Maybe talking to Davis would help her work through the decision-making process. He was coming over to the house in just a bit, and as her boyfriend of eight years, she valued his thoughts and opinions. The decision would affect him, too, after all.

* * * *

"So, what do you think?" Evie asked Davis once she'd told him everything Moira had shared with her earlier about the *Song & Dance* opportunity. Seated on the cushy outdoor sofa together, Evie burrowed into his side. Although they were stationed in front of the fire burning in the back porch's stacked stone fireplace, the March winds blew forceful and frigid, especially since the sun had sank well below the horizon. Only vivid streaks of pinks and purples were left in the twilight. They weren't going to be able to stay outdoors too much longer—the tip of her nose felt like an ice cube despite the fire.

She took a sip from the toasty mug of hot chocolate she held in her hands as she snuggled closer to Davis. With his muscular build, blonde hair, blue eyes and year-round tan skin—thanks to all those college football practices and regular fishing trips—not to mention his full lips and easy smile, Davis was the epitome of the handsome, All-American, guy-next-door. No doubt about that. And as a starting player for Auburn, he held quite the appeal to fans. Girls wanted to date him, guys wanted to be friends with him, alumni wanted to have him in their pocket for future use. All Davis wanted was for the NFL to want him.

Evie took in the sight of him beside her, the firelight providing a warm, romantic glow. He'd gotten a haircut the week before and it was just a little too short for her taste. She liked it better when he let it grow out and it curled at his collar—she found him downright irresistible with floppy hair. Tucking her legs up and sliding her feet, clad only in fuzzy socks, beneath his solid thigh, she waited for him to answer her, trying to dissect the pensive look he wore.

She cared what he thought about her next move. After all, they'd been together for over eight years. Eight years! It sounded so crazy to most people outside of the small-town South that at 22 years old, they'd been together that long, but they'd grown up together —same town, same schools, many of the same elementary teachers, their families were close friends, and they'd attended the same church since birth.

They'd always been around each other, and when middle school and hormones kicked in, "feelings" kicked in, too. But, they didn't start "officially" dating until ninth grade.

Davis and Evie. Evie and Davis. To everyone in Thompson and pretty much all of Alabama, Davis Anderson, Auburn's starting tight end, and Evie Michaelson, reality show star, were a celebrity couple. #Devie. Evie stopped counting the times she was asked if Davis had proposed yet. For her, their relationship felt comfortable. Natural. But ever since her stint on *America Sings,* things hadn't been peaches and cream between the two of them.

Time and distance apart took a toll on what had been an easy and amazing relationship up until six months ago. However, she loved Davis, he meant the world to her, and that wasn't about to change. After all, she had very few memories in which he hadn't played a pivotal part. What they had together was priceless.

"Geez, Evie. I don't know," Davis interrupted her thoughts, rubbing the back of his neck. She sensed the frustration in his voice; saw it in the tense set of his shoulders and that indeterminable look on his face. Evie sat her mug on the table beside the sofa and put her hand on his neck, massaging gently.

"Please tell me what you're thinking, Davis. I need to know how you feel because this affects you, too," she reminded him. He turned to face her.

"I'm not going to tell you what to do, Evie. This is your decision—not mine. I'll admit, it was hard on us when you were gone for a solid four months. Don't get me wrong—what you did, how far you went in the competition—it still blows me away and I'm so proud of all that you've accomplished. But think about how it's already hard enough on our relationship with me being two hours away at Auburn. And now I'm about to graduate. Have you already forgotten how we're supposed to be doing that together, but that all changed when you left and went on that show?"

She cringed at his words lined subtly with bitterness and accusation, especially since it was her fault things didn't pan out the way they'd originally intended. Davis never outright said it, but she felt like deep down he blamed her for throwing a wrench in their pre-*America Sings* plans.

Their time at Lumpkin County Comprehensive High School was a typical story—he'd been the handsome, all-star football player, and she the perky cheerleader always happy just to be on his arm and along for the ride. Life was simple and so much fun, and no surprise—they were voted prom king and queen. Then, they'd headed to Auburn together four years ago with him on a full ride, football scholarship, and her, the doting girlfriend, following along as his biggest fan not even sure what her major would be. In his mind, everything was perfect and she messed it all up when, at the start of their senior year at AU, she'd auditioned and subsequently competed on *that show* as he usually referred to *America Sings*.

As much as Evie loved Davis, she worried that the more she found her voice and liked who she was becoming as both a person and an artist, he found her less appealing. She regularly assured him that she would always be his biggest fan, but she had other interests, too. That hadn't been a problem for them until *America Sings* entered the picture. According to Davis, she'd changed. Sure, she looked no different than before with the same honey-blonde hair that couldn't decide if it was straight or curly and sea green eyes framed with thick, dark lashes she'd inherited from her Daddy's trace of Cherokee Indian blood. But inside? Well, she was no longer the naive, bubbly coed who thought that her handsome, Ken doll of a boyfriend was her entire world. And she was fine with that. She adored Davis, but she'd experienced an exciting city and a new culture—she'd discovered how people who were different from her lived their lives. The simple, Southern bubble surrounding her had popped, and now she wanted even more of what the great big world had to offer. Was that such a bad thing?

A couple of weeks earlier, Davis had raised his eyebrows and proclaimed that maybe she was getting just a little too edgy when she wore Chuck Taylors and high-waisted jeans with a bandanna tied in her hair on their date. The outfit did look strange next to the polo and khaki shorts he wore everywhere except to church and the football field.

He would roll his eyes whenever she talked about getting a tattoo—even though all she wanted was a tiny flower or cross on the inside of her forearm. To her frustration, Davis would've probably sighed in relief if she just went ahead and raided her mother's Lilly collection, popped in a pair of pearl studs and started wearing her hair in a perky, Barbie-style ponytail like most of the sorority girls on campus did.

He didn't understand that she was finally comfortable being herself instead of complying with the rural Southern expectation of young women to which she'd mindlessly adhered since her birth. For years, she couldn't put her finger on why she'd felt so strangely stifled. She still loved to dress up for football games, shopping was one of her favorite past-times, and she was all about manicures, pedicures, and keeping her eyebrows waxed. Monograms, pearls and big bows were as much a part of her wardrobe as the next Southern girl. However, she hadn't and wouldn't be interested in pledging her mama's sorority or having the singular goal of getting married and having babies as soon as Davis graduated and started his career in the NFL or at his dad's insurance company.

One of their biggest points of dissension was that Davis firmly believed her singing career shouldn't be anything more than just a fun hobby. He felt that a professional singer's schedule wouldn't work for a marriage and family—especially if he was drafted—and he'd brought it up more than a few times over the past couple of months. While she understood his point to a tiny extent, she refused to even think about marriage yet—she wasn't ready! How her singing career could eventually affect a hypothetical husband and children didn't matter to her at this particular stage in her life. In her opinion, this was the perfect time in their lives to be pursuing their dreams as individuals. And even if it did matter, why was it okay for him to have the career of his dreams, but as a woman and future wife and mother she would need to sacrifice hers?

Despite his subtle objections, Evie's desire to pursue her career and capitalize on her growing fame while she had the chance hadn't wavered. Was there anything wrong with that? Not in her opinion. *Song & Dance* provided the perfect opportunity to gain momentum and grow her fan base, and she really hoped he would have a change of perspective and eventually understand that.

"Davis, you know I'm sorry if I let you down when I decided to leave Auburn, but I had to follow my heart. I wasn't even sure why I was majoring in business administration or what I would do with it when I graduated. You know how much I hate office work! And now I'm starting to make a good living doing something that I absolutely love! This show is probably going to take my career a lot further than I could ever take it on my own, and I can still finish my degree down the road if I choose to do so. What if I never get another opportunity like this one? Can't you just be supportive? Please?"

He sighed and leaned forward. "I'm sorry, Evie. I didn't mean to come off as unsupportive. It's just that I don't like knowing you're going to do this no matter how I feel about it, and I hardly ever get to see you as it is. But hey, when you think about it, what's another three months apart in the grand scheme of things?" Davis asked, shrugging as leaned back and put his arm around her, pulling her back close to his side.

They sat in silence for a minute or so, the matter apparently dropped. She wasn't about to bring up the tour that would immediately follow the wrapping of *Song & Dance*. No need to spark another argument. This wasn't how she wanted things to go—him basically relenting that he'd be cool with her deciding to do the show, even though that wasn't how he really felt. However, continuing to talk about it would probably make matters worse, and they didn't need all that tension ruining what little time they did get to see each other.

Evie laid her head gently against his shoulder and watched as the flames flickered in the outdoor fireplace. The way a good, roaring fire burned captivated her. The wood had to be super dry, and someone had to be constantly watching it, poking the logs and feeding the flames. Otherwise, the fire would just peter out into a cold pile of ash before you realized what happened. It could be roaring white hot one minute, but the second you weren't paying attention, it would simmer down to a pile of charred ashes.

As they snuggled by the fire, she imagined the picture they painted sitting there under the stars resembled something plucked right out of one of the good parts of a romance movie. She kissed his cheek, desperate to re-ignite their spark again—to feel that rush of excitement and fluttering butterflies whenever they kissed, or heck, even sometimes when he just looked at her. She couldn't recall when she'd last felt that way around him.

The last thing she wanted was to be the cause of their solid relationship dwindling away to nothing but a cold pile of gray ashes. If they wanted to rekindle their spark, they were going to have to work for it, especially given their unique circumstances. Maybe, they'd just hit a little bump in the road. She'd heard people say that when you've been together for a while, you go through seasons of good and bad, and maybe this was a not-so-good season for them. Everything couldn't be sunshine and roses all the time, could it?

No matter where their relationship stood, as far as her career decisions were concerned, those feelings had to go on the back burner during her decision-making process. Changing her plans just to appease Davis wasn't an option. The last thing their relationship needed was simmering resentment or regret that would fester into an even bigger issue down the road.

"I'll miss you, Davis, but you know we can visit back and forth," she quietly reminded him, pushing past her less-than-chipper attitude. He nodded but said nothing in return.

They continued to sit in heavy silence, listening to the familiar sounds of the night. Crickets chirped, the fire sizzled and wind whistled through the pine trees creating a subtle, nighttime symphony as her mind struggled with what else to say. Why couldn't she let it go? Why couldn't she stop worrying about what she couldn't change, and simply live in this beautiful, romantic moment?

"So who do you think you'll get as a partner?" Davis finally asked after several more minutes of silence. The sound of his voice startled her, and she jumped in surprise.

"My agent is pushing for Grant or Adam," Evie told him, shivering as the temperature continued to steadily drop.

"So, let me get this right, my girlfriend is about to get up close and personal with one of the two guys that all the girls go crazy over for the next three months?"

"I guess you know the show better than I do," Evie replied ruefully with a playful elbow to his ribs. She ignored the jealousy in his comment. He did not need to start with that junk before she'd officially made a commitment to do the show. He should've known better than anyone that the close, physical contact with a virtual stranger made her so nervous. What if she looked awkward and uncomfortable the entire time she danced with someone?

"I don't live under a rock the last time I checked," he said, winking. Thank God his moody spell had ended.

They stayed in front of the fire until it burned low and the cold pushed them back into the house. Inside the warm, cozy farmhouse, a solitary lamp cast shadows throughout the hall and kitchen. Her parents had already called it a night and retired to their room.

"Do you want to watch a movie?" Evie asked, her voice breaking the weighty silence as they tiptoed into the family room.

"Sure, you pick," he murmured against her ear, snaking his arms around her waist. Evie grabbed the remote and flipped through the movie channels until she landed on a romantic comedy from the 80s she'd already seen at least five times.

"Really?" Davis asked warily as they plopped onto the leather sofa together.

"You told me to pick," Evie shrugged. He rolled his eyes and laughed.

"I forgot how different our tastes in movies are." He yawned while tossing his arm behind her shoulders and pulling her close.

"That's your own fault. As many movie nights as we've had since ninth grade, you should definitely know better," she winked and gave him a quick kiss before settling in and getting comfy. He leaned down and returned her kiss with enthusiasm.

"Don't forget that my parents are upstairs," she reminded him.

He nodded, disappointed acceptance on his face as he pulled back and rested his head on the back of the sofa. She dozed off at some point, only waking when Davis stirred beside her.

"I'm going home now, sweetie," Davis whispered as he got up, turning off the television with the remote as the credits rolled. She sat up and stretched sleepily.

"Thanks for letting me take a nap on you," she yawned, smiling. Rising from the sofa, she wrapped her arms around his neck hugging him close before walking him to the door.

"Anytime. It was nice to just be with you tonight. It's been a while and I've really missed you, Evie," he told her before giving her a lengthy goodbye kiss. "Love you," he added, his forehead against hers.

"I love you, too, Davis," she replied as he lifted his lips from hers. She squeezed his hands before he finally walked out the door and into the pitch-black country night.

She double-checked that the house was locked up before padding upstairs to her room after hearing the familiar sound of Davis cranking up his Jeep and heading down the long, graveled drive faded to the stillness of midnight. That Sunday, he would head back to Auburn when his spring break ended. Her heart tugged—she missed him already. She sure was glad he'd been at home in Thompson when she received the show offer, and that they'd had the chance to talk about it in person, rather than having to attempt the conversation over texts and a long distance call. They'd also needed to spend quality time together like they did that night. It had been far too long.

Evie changed into her warmest pajamas and scooted between her chilly sheets, but sleep evaded her —thanks to a huge decision to make combined with a late-night nap. After half an hour of counting sheep and restless flopping from side to side, she pulled out her laptop and settle in to watch episodes from the past seasons of *Song & Dance* propped up against her pillows. In the wee hours of the morning, as her eyes grew bleary and her neck stiff, she pulled the bright patchwork quilt her grandmother made years ago over her shoulders and fell into a deep, dreamless sleep.

When she rose late the next morning, she hopped in the shower and drank a quick cup of coffee before pulling her phone off of the charger. The *Song & Dance* episodes she'd stayed up watching before catching a solid few hours of sleep were all the convincing she'd needed. Evie pulled up her recent calls list. It took her no time to locate the contact she needed.

"Moira? I'm all in," Evie's words tumbled out as soon as Moira answered.

"Good, Evie! Great, in fact. I'll get on the phone with the producers right now and push for Grant or Adam. There's no guarantee that you'll end up with either of them, but I'm going to do all that I can to give you an edge." Moira had no problem jumping right to work.

"Thanks, Moira. It doesn't matter to me who I end up with as a partner, but it's nice to have you in my corner. I guess I'll be seeing you soon."

"Just doing my job, but as always, it's a pleasure working with you," Moira added, going over a few more mundane details with her before ending the call.

CHAPTER TWO

Still waiting for her delayed plane to board, Evie and her father both shifted in the small airport's uncomfortable plastic seats as her mother packed Evie's carry-on bag with an overflow of snacks. Finished with stocking the bright blue suitcase with a six month's supply of trail mix and cheese crackers, she checked over Evie's packing list for the third time that morning, making sure she hadn't missed or forgotten anything.

"Do you have all of your emergency contacts listed separate in your phone?" Evie's dad asked her while her mom continued to fuss with her luggage.

"Yes, sir, listed just like you told me," Evie supplied.

"And you have them written down on paper somewhere, too, right?"

"Yep, in my wallet behind my license."

"Do you have all your chargers? Phone, computer, that little thingy you listen to music on..."

"Yes, Dad, I have them all. We went through this same checklist last night," she assured him, patting his arm.

Before her dad could respond, the airport's loudspeaker boomed the announcement that her flight was finally going to start boarding passengers.

"Alright, I guess it's time for you to get going then. If you change your mind and you decide that you, in fact, do need your mama, at any time—day or night—call me and I'll be there as fast as lightning on a June bug," her mother informed her, choking up as she pulled Evie into her tight, familiar embrace. Evie breathed in her mother's comforting scent—fabric softener, bright floral perfume, and a faint hint of lavender soap—as her cheek pressed against her signature Lilly Pulitzer sweater.

"She's right, sweetie. One call and we'll be there in the blink of an eye," her dad added as her mom passed Evie into his waiting arms. Evie's chest tightened and her throat constricted as her father wrapped her up in one of his bear hugs. He was a man of few words, but his hugs said everything she needed to know. As the tears pooling in her eyes threatened to fall and turn her into a sobbing mess in the middle of the airport, she left their circle of goodbyes, straightening her shirt and jacket, and attempted to smooth her wits, too.

"Got it. I'll call y'all as soon as I land in LA, I promise. Keep me in your prayers, and don't forget for even one second how much I love you both." Evie's voice quivered as she reined in the tumultuous flood of emotions threatening to overflow and break through her calm exterior.

Picking up her bag, she marched towards her flight gate with her boarding pass in her shaking hand, compliments of that third cup of coffee she'd downed right before they'd left the house. As excited as she'd been all week, looking forward to this journey and all, now that the moment had arrived, it wasn't at all what she'd expected.

She suddenly realized the depth of how much she'd miss her parents, and it upset her that Davis hadn't been able to be at the airport to say goodbye. He'd *had* to be present for some lecture that accounted for a big portion of his grade. At least their date the other night went well, and after she'd finished packing last night, they'd talked on the phone for a couple of hours while she lay in bed, just like they used to do all the time. Things had thankfully gotten better between them since that first moment she'd told him about doing *Song & Dance*.

Before Evie handed her pass to the boarding attendant, she looked back at her parents one more time to where they stood hand in hand, watching their only child leave them for the second time in less than six months. They'd proven to be unconditionally supportive of her, keeping her grounded and always reminding her of what was most important if she ever started to forget. What would she do without them and their amazing guidance? They wouldn't let fame, careers, or dance shows go to her head, or to theirs.

Evie blew them kisses, and with one final wave, headed toward her newest adventure, clueless as to what her expectations should be. Bright-eyed with suitcase in hand, she boarded the plane trying to keep from throwing up from jittery nerves. The flight from Dothan was a quick and bumpy one hour trip to

Atlanta, where she hastily boarded her nonstop flight to LAX.

She settled into the comfy leather seat, glad she purchased a first-class ticket for the almost five hour flight. Closing her eyes, she slipped her earbuds into her ears, and clicked on the playlist she'd compiled for the flight. Flying didn't really bother her all that much, but knowing all that waited for her when the flight landed weighed heavily on her mind.

She'd made arrangements to pick up her leased car at the airport before heading to the apartment that the show graciously provided for her. Most of the contestants lived in or near LA, but there were a few from Nashville and New York, and then there was her, Evie Michaelson, still hailing from the grand old state of Alabama. After she handled the car and living situation, she still had a bunch of calls to make, groceries and supplies to purchase, and she wanted to unpack before meeting her partner and rehearsals started in earnest tomorrow. Things were about to get real. Jet lag was no friend, but the extra hours she gained flying cross country would help in accomplishing all four million items on her to-do list. As she waited for the rest of the passengers to finish boarding, she tried to relax and forget about all she needed to do when the plane landed. Her eyes grew heavy even as her mind worked in overdrive.

Just as she dozed off, an energetic tap on her shoulder startled her awake. Evie's eyes flew open, meeting a pair of big, excited ones peering over the edge of the seat at her.

"Can I get your autograph?" a young girl, the owner of the big eyes, chirped as she stood in the aisle, leaning against Evie's seat. Evie blinked a few times, trying to remember where she was, her brain still fuzzy with exhaustion.

"Yes, of course," Evie said, smiling at the girl who couldn't have been a day over ten. The girl handed her a hot pink pen and a piece of flowery notebook paper, and Evie scrawled out a little note and signed it with a flourish.

"Thank you so much, Evie! I can't believe I'm on the same flight as Evie Michaelson! I voted for you, you know!" She squealed before bouncing back to her seat two rows in front of Evie. She waved and smiled at the girl's parents as the little girl told them about her encounter. It was moments like these that made Evie's heart swell with gratitude. There's no way her life could ever be the same. Not since Fate had smiled down at her and taken over.

Shortly after the encounter, the plane took off, and she spent the entire flight drifting in and out of sleep. From what she'd gathered, the rehearsal schedule for the show would be no joke. The thought of all that energy being exerted must have worn her out, because the next thing she knew, she woke up and the plane was beginning its descent over sunny Los Angeles.

* * * *

Evie sucked in a big gulp of air and popped open a bottle of water in the dim apartment. After the last of the three trips it took to get all of her luggage from the parking deck below the building up to the fourth floor apartment, she was worn out. Bottle in hand, she sank onto the charcoal gray sofa and surveyed the small, but stylish, space she would call home for as long as she competed for the *Song & Dance* championship trophy. Everything about the space screamed modern and sleek. A far cry from her family's quaint, rambling farmhouse back home, she loved the luxe, urban vibe of her surroundings and what they represented. This was the fresh change of scenery she needed—the jump start to her career and her life as an independent woman.

After a few moments of rest, she leapt into action, hauling her bags to the bedroom area, separated from the rest of the studio by a loft-style wall. Trying to tuck the large suitcases and their contents into the tiny closet proved to be a challenge, but she managed to get everything somewhat organized in a short amount of time. Once she'd unpacked most of her stuff, she jotted down a quick grocery list before heading to the closest supermarket to stock the empty galley kitchen.

Her jaw dropped when she walked into the gourmet grocer. Memories of her trip last week to the cracked and crumbling grocery store in Thompson with its bright orange sale stickers and the distinct smell of "old" permeating the air were a stark comparison to her present surroundings. She now pushed a glossy black cart down lovely, organized aisles with soft lighting, polished concrete floors and dark wood shelving.

"Toto, we're not in Kansas anymore," she whispered under her breath as classical music played softly over the speakers. Everything sold at the market looked locally harvested and beautifully packaged, and handwritten chalkboard signs were everywhere as far as the eye could see.

Evie took her time getting the items she needed, never enjoying a mundane errand the way she enjoyed this fancy grocery store visit. She picked up much more than the list of items she'd scribbled on her notepad, simply because some things sounded too interesting to leave on the shelves. When she pushed her cart out of the store an hour later, it overflowed with reusable bags full of wheat bread, yogurt and other staples along with interesting stuff like hemp milk, sprouted almond butter, and chocolate-covered acai berries.

After getting her abundance of groceries sorted and put away once, and with most of her other tasks finished, Evie tossed together a colorful salad and planted herself on the sofa with the bag of chocolate covered berries close by. Her dinner was interrupted when Moira called, ready to conference in the production team and go over last-minute details before she met her partner and their practices started the next day.

"How's LA treating you so far, Evie?" Moira asked at the start of the call.

"Pretty good. I haven't been here but a few hours and I'm already settling in nicely."

"Hopefully you'll be calling this city home for a solid three months. I'm already rooting for you and ready to vote!"

"The show hasn't even started yet—I could very possibly totally suck," Evie pointed out as she grabbed a pen and paper.

"You could fall flat on your face and I'd still vote for you, hon."

"Thanks for the vote of confidence."

They chatted for a few moments before Moira conferenced in Kim, one of the show's producers. Moira and Kim did most of the talking while Evie tried to keep her eyes open and take notes about security clearances and practice schedules.

After the call ended, she watched a couple of reruns on television, trying to stay awake so she could get used to the time difference, but before nine, her eyes couldn't stay open any longer and she hit the hay.

* * * *

The next morning, as Evie pulled into her assigned spot amid the row of shiny cars parked neatly in front of the booming dance studio, she glanced at the time. She didn't want to be too early. She took in a shaky breath. Her nerves were getting the best of her and she hadn't pulled the keys out of the ignition yet.

What was she doing here again? Nothing had prepared her for the hands sweating, knees shaking, nauseating anxiety that hit her the moment she drove into the parking lot. This was new. She'd never been overwhelmed like this by nerves before—not even during the live finale of *America Sings*, which was broadcasted nationwide to over 20 million viewers. But then again, she felt comfortable singing. Dancing? Not so much.

Evie checked her reflection in the rearview mirror—her blondish-brown fishtail braid hung over her shoulder, a little lip gloss adorned her lips and of course she'd made up her eyes to look as natural as possible using six different products. Wearing her tank top, leggings and running shoes, she appeared casual, but coordinated. Maybe if she dressed for the part of being a pro, she would feel like one.

From her spot inside the car, she spied a small knot of photographers and maybe a few fans hanging out on the edge of the privately-owned studio lot. With a deep breath and renewed resolve, Evie tossed her gym bag over her shoulder, grabbed her water bottle and hopped out of the car. The sun beat down relentlessly, baking everything atop the asphalt, but she threw her hand up and waved happily to the little flock as their cameras furiously clicked away. Thankfully, she'd taken extra care in selecting her matching coral, mint and gray workout clothes keeping in mind that she'd end up with her picture all over the internet today. After acknowledging the photographers and fans, she walked to the locked studio door and punched in the code she'd saved in her phone last night during the production call with Moira and Kim.

Stepping inside the overly air-conditioned building, Evie's eyes took a second to adjust to the darker interior. Three people were in the small lobby awaiting her arrival.

"Hello, I'm Kim, the production director assigned to you and your partner. We spoke last night over the phone," a woman in her thirties with closely cropped, copper hair said warmly as she stuck out a hand in greeting. She wore ripped jeans, a black tank top, and a headset, and in her un-offered hand, she held a clipboard. A sleeve of tattoos covered Kim's arm.

"Nice to meet you and put a face to the voice," Evie smiled her biggest, Alabama sorority-girl smile in her arsenal, and shook the woman's extended hand, taking in a portion of her tattoos that featured a mermaid and numerous stars.

"The man holding the camera over here is Steve, and this other guy beside me is Harper—he's my assistant. During filming, one of us will be with you at all times," she explained as Evie shook hands and greeted the two guys. Steve was significantly older, maybe late fifties? He wore khaki cargo shorts with tennis shoes much like Evie's dad wore to go to Home Depot and Applebee's on Saturday afternoons with her mom, while Harper, with his dreads, chunky black glasses, ironic tee and unlaced work boots, epitomized a young LA hipster working on a studio set.

The trio escorted Evie down a long hall and into a large, empty studio. Upon entering the practice room, stuff started happening so fast that Evie didn't fully process anything until it had all unfolded. Instructions were barked, lighting adjusted, and Kim attached a tiny microphone to the inside of Evie's tank top. Evie watched, wide-eyed, as the team hustled in a chaotic, yet seamless, whirlwind.

"In a few minutes, your partner is going to come in and we're going to film your first meeting. Make sure you act completely natural. Try to forget that we're even here," Kim told her as she secured the mic in place. *Forgetting all this is here won't be easy,* Evie thought, peering around at the various recording equipment, sound booms, and people milling in and out of the room as her team prepped for filming.

The production team seated her in a folding chair smack dab in the middle of the open room. Goosebumps broke out on her arms when they brushed against the cold metal chair, adding to her heightened vulnerability. Evie studied the dark gray wall she faced with its multiple framed live shots featuring couples from past *Song & Dance* seasons. The artistic photos mesmerized her, and she briefly wondered if any of the guys in the pictures would be her partner. Beneath the shots, benches, a table with a small sound system and random mats filled the empty space.

A wall of mirrors was to her left, and a blank, pale gray wall with high set windows letting plenty of natural light stream into the studio to the right. Evie's back faced the double doors that led out to the main hall. As she sat in the middle of the room nervous and frigid, Steve, the camera guy, circled around her, getting shots from every possible angle.

Singing on national television, performing in front of huge crowds—those experiences were walks in the park compared to how she felt peering at the clock above the long wall of mirrors waiting to meet a stranger. This stranger was someone she would be working with closely for the next three months, and she didn't have a clue as to their identity. Even though Moira had pushed for Evie to be paired with specific partners, that didn't mean she'd actually end up with either one of them.

When she'd spoken with Moira earlier that morning, her agent had nothing new to report, much to her frustration. The show thrived on the element of surprise, especially when it came to partner reveals. A special show would even air on the network featuring partner reveals the next evening to create hype for the following Tuesday night's live premiere.

She cracked her knuckles out of nervous habit and checked the clock again. Waiting around drove her nuts. Her partner seemingly didn't mind keeping people waiting. Seeing as that was one of her biggest pet peeves, it didn't bode well for their partnership. Evie rubbed her temples. She had a bad habit of overthinking and making situations out to be worse than they really were. If he would go on and get here and they could get this first meeting out of the way, her nerves would calm considerably.

Just when she was about to hop up and stretch, unable to stay still in the uncomfortable seat a second longer, she heard one of the crew members whisper, *"he's here,"* to the other two seated on the bench. Evie sat up a little straighter and smoothed her mint tank top while the crew members scurried into action again, getting ready to record her and her partner's initial reactions to one another. Her stomach did somersaults, but she kept her outward composure.

The jarring sound of double doors squealing in protest as they swung open interrupted the silence hanging over the studio. In her anticipation to finally see her partner, Evie hopped up from the metal chair and with a "company" smile in place, she whirled around to introduce herself, but the toe of her sneaker caught on the glossy wood floor with a squeak.

As she fell face first, unable to stop her momentum, the thought raced through her mind that her worst nightmare had become reality. Lying on the ground, surely managing to give her professional dance partner the first impression of his own nightmares, Evie kept her eyes on the woodgrain of the floor inches from her face, trying to hide her utter mortification.

CHAPTER THREE

From her face-planted position, the clacking of her partner's dance shoes grew closer as he rushed across the studio to help her to her feet. She dreaded facing him now, absolutely positive that her cheeks were crimson, her hair a hot mess, and her dignity gone.

"I guess you have your work cut out for you," she semi-joked, smiling uncertainly as she pushed up from the floor and took his offered hand, making the best of a situation and saving what little face she had left. Her "little slip" would be included in their partner reveal package. No doubt.

Evie grasped his hand and his firm grip lifted her up as if she weighed nothing, and as he let go and she stood upright, adjusting her clothes and wires, she looked up and found herself staring into the most handsome face she'd ever laid eyes on in all of her 22 years. Dressed in a black shirt and dark pants, Grant Merritt was even more handsome in person than on television. With nearly jet black hair, a strong jawline and blue-green eyes, similar to her own, but maybe a little more on the blue side, Grant was gorgeous in a way all women, no matter what their "type" was, found irresistible. When his face lit up with a broad, welcoming smile, the tiniest hint of a dimple flickered in his left cheek, and she went a little weak in the knees. It wasn't his smile, she told herself, she was just a little off-kilter from her recent fall.

To his immense credit, he laughed at her corny joke before officially introducing himself. "I would say so," he said with an easy smile, sticking out his hand for her to shake.

"My name is Grant Merritt, I'm a three-time champion on *Song & Dance*, and I'm excited to be your partner this season," he said, sounding rehearsed. Before she had a chance to answer, he dropped his voice and asked with genuine concern, "Are you okay?"

"Yes, I'm fine," she told him, nodding her head and smiling, before admitting, "I'm more embarrassed than hurt." She didn't add that her hands smarted angrily from where they'd caught most of her fall.

"I'm glad you're alright, and truthfully, I'm excited to have you as my partner, Evie." He wiggled his eyebrows.

"I thought you weren't supposed to find out who I was beforehand," she said, puzzled. The laughter echoed around the room.

"We aren't, but I immediately recognized you from *America Sings*. I'm a big fan of the show. I'm just going to go ahead and say it—you should have won last season. I voted for you, so I'm thrilled to have you as my partner!" he told her before scooping her into an enthusiastic embrace. She froze, her arms sticking out awkwardly as this stranger hugged her. In the back of her mind, she vaguely recalled someone warning her that dancers were extremely touchy feely, but no amount of warning would've prepared her when Grant threw his arms around her and lifted her off her feet with grandiose.

When her brain began firing on all cylinders again, she returned his hug by sort of patting his back with one of her hands. She didn't know what to do with her other hand that still hung mid-air. Everything felt so awkward.

"You've got to relax," Grant whispered in her ear, barely audible so that it wouldn't pick up on their mics.

She gave him a slight nod as they broke apart. She followed him as he walked over to one of the benches and took a seat, patting the spot beside him.

"So, Evie, tell me about yourself," Grant said when she'd taken a seat beside him and the cameras and crew were situated.

"Well, let's see—I'm from Thompson, Alabama, I'll be 23 in August, and I placed 2nd on *America Sings*, but you knew that already. Your turn. Tell me something about yourself," Evie rambled off.

"I was born and raised in Northern California, and my birthday is in August, too."

"Really? What day? Mine's the 24th. How old will you be, if you don't mind me asking?"

"Wow, that's crazy—mine's the 25th and I'll be turning the big 3-0. So, what sort of dance experience do you have?" He asked, changing the subject. She really wanted to ask more about where he grew up, but talking about dancing made a lot more sense.

"Very little, honestly. Of course, I danced at prom and stuff, and I had to do an tiny bit of simple choreography in a couple of my performances for *America Sings*, but that's about it," she admitted.

"Okay, that's good. We can work with that. I've had a couple of partners who literally had no experience whatsoever. I saw your performances on TV, and from what I can remember, you have pretty good rhythm."

"That's what my agent said, too, but my boyfriend would probably disagree with you. He says I have two left feet!" She laughed.

"You did just take a spill on the floor a few minutes ago," he teased. "Is your boyfriend a musician, too?"

"Lord, no. Davis is an athlete. He's hoping to be an early draft pick for the NFL," she said proudly.

"Football player, hmm?"

"Yep. Davis and I have been together since the ninth grade. I was a cheerleader in high school, too. I guess that'll help us a little with the whole dancing thing, right?"

"It doesn't hurt. When did you start your singing career?"

"I've sang at church since I was like, no joke, a toddler. I took piano lessons, joined chorus in junior high, and of course, did the high school musical thing. I auditioned for *America Sings* on a whim but look where it's taken me." She gestured to the dance studio. What she was doing still felt so surreal.

"Wow," Grant replied, his eyes wide, jaw slack. "Your talent—Evie you were born to sing. I'm surprised to hear that you weren't already seriously performing prior to *America Sings*—you're a natural."

"Thanks," she said, feeling shy and smoothing her braid as he smiled at her. "How about you? What's your story?" She asked him, ready to change the subject from herself.

"I started dancing when I was eight—my grandmother was a ballroom dance teacher, so I didn't have much of a choice in the matter. I realized I was pretty good at it, and started competing and ended up winning a few championships, which led to being offered a spot on this show."

"Cool. So musically . . ." she prompted.

"I can carry a tune if that's what you're asking. I play the guitar and a little piano, too. Speaking of piano, I could listen to you play all day."

"Stop with the compliments, you're making me blush," she laughed, rolling her eyes and playfully hitting his arm.

"Hey, I'm just speaking the truth." He winked and smiled. Evie bit her lip, avoiding eye contact with the almost too handsome man beside her. It was hard for her not to stare at him, which was saying a lot as her own boyfriend was featured as one of *Teen People*'s 30 Hottest College Athletes.

"Okay, guys! That's a wrap!" Kim, the producer, called out thirty minutes later. In the middle of telling Grant a story about her trip to Mexico last July, Evie looked up, startled. So enrapt in their conversation, she'd totally forgotten the camera crew was actually there to film them.

"Are you free to meet me back here in about an hour to start practicing?" Grant asked as they took off their microphones.

"Yeah, sure. The sooner we get started, the better," she told him.

"I agree."

"I bet you do," Evie muttered under her breath and shook her head, cringing at the fresh memory of her up close and personal view of the studio floor.

* * * *

An hour into their first official rehearsal, sweat trickled down Evie's face, getting into her eyes and sliding off her chin. Dancing was hard work, and truth be told, it had been awhile since she'd last hit the gym. The jive, the dance they were assigned to perform for the premiere, was one of the hardest styles to learn, according to Grant, and although she had little knowledge in the matter, she absolutely agreed. Over and over, he showed her the steps until she was out of breath and wanting to lay down and die or puke or both, but she pushed through it all as she tried to keep up with his barely breaking a sweat self.

"You're doing great—you're a fast learner, Evie." Grant encouraged her with a smile.

"Really, you think? This is so hard for me!" she said through ragged breaths, wiping her forehead. She expected a lecture on what she could do to improve.

"You're picking up these steps as fast as any professional, and I'm not just saying that," he emphasized. Her cheeks grew hotter than they already were at another of the compliments he gave so liberally.

She started from the top again, and Grant walked around her as she practiced her kicks and flicks in time to the beat.

"Am I doing this right?" Evie asked, frowning at her reflection. Everything felt foreign and uncomfortable to her.

"No, but you're really close. Just remember, it's not going to feel normal—your body is doing something out of the ordinary," he replied, standing in front of her so that she could mirror his movements as he did them with her. They repeated the moves several times, until she felt completely comfortable doing the steps again on her own.

"What's our song for this dance?" she asked as she continued to flick her feet and watch them in the mirrored wall.

"Are you familiar with 'Going to the Chapel'?"

"Who isn't familiar with that song would be a better question."

"That's the song we were given."

"Okay, cool," she replied nonchalantly, but a bunch of different scenarios popped rapidly into her head.

"What's wrong?" Grant asked, staring at her face in the mirror. "Your face is saying that something is wrong."

"Nothing. Let's practice." She tried to shrug off her uneasiness. He'd unfortunately read her initial reaction with ease—she would have to watch her facial expressions around him.

"As soon as you tell me what you don't like about the song choice." He folded his arms. He wasn't going to let the matter rest.

"I love the song. I really do," Evie deflected. That wasn't a lie.

"But . . ." he prompted, waiting for her to continue with an explanation. He wasn't budging until she gave him a satisfying answer.

"But the theme . . ." she paused before continuing, "The best way to work with the theme is for me to dress as a bride and you as a groom, correct?"

"Yes, that would be the most likely plan," he agreed.

"That's the problem. I know how fans get about 'shipping' people, and if we come right out of the gates in wedding garb, we're just setting ourselves up for it. They're going to want us to legit head to the altar right after watching a performance like that, and not only can that get awkward, but my boyfriend is going to freak the flip out," she admitted with an exasperated sigh. Honestly, she loved the whole concept—what girl wouldn't want the opportunity to wear a fun wedding dress and dance—but it would lead to a lot of unnecessary and unwanted speculation for them to immediately have to combat.

"That's what bothers you? People will actually think we're getting married? The opinions of strangers matter that much?" Grant asked, brows furrowed, arms still folded across his chest.

She nodded, fidgeting from side to side, wishing the floor would swallow her whole. What an awkward conversation to have with someone she'd known for a total of three hours. "It's not so much that they matter to me, but they will matter to Davis."

"Evie, it's just a performance. Think of it like a play and we're the actors. That makes it a lot less strange, doesn't it? 'Going to the Chapel' is a popular dance recital song, in fact. I think if you explain all of that to him, your boyfriend will be fine. The producers probably picked this song for you to play on that wholesome, fresh-faced beauty thing that you have going on. It really is the perfect choice for you. And to be honest, if the fans and press thinks there is a little something between us, you know it won't hurt us in votes," he said with a wink.

She rolled her eyes, but he spoke the truth. "You're right, and I do love how fun the dance is that you're showing me," she told him.

Grant held out his hand to her. Now that she'd learned the basic steps of the routine, they dove into working on proper hold and a few other techniques. As she bounced around the room in his arms, a twinge of guilt kept plaguing her. Evie didn't want to admit that she liked the way his hand on the small of her back held her snugly against him just a little too much. She tried to separate herself from the feelings, tried to view it as just part of the routine, but putting so much focus separating her mind from her body made her confuse turns and misstep repeatedly.

Suddenly, without warning, Grant broke their hold and took several steps away from her. He studied her with steepled hands beneath his chin and didn't say a single word as the minutes passed by slowly. She shifted her weight under his microscopic gaze.

"Okay, Evie. We have to talk. What's your deal? Why are you freezing up every time I put my arm around you?" His voice was soft and soothing as his eyes trained in on her, waiting to assess her answer.

She shrugged as she played with the hem of her tank top, studying her reflection in the mirror as she avoided his intense stare.

"Um, I'm not freezing up. Why do you say that?" Her voice squeaked a little as she threw a question back at him. Deflection was her only defense.

He rolled his eyes and waited for her to give him a better answer. Clearly, he wasn't having it.

She sighed, giving in so the standoff would end, and they could get back to practicing. "Okay, geez, I'm sorry. I can't help it. I keep thinking about how much it would probably bug my boyfriend to know that I was in the arms of another guy as stupid as that sounds. This is all new and totally different for me, you know." The words tumbled out of her mouth. She didn't want to be one of "those girls," constantly bringing up her boyfriend, but he'd wanted the truth.

He shook his head and smiled down at her. His bemused expression didn't appear to be laced with impatience or annoyance. She'd have been both if she were in his shoes listening to her silly concerns. He had to think she was silly at the very least.

"Evie, your boyfriend has nothing to worry about, I promise. I'm a professional, and this is my job. Of course, it helps if we bond and develop good chemistry, but there's no need to stress out or feel guilty about it. That's normal. It would be bad for us not to enjoy being around each other or not find one another appealing. But for the record, I wouldn't dream of putting you in any sort of situation that made you feel uncomfortable being my partner. You're my top priority for the duration of our time on this show, and besides, I'm seeing someone. Make sure to mention that to your guy back home."

Grant mentioned his seeing someone as a side note, but that would help matters more than he knew. Conversations with Davis needed to be the least of her concerns at this particular moment anyway. It was time to just relax and focus on doing her best.

"Well now I guess we've got our work cut out for us!" She pretended to wipe her brow with an exaggerated gesture before he took her hand back in his. This time, when Grant put his other hand low and secure on her hip, it didn't phase her.
One thing was clear—Grant and she would not lack in the chemistry department. Although she'd only been around him for a handful of hours, the way they chatted and joked combined with the close physical proximity the dance required helped them get acquainted fast.

After they ran through the basic routine several more times, Grant turned the music on, and a thrill of excitement shot up her spine. This finally felt real. Besides, the cheerful song conjured up memories of weddings and scenes from some of her favorite movies. Who really wouldn't want to perform this song?

As the peppy notes filled the studio, Evie did some happy, freestyle dance moves, snapping her fingers and swaying to the beat. She smiled wide—how could anyone keep still with the cheerful beat blaring through the studio?

"What are you doing?" Grant asked, hand over his mouth, masking a laugh.

She froze in place, arms splayed, one leg kicked out, and stared at him.

"I'm just, you know, dancing," she said with a playful shrug.

"Let's just stick with the moves I showed you for now," he replied slowly, clearing his throat and stifling laughter. Evie returned to his arms, straightening her back, pulled her shoulders down.

"Nice," he said, nodding his approval at her dance posture.

They took a few more turns around the studio, trying to get a good feel for the rhythm of the song. The doo-wop vibe meshed perfectly with their jive routine and turning the music on really helped Evie with rhythm and timing.

"We'll have your dance shoes at practice tomorrow. The heels will take some getting used to, so it's good to start practicing with them as soon as possible," Grant told her as he whirled her across the floor.

Feeling accomplished, since she had nearly every step already memorized and it was just their first practice, Evie smiled to herself as they picked up the pace. Sure, her moves still felt like a hot mess to her personally, they would get even more so when she did them in high heels for the first time, and there was no way she had all those tiny details down that would really make the dance, but at least she had the basic concept under her belt.

After they'd practiced for another solid hour, Grant clapped his hands and called out, "That's a wrap for the day," and turned off the music.

"So how'd I do?" she asked as she walked over to her pile of stuff, wiped her face with a towel and picked up her hot pink water bottle. She took a hearty swig as he answered her.

"Evie, you did awesome—I'm really impressed. We've still got our work cut out for us, but you've got the choreography down pat. I'm going to have to increase the skill level of the dance if we make it through to week two." He reached out to give her a high five, clasping her hand firmly.

"Wow—harder steps? You think? I don't feel like I've got these down yet, and I can only focus on getting through the current week right now—I can't even process the idea of another week," she said, continuing to blot her sweaty face with a towel, and calm her breathing.

"So, where's your entourage?" he asked, looking around before he grabbed his own bottle of water.

"What are you talking about?" She tilted her head, confused.

"You know, your friends and family—all the people that are staying with you while you're in LA. Usually, my out of town partners have the most bystanders," he explained.

"I'm here by myself. Everyone has lives going on back home, and it's not the first time I've stayed away from home anyway. I lived with other contestants during *America Sings*, and I was on my own at college just before I was on that show," she explained. Evie didn't know why she was defending her reasons for doing this solo—it's not like it was his business anyway.

The conversation paused.

"Don't you think you'll get lonely being here by yourself?" he finally asked her. They hovered near the double doors, neither of them making an attempt to leave just yet.

"Nah, I like being alone sometimes. My mother would have came with me, but I insisted she stay home. Besides, I have a couple of acquaintances around town I'll connect with at some point, and I figure I'll make new friends while I'm here," she shrugged as she started gathering up her workout bag and purse. She wished he would drop it. She was fine.

"Well, you've already got one new friend," he said as she pushed the door open. With one foot through the door, Evie looked back to see him, handsome and muscular, shuffling his feet, far too adorable for his own good.

"Well, thanks," she commented, laughing. She didn't want him to think for one second that she was the least bit unhappy about being here on her own. The experience excited her, even if it did make her nervous at times.

"No, I'm being serious, Evie. Are you busy tonight? Do you want to maybe grab dinner later?" he asked casually, stepping toward her.

"I'm sure you have better stuff to do than babysit me, Grant. I promise, I'm not kidding when I say that I'm perfectly fine on my own." Why wouldn't he believe her?

"You're taking it the wrong way—I don't have any plans for the evening and it wouldn't be babysitting—you're a grown woman. Come on, let me take you to dinner, and then I can show you around a little. It's more competition related than anything—I think it would be good for us to get to know each other better."

Evie hesitated, but nodded her assent. He made a good point, and it wasn't like a date or anything—he was her partner and she needed to get to know him for the sake of the show. Plus, she didn't want to be downright rude and not accept his second offer of hospitality. That wasn't the Southern way of doing things.

"Okay, great. Are you staying in one of the apartments the show provides?"

"Yes, but you don't have to come pick me up; I can totally meet you somewhere."

"My apartment isn't far from there, and I'd be happy to swing by and pick you up. It's easier than trying to explain directions or having you pay for an Uber. How about I pick you up around eight?"

"I suppose I can pencil you in," she joked, tossing him a friendly wink.

"Thanks, I appreciate it," he teased back. As they stood there, grinning goofily at one another, for a second, she totally forgot that the cameras were still rolling. She breathed a sigh of relief—despite a crew member's constant presence with them, she acted normal. Hopefully, they wouldn't use any of that stuff they'd been talking about earlier. It really wouldn't fit in the narrative the producers were surely bent on creating. Them going out for dinner though and getting a bit flirty? Yeah, millions across America would probably see some of that exchange. Nothing too personal, but enough of their conversation would be shared to spin a story.

"See you later," she waved at Grant before heading to the lobby, dropping off her mic and heading into the warmth of a late afternoon in LA.

On the short drive back to her temporary apartment, she laughed out loud, downright giddy. Despite her initial trepidations, she thanked her lucky stars she'd decided to do the show after all. She'd had no idea how much she would enjoy dancing! Even before the music ever got involved, she'd been having a blast. When she was fighting the endurance throw ups and sweating profusely, it was still exhilarating. Grant was the perfect partner for her thankfully, and she would just have to trust his methods—even when it was the twentieth time they ran through four easy steps and she huffed and puffed to keep up with his pace.

At the thought of Grant, she sucked in a sharp breath. She'd made several conclusions about him in the past few hours. First of all, he intimidated her a little. Well, in all honesty, a lot. He was one of those guys where when he walked into a room, he owned it. He had that intangible quality she couldn't name, and it wasn't just because of his ridiculous good looks that a lot of the pros on *Song & Dance* had anyway and were evident to anyone with eyes. Grant's strong, masculine features and very nice build made it hard not to simply stand and gape at him, but when he started dancing or talking or moving—he was off the charts attractive. Whew. She subconsciously wiped her brow just thinking about him.

Although Grant had been nothing but a perfect gentleman, his confident, mysterious air could leave a girl—even a taken girl like herself—more than just a little intrigued. He wasn't just an attractive celebrity, he was a work of art, and in barely a week, she would be dressed as a bride and dancing with him as her groom on live television. Women all across America would be super jealous of her, and she wouldn't blame them one tiny bit. She just hoped they would live vicariously through her and end up voting for them.

Adding to his allure, Grant exuded confidence in his every move and gesture. He wasn't arrogant—that would've been annoying and gross and far less attractive. What Grant possessed was a self-assurance that could only be obtained when you had the perfect balance of both confidence and humility. If she ever got used to his crazy hotness and could simply think of him as any other average human being, she'd be able to learn a whole lot from him. Especially since she had a tendency to worry that people would think she was being prideful or conceited when she talked about her accomplishments in front of them. No matter how she tried, she'd get shy, blush and downplay the pretty awesome stuff she'd managed to accomplish in such a short amount of time at 22 years old.

Grant possessed the suave ability to rattle off details about his skills without appearing the least bit prideful. To him, it was simply a matter of fact. He was secure in who he was. He couldn't be all that perfect, right? He had to have some sort of major character flaw —or at least a little one. Too much perfection would be boring. Maybe she would find out if Grant hid any terrible character flaws tonight. Tonight. Her traitorous heart raced when she pictured spending the evening with him. She shouldn't have been nervous, but, oh boy, was she.

The evening's purpose found root in Grant taking her under his wing—kind of like a big brother. She assumed that's how he saw it since that was how she saw his gesture of kindness. But, Davis, no matter what innocent purpose was behind her evening out, would freak out when he found out that she was going to dinner with Grant, and it didn't help her case that

Grant looked like he stepped right off the cover of *GQ*. She weighed her options. Maybe it was best to not mention her plans for the night to Davis. She didn't want to make things worse between them, and based off past experiences, he would end up accusing her of cheating on him right off the bat and that held no appeal whatsoever.

"Stop overthinking all of this crap!" She yelled at her reflection in the rearview mirror.

To be honest, she wouldn't have liked it either if Davis hung out with a co-ed all evening, but the difference between the simple jealousy to which she'd fall prey and Davis' likely accusations of cheating was a major trust factor. She trusted him to make the right decisions, but since her first trip to LA, Davis seemed wary of trusting her in pretty much any new situation.

After sitting through way too much LA traffic and taking too long to figure out the still confusing, keyless entry to the building, she raced up to her apartment. Throwing her stuff in a pile as soon as she dashed through the door, her eyes caught a glimpse of the vivid numbers blaring from the oven's digital clock. It was already half past six! She had to get a move on it and jump in the shower if she wanted to be ready before Grant arrived to pick her up.

Picking through her clothes hanging in the bedroom's infinitesimal closet, she wondered what in the world was she going to wear. The weather was warm, especially for March, but it could get a lot cooler once the sun set. After leaning hard toward a chambray shirt and leggings, she settled on a pair of nude lace shorts and a mint blouse. She rummaged around a little more and found a bleached linen blazer and nude ankle boots that would finish out the look and keep her from freezing to death if the night air took a chilly turn.

She selected jewelry, too. She liked to have everything picked out before she started getting ready so she wouldn't get all frantic and start sweating makeup off when she couldn't find anything that she needed. Unrolling her jewelry travel bag, she pulled out a long gold and pearl necklace and a skinny gold chain with an antique locket that paired nicely with her neutrals and the mint top. A pair of classic pearl earrings was all she needed to go with the intricate statement necklaces.

Once she'd laid everything out on the bed, she ran to the bathroom "conveniently" located on the other side of the apartment, peeling off clothes and tossing them wherever they landed on the way. She showered, blow-dried her hair, and proceeded to the beauty routine she dreaded the most—hot rolling her hair. In the midst of the tedious process of covering her head in thick rollers, she never failed to make a mental appointment to get her hair chopped off, but the end results always changed her mind. Hot rollers may have been old school, but they gave her bouncy, even-curled, Victoria Secret model hair in a way no wand, curling iron or other hair tool ever could.

While the rollers did their thing, she did her makeup. Going for a natural look, she added neutral, shimmery eyeshadow to her lids, and went only a little heavier on the eyeliner than normal. A little illuminator, lip tint and some shiny gloss and she was done.

Sticking her phone in the speaker dock, she turned on her "Going Out" playlist. With the rollers still in her hair, she sang and danced around the bathroom in the short robe she'd gotten two Christmases ago from her mom. The plush gray robe with her initials monogrammed in a blush pink went everywhere with her. As she swung her arms up in happy abandon, she caught her reflection in the mirror and laughed out loud. Grant was right—she'd just stick to the steps they rehearsed from that point forward.

Evie pulled out the rollers and watched in awe as the curls bounced down her back after she finished her impromptu dance party. Hot rollers had to be made of magic or fairy dust. Something along those lines anyway. Once she was satisfied with her face and hair given her time constraints, she crossed the living area and headed back to the bedroom. She shouldn't be so worried about what she looked like, but on some subconscious level she cared way more than she should and there was nothing to be done about that. Subconscious thoughts were hard to control.

In her tiny, temporary apartment, the sleeping area was separated by a half wall from the rest of the home, affording a modicum of privacy. She dressed quickly in the outfit and shoes waiting for her, spritzed perfume into the air, and walked right through it.

Checking her appearance one more time in the mirrored closet doors as the fresh scent of crisp apples settled into her skin, she was pretty sure she'd covered every detail from the top of her long, bouncy tresses to the bottom of her ankle boots.

"You'll pass," she teased, winking at her reflection. Now she was talking to herself. Oh Lord. Maybe Grant was right. It might not be too good for her to be by herself all the time.

Another song filled the air as she transferred everything she might need for the evening from her big Kate Spade bag into a small leather clutch. She busied herself checking over the contents of her bag while waiting for Grant, trying to dispel that "waiting on a hot date" feeling she couldn't seem to escape.

CHAPTER FOUR

Checking out her new surroundings accompanied by Grant, who had offered himself up as her personal guide, filled Evie's veins with excited energy. She couldn't keep still—nervously pacing the small apartment as her ears listened closely for the sound of the buzzer. She'd stayed in LA a few months ago, but the schedule and tapings for *America Sings* were rigorous—allowing for very little down time or nervous pacing and offering her no chance to explore the city.

Besides, she'd lived in dormitory style housing, rooming with the other female contestants. She and the other girls were young and generally stuck together— never venturing too far from their dorm or the network's studio, which was further off the beaten path than the *Song & Dance* taping locations.

The loud buzzing noise filled the apartment and jarred her senses. She hurried to press the button, allowing Grant entrance to the building. A moment later, she rushed to the door, and opened it to a smiling, dapper Grant standing on the rubber welcome mat. His smile faltered for a fraction of a second when he caught sight of her, but then he swallowed, and it was back in place, showing off his pearly whites and that cute little dimple of his.

"Hi, you. Long time, no see," he joked.

She laughed. "It has been ages, hasn't it?" He brought out the silly side of her.

"Far too long. By the way, you look amazing, Evie. Are you about ready to get going?" he asked, still standing in the corridor.

"Yes, pretty much. Do you want to come in for a second while I grab my stuff?"

Grant nodded as he stepped into the apartment, looking around the small space.

"It's little, but it's home," she explained in a singsong voice as she headed back to the bedroom to grab her phone from its charger.

"Somehow, you've managed to make it very girly in here." His deep voice called out from across the apartment.

"Weird. I haven't added or moved a thing," she said with an eyebrow arched, returning to where he stood by the door with his hands thrust into his pockets.

"Maybe, your girliness just permeates the air around you," he teased.

Evie threw her head back and laughed freely. "I'm not all that girly," she defended.

Grant raised his eyebrows. "I beg to differ."

She'd never thought of herself as being super girly. Feminine, yes, but not girly. Maybe Grant saw her that way since he was older and seemed to be wise in the ways of the world. Or maybe it was just her Southern roots showing? In the deep south, she didn't seem all that Southern, but in LA she'd already noticed her own differences in comparison to those around her.

"Ready to go now?" he asked again, offering her his arm. As she linked her arm through his, the familiar shiver of excitement raced up her spine the way it did every time her skin touched his would hurry up and fade on away. She had to get over it. The sooner the better.

Keeping that theory in mind, she squeezed his arm and nodded.

"Where are we going?" she asked as they walked in tandem to the elevator.

"We're having dinner with a few other cast members, and then we're going to this great place for karaoke if you're up for it."

"Ooh, that sounds like fun!" she exclaimed. Dinner and singing? What could be better?

They stood close as they rode the elevator down to the parking deck below her apartment building. Just as Evie decided it best to put some additional space between the two of them, Grant turned to her.

"Have I told you how nice you look this evening?" Grant asked, picking up one of Evie's bouncy curls from where it hung over her shoulder, playing with the silky strands between his fingers.

"Anything is an improvement from being sweat-soaked like I was earlier at practice." Her face grew red as she felt the hair fall from his hand and brush against her neck. She shivered again at the close contact. Did he feel this? Did he think that she was being flirty? She'd wanted to dress to impress, but maybe he thought that she was trying to allure him. That was in no way the message she wanted to send.

When she looked down, studying her shoes with intense scrutiny, he tilted her chin up with his hand, forcing her to look at him.

"Evie, you're drop dead gorgeous, and we've got serious chemistry. Don't worry, it's a good thing. Don't be shy about it, we have to own it," he said, searching her eyes. Her breath caught in her throat.

"Okay," she half whispered, her voice cracking. The elevator doors opened silently, breaking whatever mystical trance Grant placed her under on their ride down. He could have told her that potatoes were brown or explained the process of osmosis and she'd want to know everything about it just to stay in that moment, under his intense gaze, his eyes locked on hers as he spoke. Like the perfect gentleman that he was, Grant waited for her to exit the elevator first.

In the parking deck, he rested a light, but secure hand on the small of her back as he guided her to his car. He opened the passenger door for her before walking around to the driver's seat of his black Aston Martin. As he started the car, a tidal wave of guilt crashed over her. Between the moment in the elevator, his gentle touches and her musings about how ridiculously hot he was, this felt a lot like a date, which added reason number 809 as to why it was best that she not tell Davis about her evening out. Feeling guilty, she bit her lip and looked out the window as the street came into view.

"What's the matter?" Grant asked as he pulled onto the main highway. Evie turned to face him, her mouth popping open. How did he figure out that something was wrong without her saying a word? She couldn't possibly be that easy to read! They'd been in the car for less than a minute—and they'd known each other for less than a day. He must have had a sixth sense or something.

"Nothing," she lied.

"Why are you lying to me?" he asked so quickly and casually that it took her a second to comprehend his words. Now, she was sure he had a sixth sense.

"Why do you assume that I'm lying to you?" she countered after a long pause ensued.

"Evie, I'm really good at reading people, and you're my main focus during this competition, which means I'm going to get really good at reading you in particular. It's not that hard anyway—your face is like an open book, and right now it's screaming that something is bothering you."

She let out a sigh of frustration. She didn't want to talk about what was bothering her, but he'd put her on the spot.

When several moments passed and she'd yet to say anything, he ventured, "Here's my theory—it's just the two of us, we have this great chemistry, heading out for the evening together feels like a date, and you're worrying about what your boyfriend will think. That's pretty much the gist of it, right?"

She stared at him, her mouth open. Grant's calm, casual delivery of his synopsis shocked her. He drove her crazy. He'd spelled out her feelings and her exact problem, all while acting as casual as if he was offering her a piece of gum. Evie cleared her throat, still taken aback at his far too accurate assessment.

"Yes, if you must know, that pretty much sums it up," she confessed, shifting in the leather seat.

"Evie, I told you already—you have nothing to be worried about. We are strictly in the friend zone where we're going to stay, and we're meeting up with other people for dinner. Quit stressing out so much." He nudged her arm with his elbow. She rolled her eyes but shook her head and smiled at him.

"I know that, Grant, but it doesn't change how my boyfriend would view the situation. I don't think I'm going to tell him about tonight just to avoid having to justify something innocent," she explained. She didn't want to bash Davis to Grant, but as her partner, he needed to know where she was coming from and why she was concerned. Evie didn't like the way it sounded coming out of her mouth—her words made Davis sound like a controlling jerk. He wasn't though, they'd just had issues, that's all.

"Not to, you know, get all up in your business or anything, but that doesn't sound like the healthiest of relationships," Grant pointed out after a moment of awkward silence.

"We have our issues, but who doesn't? Is everything always rosy with . . . Kacie, that's her name, isn't it?"

"I see someone did their homework," Grant said, raising an eyebrow. Evie knew exactly what he was doing—avoiding answering the question about his own relationship. So, she used one of his tactics and settled in to wait out an acceptable answer.

However, her question remained unanswered since they'd reached their destination. Evie assumed they had, anyway, since Grant pulled the car into a circular valet drop off in front of a fancy-looking outdoor mall.

"Where are we?" she asked, but before he told her, a valet attendant opened the car door for her.

"Welcome to The Grove, ma'am," he said as he helped her out of Grant's car.

She waited on the cobblestoned walk for Grant while he spoke briefly with the valet. When Grant finished, he strode over to where she stood. A light, but crisp, breeze hit her bare legs, causing goosebumps. Despite the warmth of the day, a distinct chill was in the air now that twilight had settled.

"We only have a short walk to the restaurant. I hope you like Italian," he informed her, putting his arm snugly around her shoulders, rubbing up and down her arm. She took advantage of the shared warmth, huddling against his side as they kept a brisk pace. Her earlier inhibitions were the least of her concerns with the nip in the air smacking her exposed legs with each step she took.

"I'm really regretting wearing these shorts tonight," she mumbled as they turned a corner and a lovely courtyard, complete with a huge fountain, came into view. She longed for the leggings and top she'd considered wearing, picturing the outfit still hanging in her closet.

"It's a little cooler than normal tonight, but if it's any consolation, every guy that's walked passed us can't take his eyes off of you," he said in a low voice, leaning in close to share the confidential information. "You've got some killer legs."

A blush crept across her cheeks and suddenly she wasn't so cold. She peered around the courtyard—just now realizing how many people probably recognize them or, at least, him anyway. As they'd been walking, her focus had been on how cold she was—she'd completely forgotten that they were in his main stomping grounds. Grant was a well-recognized television personality and people took notice when he walked by. Sure enough, as she looked around, she saw people from every direction staring at them—some casually, while others outright gawked.

It still felt weird to her that she was a little bit of a "star" in her own right. Just seven months ago, she was a basic college girl starting her senior year. Now, she walked through The Grove in LA with Grant Merritt's arm around her headed to dinner on a weeknight like it was par for the course.

"Let's hurry and get inside—we're running a few minutes late," he said, pulling her across the courtyard before scooting inside a crowded Italian restaurant. Grant grabbed her hand and pulled her through the crowd, making his way to the hostess' stand.

"We're with the *Song & Dance* party," he told the sophisticated brunette wearing a black suit. Her eyes lit up immediately at the sight of semi-celebrities.

"Why, hello! Grant, we're so glad you're here! I must tell you—I can't wait for the season to start! This must be your partner. . ." she trailed off in her faint exotic accent as she took in Evie.

"Yes, this is Evie Michaelson," Grant filled in the blanks for their overly-friendly hostess, putting his arm lightly around Evie's waist with the introduction. Touchy feely was an understatement. Dancers were the touchiest feeliest. Evie smiled brightly at the hostess.

"Nice to meet you, Evie," the hostess replied, studying Evie as if still trying hard to place who she was.

"I've got it! You were on that singing show, weren't you?" she exclaimed, snapping her fingers when it finally came to her.

"Yep, that would be me," Evie admitted, looking away once she noticed the hostess making suggestive eyes at Grant even while she'd addressed Evie. What else was she supposed to do? Stand there and stare awkwardly as the lovely dark-haired girl ogled her partner?

"Do you mind showing us to our table?" Grant asked. Evie silently thanked him for getting the hostess back on her task. Clearly, the woman had a thing for Grant, and although Evie understood, it didn't make it any less weird. The hostess continued to eye Grant down like he was a slice of cake and she hadn't had a carb since 2013. Her sleek ponytail bobbed up and down as she motioned for Grant and Evie to follow her to their table.

"Thanks for putting an end to that," Evie said softly. This time, she was the one whispering in his ear. Except, it wasn't all smooth like the way it was when he did it. Grant was at least six inches taller than her, so she was eye level with his lips in her low-heeled boots. She had to lean up and balance herself on his shoulder to get close to his ear.

He smiled and leaned down to her. "No problem, anytime," he whispered back with exaggeration, patting her hand and sharing a secret smile between the two of them. For the first time, she noticed his eyes crinkled when he smiled.

When they made it to their table at the back of the dim restaurant where the crowd thinned, the scene caught her off guard. She'd been expecting more people to be at dinner. Only two men and two women were seated at the round table.

As soon as they took their seats, Grant went around the table and introduced everyone to Evie. "Evie, I'd like you to meet my good friend, Jared, his partner, Amelia Berry, and to her left is my buddy, Adam, and his partner, Nell Fielding. Everyone, this is Evie Michaelson, my lovely and talented partner this season."

Evie smiled at everyone, trying to study faces and make eye contact, but it was hard in the candlelight and recessed lighting to do so. Jared and Adam were familiar faces from the show, and she liked that Grant introduced them as his friends, especially since it seemed genuine. The two guys were both attractive, but not in the dark, muscular, smoldering Grant way.

She also recognized Amelia Berry. Back in Evie's middle school days, Amelia was the reigning queen of pop. Even though she'd never owned any of Amelia's albums, she had downloaded a few of her hit songs over the years. Her song, "Get It, Girl," had been her seventh-grade jam.

Amelia, in her early thirties, looked prettier to Evie now than she did back at the height of her popularity. She'd been known for a severely short bob that was always changing from neon pink to electric blue to highlighter yellow to match her flamboyant clothes and fluorescent shaded lipstick. However, the demure woman seated across from Evie smiling sweetly to those around her had pale, blonde hair cut in an adorable, soft style that framed her face, and she was wearing a classy black blouse with pearls.

Evie couldn't place Nell, but she sensed that Nell would be her fiercest competition. They had to be roughly the same age, and with her jet black, glossy hair and hourglass figure, Nell possessed magnetism and she knew it. Her striking blue eyes were identical to the vivid, cobalt dress she wore, which happened to have a plunging neckline that came to a stop somewhere near her belly button. It wasn't a surprise that much of the wait staff and restaurant patrons couldn't keep their eyes off her, but it made Evie super uncomfortable. What if the dress slipped? Evie worried for Nell's sake about a wardrobe malfunction, even though Nell wasn't the least bit concerned.

Out of curiosity, Evie studied Grant's reaction to Nell. Sitting back quietly, she observed as Nell tried to strike up a flirty conversation with Grant the second they were settled, making sure to lean forward so that it would be impossible for him not to be aware of what she had on full display.

"Grant, I've heard so much about you," Nell purred seductively. Evie nearly gagged at having to watch yet another obvious attempt to pick up her partner. Distaste was written all over her face if Grant was right about her expressions being easy to read.

"Well, I hope it was all good," Grant chuckled. As the words left his mouth, he slung his arm across the back of Evie's chair and rested his hand on her shoulder, turning slightly away from Nell to focus on the animated story Jared was sharing about his and Amelia's reveal taping. Grant's blatant brush off didn't sit well with the vixen apparently used to being the center of attention and getting any man she wanted.

"Well, well. You must be pretty good on and off the dance floor, hmm?" Nell queried with an arched eyebrow directed at Evie. She then had the audacity to snicker at Evie's startled look. Was she assuming that she and Grant were . . .?

Oh goodness, Evie looked down at her lap, mortified and growing red. And angry. Hot tears pricked her eyes, making her even angrier at herself for letting the catty girl's insults embarrass her. She was implying…good grief! What if others thought that? Maybe she should announce to the table that she was still a virgin. She cringed at *that* thought and the fresh assault it would bring. Her own chastity aside, what gave this girl the right to accuse her of anything even if she and Grant were in a relationship? Not that they were. They each had their own relationships. Separate from each other. How dare Nell imply that she would… that he would…ugh! In less than a day of knowing one another at that! To make matters worse, Grant overheard Nell's inappropriate and embarrassing dig.

Angry tension emanated from her partner. His arm swung off the back of her chair and he leaned over the table to look Nell straight in the eyes. His hands clenched the edge of the farmhouse style table. Evie was glad she wasn't Nell. She touched Grant's arm lightly, hoping he'd calm down a bit.

"Look, Nell, I don't know what you're over here trying to insinuate to my partner, but just in case you're not aware, you've crossed a serious line," Grant warned her in a low, cold voice. Everyone at their table fell silent, watching the exchange. Nell sat dumbfounded as Grant stared her down. She looked ashamed. Served her right for trying to start something.

"Why don't we order some drinks?" Adam asked, waving their server over, breaking the heavy tension that his partner instigated.

"I think that's a great idea," Amelia chimed in sweetly. The awkwardness slowly dissipated as small talk filled the silence at their table once again. Everyone started sharing their back stories and what led them to the show, and soon the mishap with Nell was forgotten.

"Did you know that you're the youngest competitor this season?" Nell asked Evie after she had finished telling her own brief story. Nell hadn't said much since Grant put her in her place, but her cold glare directed at Evie said everything. Waiting for Evie's response, Nell took an exaggerated sip of her gin and tonic. Evie's brow furrowed in confusion. Was that supposed to be an insult?

Evie sipped on her water, dragging out her response to Nell's question. Why Nell chose to single her out, she had no idea—other than the fact that she had the hots for Grant, and perhaps she thought Evie put a kink in her plan to hook up with him. If that was the reason, Nell needed to get over that fast and realize the truth—there was nothing but friendship between her and Grant. The next few weeks or months of competition could be enjoyable for all involved if it didn't get vicious.

"I didn't know that, but it doesn't bother me," Evie finally replied with a small shrug. What else she could say since it wasn't really an insult? Sure, she personally felt the sting since what she wanted more than anything else was to be considered a legit artist, and not a naïve kid who didn't know what they were doing, but Nell didn't know that, nor would she ever find out. Nell's attempt at age discrimination really could've been viewed as a compliment if someone else would've said it. Her youth was a strength, not a weakness in this competition, she reminded herself.

Thankfully, their entrees arrived before any other barbed remarks or questions slipped off the tip of

Nell's tongue. As everyone ate, the conversation flowed smoothly as the pros told interesting stories from previous seasons of the show, mixing in helpful tips for their partners this season. The rest of the table had picked up on the way Nell continued to try and bait Evie every chance she got, so they made pointed efforts to keep Nell from spinning the conversation out of control again. They couldn't, however, stop the icy glares Nell shot in Evie's direction throughout the rest of the meal.

Once plates were cleared, their waiter stopped by the table to ask if any of them wanted to see the dessert menu, but the poor guy was met with a resounding, "No, thank you," from the entire group. The dinner she'd anticipated with excitement ended up being a ridiculously stressful experience. It would take a while for her stomach to unknot—she'd only managed to eat a few forkfuls of the delicious eggplant lasagna.

"May I please have our check?" Grant asked the server, pointing to himself and Evie. Normally, she would put up a fight about him paying for her meal, but she didn't have the energy to do so. The less she said in front of Nell, the better.

The waiter nodded and hurried off to get their check.

"So, are we headed to EB's for karaoke?" Jared asked the rest of the table, trying to lighten the mood. Oh my. So wrapped up in the uncomfortableness of dinner, she'd forgotten about the plans for the evening to continue on somewhere else. Her shoulders slumped. Why had she decided to leave her apartment tonight?

"Actually, Evie and I probably need to call it an early night—we have a lot going on tomorrow and need to get some rest," Grant said with hesitation in his voice, "If that's okay with you," he added, shooting a questioning glance at Evie.

"I'm sure she's ready to call it a night with you," Nell remarked, implying that Grant was being suggestive. Either Nell had had one too many drinks, or she was just plain stupid.

"That's fine with me," Evie replied, looking directly at Grant and ignoring Nell. She nudged Grant's knee beneath the table, hoping that he would catch her hint and ignore Nell, too. It wasn't easy for him—his jaw clenched again, and his eyes darkened, but he kept his mouth shut.

"I get it, no problem, man," Jared said, casually rolling his eyes and nudging his head in Nell's direction.

"I'm in if you're in," Nell told Adam, and he half-heartedly nodded his agreement, which meant Grant and Evie were the only ones bowing out of their pre-arranged plans. Evie didn't feel bad about it, though. Even if the evening was coming to an early close, at least she didn't have to go anywhere else with that intoxicated girl hell-bent on getting under her skin. Nell would've turned a fun night of karaoke into a ridiculous, cutthroat competition before the night was over.

After everyone settled up with their server, they left collectively as a group, but as soon as the group reached the outdoor courtyard, Grant and Evie said a brief goodbye to the others as they headed in the direction of the karaoke bar.

When they were out of earshot, Grant turned to her and put his hands on her shoulders.

"I'm so, so sorry," he said, his eyes full of regret.

"What do you have to be sorry for?" she asked, perplexed. She searched her mind, trying to recall him doing something that would've offended her.

"Dinner was a train wreck. I have no idea why Nell felt the need to single you out and make those kind of comments, but it wasn't right or fair of her," he explained.

Evie shrugged. "You're right. Dinner was awful, and Nell wasn't nice at all, but there isn't anything I can do about it, and it sure wasn't your fault. I think she's jealous because she has a thing for you."

"I agree with the jealousy thing, but I don't think it has to do with me. Her career has kind of stalled, and I've heard a few rumors swirling that you're the next big thing, a breakout star, up and coming—all that good stuff. You're her competition—both on and off of the show," he said as they started walking again.

"I didn't recognize her, but she sure is gorgeous. She has that going for her, and she doesn't have any reason to be jealous of me. Also, someone needs to let her know that you have a girlfriend who isn't me."

Grant shook his head. "I don't think you're getting it. Yeah, Nell looks good, but you don't see yourself the way others do, Evie. When you walk by, people can't help but stare. You have this . . . light about you that draws people to you like a moth to a flame. Nell does not have that."

Speaking of flames, her cheeks were on fire. He'd made her blush . . . once again and evaded talking about his girlfriend . . . once again.

"Once you figure it out, you'll be unstoppable," he added before completely switching gears as he peered around at the still crowded courtyard. "We don't really have to call it a night, you know. I just knew karaoke with Nell would have been supreme torture for you."

"I appreciated that. Nell was going to use it as another opportunity to make me miserable."

"Yep, I figured that, but since it's not even ten yet, do you want to do something else instead?"

"What do you have in mind?"

"We didn't have dessert."

"That's true, we didn't, and it's a shame. I have a huge sweet tooth," she confided, nudging him. He put his arm around her, rubbing up and down to ward off the chill again, and she burrowed into his side. Figuring out the weather and how best to dress for it would take a minute.

"There happens to be a cupcake shop not too far from here," he said with a surprising amount of enthusiasm while turning them around and heading in the opposite direction.

"Cupcakes sound much more exciting than karaoke, anyway," she said, the spring in her step returning.

"I couldn't agree with you more after that dinner we just suffered through. It wasn't the best representation of how the cast usually treats one another. Jared and Adam are both good friends of mine, and from what Jared's told me, Amelia is a lot of fun. Nell, on the other hand, put a bad taste in my mouth right from the second we sat down," Grant told her candidly.

"Yeah, she was my problem, end of story. I'm not going to hold it against her, but I'm not going to seek out a friendship with her, either. I think it's best if I just avoid being around her as much as possible."

"That's easier said than done. After morning rehearsals and our wardrobe consult tomorrow, we have a group practice for the show's opening number," he informed her as they walked.

She frowned.

"Hey, it isn't all that bad. I'll work with Nala, the head choreographer on the number, and see if she can place you in formation far away from her," he added as they approached the tiny, fragrant shop. Evie inhaled the sugary scent of frosting and cinnamon floating in the air and instantly felt better about life.

"When's our first song rehearsal?" Evie asked him as they scoped out the selections in the bakery case. After a quick skim, she decided to go with red velvet—a classic that never disappointed.

"Tomorrow evening, if that's alright with you. I try not to have sessions scheduled past five or six if we can help it, but I think we'll both feel better once we get a vocal practice under our belts, too," he said and she nodded her agreement. Between practicing and consults, they were going to be together from sun up to sun down the following day. "I think I'm going with the chocolate hazelnut," he added.

They stepped in line behind a couple of people to place their order. While they waited, a young girl walked up to them. Her high ponytail bounced with excitement.

"Oh my gosh! You're Grant from *Song & Dance*! I am your biggest fan! Will you take a picture with me?" Her words tumbled out, all bubbly and adorable. She couldn't have been more than twelve, reminding Evie of the fan on her flight the day before.

"Of course, I'll take a picture with you. Would you also like to meet my partner for this season? The season starts back up this Tuesday night, you know. I hope you'll be watching and rooting us on," he told the tween while she waved her camera-holding mother over. Grant put an arm around the girl's shoulders and smiled.

"I sure will! You can always count on our votes, Grant." She beamed up at him. Grant was this girl's celebrity crush—maybe her first one ever—and the way he was so genuine and kind as he took his time to chat with her was incredible. The girl would remember that moment for the rest of her life. Evie would've been the same way had it been Zac Efron, her first big celebrity crush.

Although Evie's heart swelled at the scene between Grant and his little fan, her mind struggled. Why did Grant keep on giving her reasons to adore him even more? That moth to a flame metaphor he said about her earlier summed up her feelings about him. Not that she would ever admit that to anyone, especially Grant! He'd just see her as a young, naïve girl with a silly crush on her dance partner. So, her number one goal was to quash the feels she had for Grant and get her head fully back in the game. He was worldly, sophisticated and was—the most important thing to remember—taken. Just like she was, she reminded herself.

Grant introduced her to the girl and her mother, and after they exchanged a few pleasantries, the mom and daughter politely retreated, letting Evie and Grant place their order. He paid once again, even though she offered to get it—especially since he'd bought her dinner.

"Evie, please, the least I can do is treat you to dinner and dessert after putting you through the wrath of Nell earlier," he informed her, brooking no arguments.

"Thanks, Grant. That's so nice of you. It isn't your fault that the evening wasn't . . . all that pleasant. At least it is now," she said, her smile broad and unapologetic, just like the younger fan's expression a few minutes earlier. No matter how much she told herself to get it under control, her ridiculous feelings sped ahead like a train with no brakes, and she'd only known him for a single day. Heck, less than a day.

Grant's company was the best and she recognized the throes of infatuation when she felt them. She could talk to him about almost anything, and he constantly made her laugh. Although dinner really had been atrocious, being out with Grant was pure fun so far.

They ordered their cupcakes to go since there were no seats open in the cramped and crowded bakery.

"Do you want to eat these now?" he asked her when they were outside again. She inhaled the scent of cake from the small white box in his hands.

"As amazing as those smell, could we wait 'til we get back to my place? It's a little too windy and cold out here."

"Yeah, you're right. We can wait."

They hurried to the valet and waited under the heated pavilion as the attendant retrieved Grant's car. Once they were all settled and on their way back to her apartment, she relaxed. Between the recent time change, and the jam-packed day they'd had, beyond exhausted didn't come close to covering the level of tired she was. She sank into the supple leather seat like it was a warm embrace. They were scheduled to be at the studio at 7:30 the next morning, and her eyes grew heavy thinking about how good her bed would feel tonight—even if she wouldn't get to spend nearly enough time in it.

"Tired?" Grant asked as they sat at a red light.

"I'm slap worn out. It's been a crazy couple of days."

"It's going to take you a while to get used to your new schedule. LA is a couple of hours behind Alabama isn't it? It feels way later than it actually is to you," he pointed out. Her eyes almost crossed, she was so sleepy.

"Mm-hmm," she mumbled, closing her eyes and resting her head on the back of the seat.

She hadn't meant to fall asleep, but unfortunately, the next thing she knew, her eyes cracked open as a hand gently shook her shoulder. Her eyes rebelled and closed tight when hit with the bright fluorescent lights of the parking deck.

"Evie, wake up, we're back." Grant's soothing voice pulled her from her solid, full on REM cycle slumber.

Evie's eyes finally opened, and she gazed around, disoriented, trying to gage her surroundings. Still in his car, dead to the world only ten seconds earlier, her mind grappled to understand where she was and what was happening. Talk about embarrassing.

"I'm so sorry—I didn't mean to fall asleep like that," she said, her voice low and throaty with sleep as she wiped her mouth. Still captured in the tug of deep slumber, her words and actions came slow and only through great effort. Everything had a dreamlike, hazy quality, which was the only reason she wasn't utterly mortified when she realized she'd been drooling.

"No worries. I know you're tired, and I honestly feel bad having to wake you up. Let me help you up to your apartment," he said before hopping out of the car and jogging around the car to open her door for her.

"Are you sure you don't want to come in for a few minutes? I can make coffee and we can eat cupcakes," she offered half-heartedly. With great effort, Evie willed herself out of the car. Her legs felt like lead and her head, foggy with fatigue. She rested heavily on Grant, her cheek against his shoulder.

"I think jet lag has caught up with you rather quick like, and you really need to get some sleep—we have a busy day tomorrow, and we need you rested," he told her as they slowly made their way to the elevator.

"I guess you're right. I probably wouldn't be much fun to talk to anyway. I'd more than likely fall asleep mid-sentence." She yawned, unable to help herself.

"I'd like to see that," he smirked.

"Ha ha. Grant, you don't have to ride up with me. I'm tired, not incapacitated," she said as the elevator opened.

"I beg to differ—you're almost completely dead weight," he argued, securing his grip around her waist before he continued, "besides, I'd never just drop you off in a parking deck and leave. I was raised better than that."

"Your parents did a good job with you, Grant. You've been quite the gentleman tonight," she said dreamily. In a state of sheer exhaustion, she questioned if maybe this was all a dream—especially since she was being held by a hot guy she barely knew, far away from her home and everything familiar.

"It's easy when you're with the perfect example of a lady."

The smile spreading across her face and the unfiltered adoration shining in her eyes as she leaned against him gave away her crush on him, but she didn't really care in that moment. Her lack of sleep lowered her inhibitions, like if she'd been drunk. She'd only been drunk once—thanks to an out of control frat party a couple of years ago, and never wanted to repeat the experience again. Grant cleared his throat and his eyes broke away from hers, ending the dreamy moment.

"Everything okay?" she asked as the tension reached a ridiculous level. She rested her hand against his chest, missing the closeness. He seemed so far away now.

"It's getting late," he replied, shifting away from her. Grant was lying, but too tired to really push for a better explanation, she kept silent. The elevator doors opened and they stepped into the fourth floor corridor.

"I can tell you're lying," she murmured as they headed in the direction of her door. She felt a little more alert, and his sudden freeze out gnawed at her.

"I don't know what you mean," he replied, feigning confusion.

"Something is wrong," she spelled out for him, wide awake now.

"No, nothing's wrong. Everything is right," Grant said with a smile, but the smile didn't reach his eyes. There were no crinkles.

"Well, on that note, I suppose we should call it a night," she replied, taking the last few steps to her door.

"Be thinking about song options, okay? We have to turn them in for production approval as early as possible tomorrow if we want to start practicing," he said as she unlocked her door.

"I will. Goodnight, Grant," she said, her voice short.

Grant nodded to himself, seeming to resolve to something of which she wasn't aware.

"Goodnight, Evie," he replied, a wistful note to his voice.

Evie closed the door, sank back against it and sighed.

CHAPTER FIVE

Grant checked his watch as he and Evie finished up lunch at the commissary on the studio lot the next day. Their wardrobe consult was supposed to start in twenty minutes and being late wasn't an option. It was an unspoken rule that no dancer ever crossed that line. Everyone—contestant and professional alike—were duly warned that being late to wardrobe was a cardinal sin.

So far, the morning after his and Evie's . . . interesting evening had been awkward at best, and uncomfortable and stiff at its worst. Grant didn't want to hold her at arm's length, but the immediate chemistry between the two of them was like nothing he'd experienced with any of his past partners, and he felt himself teetering dangerously on the edge of full-fledged falling for Evie.

That was not acceptable.

Nothing like this had ever happened to him before, and he had to cool things down pronto. Especially if they were only half way through the second day they'd ever spent together.

For crying out loud. He was a professional and a well-adjusted, grown man and he needed to nip this in the bud. Evie was young, innocent and had a lot to learn regarding the ways of the world—especially the world of entertainment.

He knew better than to spend even a second entertaining the feelings that stirred inside of him last night in the elevator when she had gazed up at him with those sparkling eyes of hers, her full lips curving into a mysterious smile.

They connected on a level that would zoom past friendship before they knew what hit them if he didn't tread with extreme caution from that point forward. He wasn't sure where Evie stood on the matter, but he'd never had feelings so fast and deep for anyone—his current, on again/off again girlfriend, Kacie included. He and Evie barely knew one another, and his feelings were already venturing into serious and dangerous territory. That scared him out of his wits, to say the least. There were so many reasons that the rapid tumble of feelings needed to be put in check before they really wreaked some havoc.

First of all, he was Evie's professional dance partner, and second of all, she had a boyfriend. Thirdly, he was a good bit older than she was. Then, there was his own girlfriend to consider, as well. He hadn't mentioned much about her to Evie, and he wasn't exactly sure why, but he cared about Kacie, of that he was certain. He enjoyed their comfortable relationship —even if Kacie had been hinting that she wanted more from him. But what she wanted was always more than he was willing to give. He wasn't interested in settling down, getting married or any of that at this point in his life. It's not that he wanted to date other women or anything, he just wanted to focus on his career, and be free to do what he wanted when he wanted. Therefore, he and Kacie cycled through the same arguments over and over, which would lead to their breaking up and getting back together at least every six months or so. The relationship wasn't something he wanted to share with his beautiful new partner.

Get a grip, dude, he thought to himself. The rampant feelings he had for an off-limits girl were ending right then and there. He would will it to be so. It made no sense for him to pine over her like a lovestruck teen. They were adults. Professionals. She was taken, and so was he. All of his very valid reasons were supposed to make the logical decision to shut down his emotions easy, but instead, unbidden thoughts popped into his mind. Like remembering how perfect her hand felt in his while they rehearsed the jive, or how she fidgeted with her shirt hem when she was nervous, and just how much he enjoyed every single moment with her the night before.

He needed to forget all that, though. Just bide his time, remain kind and civil, but hope that the infatuation with this beauty would hurry up and get out of his system before it messed with their partnership dynamics. Their chemistry would make or break them—kept in check, it would send them easily to the finals, allowed to run wild, there would be an explosion. With casualties. He resolved to view her as a student, someone he could mentor going forward. That would be best for the both of them.

"I hope production approves 'Say Something,'" he remarked, taking a sip of his iced green tea.

"Me, too," she replied, a flicker of life in her eyes at the mention of their proposed song. If they couldn't talk about a myriad of off-limit issues, at least they could discuss their work. That was what truly mattered anyway.

"Here's my ideas so far—I think it would be great to start out with a single, warm spotlight on just you at the piano. We'll stay true to the essence of the song, so I'll stand to your side, but kind of behind you, like I'm singing to you without you knowing," he spouted off quickly. His eyes were bright with excitement as he shared his plan for the song. Evie leaned forward in her seat, mesmerized, as he painted the scene.

"Ooh, yeah. I like where this is going. I think there should be lots of Edison bulb pendant lights hanging from above, but other than that, no props or sets. Don't you think?" She added.

He pointed with both fingers at her across the table in excitement, "YES! You are completely right. That's all we need."

She continued, excited, "Even though the chords are simple, I still need to start practicing as soon as possible."

"I'll go over what we've talked about with the set designer later, but I'm sure they'll clear our ideas. Basically, all we're going to need is a baby grand, a little foggy mist and some lights," he told her as she forked up the last few bites of her Greek salad.

"I like how this performance will be a stark contrast from our jive. It will show versatility," she pointed out as she gathered up the remains of her lunch.

"Insightful, Evie. It will give you a definite edge in the competition. We don't want to hold anything back, period. If we want to win, we've got to give it everything we have, no holds barred, each and every week." His intense and motivational words affected Evie—she sat up straight in the wooden seat and pushed her shoulders back.

"I'm not even going as far as to think about winning. I just don't want to be eliminated the very first week," she admitted before taking a sip of water. Grant shook his head.

"I'm not even worried about that at all. Trust me, we aren't going to be eliminated this week. I'll be more shocked if we don't make it all the way to the finale," he confided, "and I'm not exaggerating," he added while she stared at him as if horns grew from his crop of dark hair.

He rolled his eyes. "We've got to hustle. It's time to head over to wardrobe," he told her, checking his watch. They made quick work of clearing off their table. Grant broke into a brisk jog once they were outdoors.

"I'm pretty sure you're enjoying torturing me!"

An out of breath Evie rested her hands on her knees when they stopped to wait at a light. He laughed and picked up his speed to a sprint before slowing to a light jog, then picking the speed back up again as they made their way to wardrobe across the lot. It never hurt to get in a little extra cardio to build endurance.

They made good time—actually arriving a few minutes early for their wardrobe consult. That alone was worth the murderous look Evie trained in his direction.

Once settled inside the wardrobe bungalow with its comfy chairs and quick-change tents, Evie struggled to catch her breath as she wiped her face with the bottom of her shirt. She scowled at Grant, who'd taken the seat across from her. He winked at her. Her scowl deepened.

"I'm so happy you've made me such a sweaty mess right before I have to try on costumes and gowns," she said testily.

He gave her a big smile, egging her on. "I knew you would be."

Their eyes darted to the door when it swung open with an array of tumultuous noise. Laine, the show's head costume designer, bustled into the room, pushing a rolling rack packed with several different costumes in an array of sequins, silks and feathers through the door. Grant and Evie had discussed over breakfast their ideas for costumes, and Grant had emailed them all to Laine, but he ultimately trusted her expertise and opinion when all was said and done.

"Hello again, Grant," she nodded at him before sticking her hand out to shake Evie's. "My name is Laine Fulcher, and I'm the head wardrobe director for *Song & Dance*. I meet with every couple each week to plan out your costumes for the live show, and I oversee the wardrobe at dress rehearsals and live show tapings.

You don't get in front of that camera until I ensure that you look like a million bucks," she explained.

"It's so nice to meet you, Ms. Laine. I can't wait to see the costumes. I'm pretty sure dressing up is going to be my most favorite part of this whole experience," Evie exclaimed, clapping her hands happily.

"That's just the kind of enthusiasm I like," Laine replied. She turned to the rolling rack and flipped through the tightly packed costumes.

Grant leaned forward, grabbing Evie's attention. "And you tried to tell me last night that you weren't girly?"

She rolled her eyes at him. "Okay, maybe I am. Just a little."

"Evie, for the jive, I'm feeling something like this right here," Laine said, pulling a short white strapless dress covered in sequins and pearls from the rack. The full skirt hid multiple layers of crinoline. "Do you mind trying it on?"

"No problem. In there?" Evie asked, pointing to one of the black paneled tents hanging from the ceiling down to the floor along the side of the room.

"Yep," Laine replied, taking the seat Evie vacated across from Grant when Evie ducked inside the quick-change tent.

"Classy but fun," he remarked about the dress as Evie changed.

"It's what you guys asked for—happy and feminine," Laine told him.

"I want the viewers to pick up on those qualities in her before anything else. There'll be more for them to discover, but those attributes will be easy to admire," Grant explained. "I've only been around her a couple of days, and it was what I noticed about her immediately."

"And who doesn't love to see a vintage bride? The producers were smart to assign you that song with the jive," Laine continued, jotting down a few notes.

"I agree with you there."

Just then, Evie stepped back into the room in her bare feet. Grant clenched the arms of the chair. Wearing the white dress with her hair pulled up in a messy bun, he imagined she would look much the same after her own wedding—tousled, but beautiful. He pushed the thought away.

"Ooh, honey! That looks gorgeous on you! Just gorgeous! I'm thinking a pair of hot pink heels and lipstick to match, white gloves and a little bird's nest veil and this dress will be perfect for that song and your jive. It will give it more of vintage feel," Laine gushed as she rose from the chair. At least Laine could think clearly. Unprofessional and out of character, Grant couldn't see past how beautiful Evie looked and view her with a critical eye on where to make improvements or changes. It didn't help matters when Laine turned Evie around and directed her to stand in front of a huge three-way mirror before zipping up the dress. No matter how hard he tried, he couldn't get his wayward thoughts in line.

As Laine tucked and pinned to mark where the dress needed altering, Grant managed to assess Evie from the viewpoint of a professional dance coach. He cleared his throat, and Laine and Evie paused mid-conversation, looking over to where he sat observing them from the plush velvet chair.

"I think the dress might be a bit too low in the neckline," he said, nodding in Evie's direction. Evie blushed, which was not his intention, but it was his job to protect their interest as a team.

Evie and Laine glanced down at the bodice, contemplating what he'd pointed out, and Laine didn't say a single word in protest, just went to work lifting and securing with a few pins. Within seconds, the top came up two inches higher. Laine caught his attention and gestured in the general direction of Evie's chest and he nodded his approval.

"It wasn't all that low before. Now, it looks like a Mennonite wedding dress," Evie called out, glancing at him icily in the mirror.

"That's a bit dramatic, Evie."

"If you say so," she huffed.

"Look, I'm not trying to be misogynistic or controlling or mean or whatever it is you think I'm being right now. The bottom line is the viewer's opinions. Their votes keep us in this competition. We must play certain parts, and I don't want you pigeonholed in the first week. If your costumes even hint at anything too this or too that, you'll be stereotyped as too boring, too slutty, too safe—you get the idea. Prime example—just imagine what Nell will want to wear and what the audience will think," he explained.

Evie assessed her reflection in the mirror. "I get what you mean now and you're right . . . thanks," she conceded.

Laine spent a few more moments pinning and making notes on the dress as Evie stood as still as a statue. Grant busied himself on his phone emailing the set producer and the lighting director with his ideas for their performances. He kept an eye out for an official song approval message, too.

"Alright, Evie. Let's move on to your outfit for the song portion. Grant tells me you'll be playing the piano and the feel is sort of other-worldly meets modern hipster romance," she said humorously, "so, I was thinking about this dress right here," she added as she plucked a long, pale peach dress off of the clothing rack, motioning for Evie to head back into the changing room once again.

A couple of minutes later, Evie pulled back the curtain and stepped into the open room once again. Grant's mouth popped open. The silky peach fabric was loose, except at the cinched waist, and didn't even show a hint of cleavage in the front, thankfully, but the back. . .

Oh, the back. As Evie walked past him towards the mirror again, the wispy train floated behind her, drawing attention behind her. Her entire back was exposed as the dress dipped dangerously low.

However, the gown managed to be tasteful and elegant, even if it had no back of which to speak. The soft peach fabric fell perfectly along the lines of her body, and in the front, the sleeveless bodice rose nearly to her collarbone and tied in a bow beside her neck, accentuating her shoulders.

She fidgeted with the dress, trying to make sure she had it on right probably, but when she spun, the fabric flared around her, and the smile on her lips caused his heart to stop beating in his chest before coming back to life with powerful thuds.

"If I actually owned this dress, I don't think I'd ever take it off," Evie said as she peered at her reflection in the mirror, smoothing the fabric beneath her hands like it was spun from magic. The elegant, serious dress contrasted well with the light and fun jive costume. Evie exuded grace and sophistication in that peach gown. Grant smiled, under Evie's spell, as she twirled in front of the three-way mirrors again before Laine got to her with her never-ending supply of straight pins. Standing statuesque, Evie caught Grant's gaze from the mirror.

"So what do you think of this one?" she asked him.

He studied her for a moment, thinking about how to convey the right words. The mix of what he should say and what he wanted to say were two very different things.

"The dress sets a more serious tone, which is good, and the train will look dramatic fanned out behind the piano bench and to be honest . . . you look like . . . a goddess in that gown," he confessed, his infatuation with her unmasked briefly as he stared at her.

To his unfortunate delight, she blushed profusely. He didn't mean to make her blush so much. With her cheeks bright pink, she glanced away from the intensity.

"Now, Grant I'd say that we need you to look like a Greek god, but you already do, so what's the point?" Laine commented with a cougar-like wink in his direction. She continued to work deftly on the gown as Evie struggled to stay still, trying not to giggle at Laine's brazen words.

"I think I could probably wear the same pants for both sets and just change my shirt," Grant told Laine, ignoring her harmless flirting.

"That would work, but I have a better idea— we'll do a white button up with a hot pink bowtie and suspenders for the jive, and we can just switch the bowtie out for a vest and tie for the song. You'll need to wear gray pants," Laine brainstormed as she finished up with Evie.

Evie glided across the room again and slipped into the dressing room to change while Laine and Grant finalized the rest of the details for their wardrobe.

"Do you need anything else from me?" Evie asked when she emerged wearing her gym clothes once more.

Grant shook his head. "Nope. Laine and I have covered it all. We're good to go."

"Well guys, it's been real, but I've got my work cut out for me, so go on and get to practice!" Laine said, clapping her hands to signal that they were finished before shooing them out of her sequined and feathered domain.

Grant and Evie walked outside, pausing on the wardrobe bungalow's porch.

"Well, that was fun. She really knows what she's doing, doesn't she?" Evie remarked, leaning against the porch railing.

"Yes, she does," he replied absently. They walked along in silence, heading back across the lot toward the show's soundstage and trailer setup. The awkwardness between them had unfortunately returned now that the wardrobe consult was over. His previous concerns had returned in earnest.

"We have about an hour before the group practice, and I need to run a couple of errands, do you mind if I meet you at the rehearsal?" he asked her when they'd reached the shuttle pickup.

"Um, sure. No problem. See ya later," she said, completely caught off guard. With a nod, he dashed off in the opposite direction going who knows where on the vast lot, leaving Evie dumbfounded waiting for the golf cart shuttle. He didn't want to run away from her, but given the circumstances, what other choice did he have?

CHAPTER SIX

Evie didn't see Grant again until exactly one minute before the group rehearsal started. All the other contestants and professional dancers were already there, paired off, chatting and laughing happily while she stood all alone, watching and waiting for Grant to arrive. The room felt like a high school cafeteria. But in high school, Davis had been the ringleader and she'd never lacked for a social life or struggled to be a part of the "in" crowd. Now, it felt like she was on the opposite side of the fence.

Grant finally dashed in, sliding his arm around her and pulling her into position beside Jared and Amelia with only seconds to spare. She was so mad, heat radiated from her fiery stare directed solely at him where he stood facing her. How dare he! This was their first practice with all of the other contestants, and he'd skimmed in at the last second, giving them no opportunity to show their solidarity as a unit or make friends with the others. The other couples had all been there for at least fifteen minutes or so, hanging out together like old friends gathering for a reunion. The common thread had been the professional dancers who worked together season after season, and Evie's pro was the only one not there. Ugh! He'd left her alone to fend for herself in a completely foreign situation.

"What the heck, Grant?" She whispered through clenched teeth. She wanted to yell, to totally go off on him for being so thoughtless. However, Nell was already staring at the two of them, the cameras were rolling, and Evie didn't want to explode on Grant in front of everyone.

Grant smiled down at Evie with that smile that didn't quite reach his eyes again. She didn't like that crinkle-less smile at all.

"I'm sorry I didn't get back as early as you would've preferred, but in my defense, I wasn't late, and what stopped you from chatting with some of the people you've already met? Be friendly," he admonished.

She stopped herself before lifting her hand to smack some sense into him. Was he really getting snarky with her? This wasn't his first rodeo—he should know why she was making such a big deal out of the issue.

"You're being a jerk. Everyone else was already here, and I had to stand there all by myself. . ." she trailed off as her voice cracked a little. "You have no idea what that was like for me, Grant." She could only imagine what had been going through everyone's minds at her lack of partner. *Poor girl. Her partner must not be able to stand being around her any longer than he absolutely has to be.* Surely, that's what they'd been thinking. Surely, Nell would plant those seeds of contention. She'd witnessed the undeserved hostility the night before.

"Oh, Evie, I'm sorry, I really am, it won't happen again," he said when he realized her struggle was legit, and his mask fell away for a moment as he touched her hand, his eyes full of real concern. She nodded at him, letting the issue go as she brushed off the emotions threatening to rise. *Keep it together, no tears, no tears, no tears*, she repeated the mantra in her head.

The cameras were rolling. She wasn't a baby and didn't want to appear as one for all of America to see. Now that Grant had apologized, she felt kind of bad for making such a big deal about it.

The rehearsal started and turned boring quickly —the only highlight was finally getting to know some of the other competitors. While the pros tweaked the choreography and went over final placement, Evie took Grant's advice and made small talk with some of the others. Her favorite chats were with Melvin McRoy, a legendary doo wop singer, and Shanda Henson, a classic country artist.

"My mother has got to be your biggest fan," Evie told Shanda as they watched the dancers do their thing.

"You gotta tell her how much that means, honey. Tell her I said hello and thank her for me. If she comes to the shows, you point her out to me now, 'cause I'd really like to meet her," Shanda gushed.

"Thank you, I'll do that. It would mean the world to her. One of my earliest memories of her is when she dressed up in a purple cowboy hat and matching boots to go to one of your concerts when I was five," Evie confided, giggling at the memory of her mother in Western wear.

"She shoulda brought you along!" Shanda laughed with her.

Evie talked with Amelia some, too. There wasn't a chance to meet the other five contestants, and she definitely wasn't going to go out of her way to speak to Nell again after her snide remarks and the previous night's dinner debacle.

The song choice for the group number pumped through the speakers, and it was one of those songs that really kept people moving when it played. Evie tapped her feet to the beat, wishing she could learn the faster, fancier footwork the pros rehearsed together. The steps for the singers were basic and simple so that they accommodated all the different skill levels represented, and the dance pros paired off for the more complex parts of the routines, while the rest of the group stepped off the dance floor and out of the camera shots. Then, they all hurried to their assigned places as the cameras did a little spotlight scene announcing each couple. Simple enough.

When the rehearsal ended, several couples stood around and made plans to go out together for the evening. Just as Shanda called out and asked if Grant and Evie wanted to join them, Nell piped up before Evie had a chance to respond.

"Oh no, Shanda. She can't go, she gets too tired —all this change and activity isn't what she's used to, you know," Nell explained in a sickeningly sweet voice to Shanda, "But, Grant could definitely come with us if he's free," she added, casting a seductive glance at Grant, much to Evie's disgust.

Grant gently squeezed Evie's shoulder before answering Nell. "Sorry, we can't come with you guys. Evie and I already have plans tonight," Grant said, his hand protectively running down the length of Evie's arm in a gesture that could be construed as intimate.

Nell glared at them, but Evie just shrugged her shoulders and leaned back against Grant. Take that, Nell.

Nell swung around and stomped out of the studio. When the door shut behind her, Evie turned around to face Grant, already forgetting about Nell and her nasty attitude.

"Have you found out about our song?" she asked as they left together. Best to let their other little tiff go for the time being.

"Yep, it's been cleared. They should have one of the practice rooms set up with a keyboard ready to go, so we can head there now and get started right away if you want," he told her.

Evie nodded enthusiastically. Her fingers itched to play; she needed to release some of the pent up emotions that had been building over the past couple of days.

They left the soundstage and took a shuttle over to a three-story building the same beige stucco as the rest of the buildings on the lot and took the stairs up to the second floor. The room to where Grant led her was a tiny space in comparison to the dance studios, but a

Nord keyboard waited for her in the center of the cramped room.

"The baby grand will be at dress rehearsal and camera blocking on Monday, but this should work fine for practicing in the meantime," Grant said as he gestured to the keyboard.

She barely heard his explanation as she took a seat, eyeing the red keyboard before her. She glanced over the chord charts, but she'd already looked up the major chords and listened to the timing of the song between rehearsals today, so as soon as her fingers began to move, the haunting melody began to fill the small room. Since the chords were repetitive, after running through it a couple of times, she was ready to add in the vocals.

"How did you want to start?" she asked Grant, resting her hands in her lap as she waited for his response.

He strolled over to stand beside her, rubbing his jaw as he contemplated the question.

"I think you should sing the first verse, and I'll come in with a harmony on the second. The rest of the song we'll stay together in harmony, and really build before finally echoing out. Basically like a role reversal of the original performance. Does that sound like a good idea to you?"

"Yes, I like it. I'll go ahead and start then," she replied, stretching her arms.

She placed her hands back into position over the keys, and closed her eyes, feeling the emotional notes as she played through the soft intro before starting to sing.

> *Say something, I'm giving up on you*
> *I'll be the one if you want me to . . .*

When Grant joined her, their voices melded together so inexplicably well, it thrilled her to her very toes. The room buzzed with a vibrant, almost tangible electricity as their voices rang out. Singing with someone and blending that perfectly—it was like riding a high and breathing in joy while her insides crushed at the overwhelming weight of emotion.

She played the last few notes and the room fell still and silent. Even Steve, their camera guy who had rode over with them to film, didn't move a muscle. It was the rawest, most emotional singing experience she'd had since she started performing at church as a child. And this had only been their very first run through of the song in a dinky little room on the second floor of a cookie cutter studio building!

Grant's clear baritone blended with her soprano like it had been fine-tuned to do so. They'd both already practiced separately, and it showed in the inflection, the pauses, and the pitch—which were already on point. If they had to perform their song for a live audience at that exact moment, Evie would've been absolutely comfortable doing so. That wasn't normal—blending so well with someone she'd never sang with before was strange, and she didn't take the phenomenon lightly.

"Wow." Grant finally broke the silence with that one, barely audible word. His eyes were wide as he stared at her still seated in front of the keyboard.

"Right?" she asked, looking up at him in awe. She'd never sung anything that moved her the way she'd just been moved. It wasn't necessarily because of the particular song, but more of a culmination of a touching song, a room with good acoustics, and the amazing way their voices sounded when they sang together.

"Guys, you know I don't normally say anything, I just try to just blend into the scenery so that you don't notice I'm here while I film, but I have to say—that was . . . awesome," Steve said with a grin.

Evie ducked her head at Steve's kind words. During the song, she'd forgotten that Steve was there—it was like she and Grant were suspended in a private bubble, and they'd been untouchable by all of the outside world for the moments the song lasted. That other-worldly experience was one of the reasons she loved singing and playing music more than anything else. Her soul could run free as the melodies touched the deepest parts of her. Emotions that she didn't even know existed captivated all of her senses, and one of her greatest joys was when her music actually helped others feel those emotions, too. But to share that experience with someone? That was a totally new and exhilarating thrill for her.

"Wow," Grant repeated.

"Is that all you can say?" she laughed.

Grant nodded.

"Well, okay then. Let's go through it again. We could've just had freak beginner's luck," she pointed out. They went through it again, then twice more. The performance only grew more intense and powerful with each run through.

"Let's call it an evening," Grant said, checking his watch after they'd practiced it for the fifth time.

"It's been a long day," she yawned and stretched her back as she stood.

"Tomorrow, we can start around nine. Sleep in a little if you can, because you're going to need the rest. Tomorrow's dance practice will be a solid six hours, and we're going to hit it hard. Then, we'll break for a couple of hours in the afternoon before our two hour song practice, after which we have about a dozen press interviews," he told her. She yawned at the thought of another action-packed day. The rest of her first week in LA passed by in a whirlwind because every day leading up to Tuesday, the day of the premiere, was a whirlwind of dance practice, interviews, song rehearsals, and then dress rehearsals and camera blocking were added into the mix on Monday.

She barely had time to meet up with her friend, Lex, who she'd grown close to during their *America Sings* season, but managed to squeeze in a quick chat over coffee on Sunday afternoon. Lex had competed with her and landed in the top five. They'd become close friends over the course of the competition and rooming in the same dorm-style complex together. Lex had stayed in LA after the show wrapped, taking any gig she could get and moonlighting as a wedding singer and bartender.

"I never thought I'd still be sharing a room with three other girls six months later!" Lex laughed, and ran a hand through her sleek, chestnut bob that barely grazed her shoulders. She was thinner than the last time Evie saw her just after New Year's when she'd been in LA taping a special with other cast members.

"At least you're doing what you love," Evie offered, taking a sip of her rose and honey latte.

"Yeah, true, but look at you!" Lex burst out, gesturing to Evie. "I would've jumped at the chance to be on *Song & Dance* and whew, Grant is hot. Is he as hot in person as he is on TV?"

Evie laughed awkwardly. "I mean, yeah, I guess, but I don't think about him like that. I'm with Davis, remember?"

"Oh, yeah. That's right. Still—you can look and admire," she shrugged, a gleam in her eye, "or help a sister out and give him my number," she teased with a wink.

"Grant has a girlfriend," Evie said quickly. She didn't know why, but even the *idea* of setting Lex up with a single Grant ruffled her feathers. Her stomach turned somersaults. That wasn't a good sign. Lex was fabulous. She *should've* laughed right along. Why on earth did a sudden twinge of territorial jealousy take over at Lex's light-hearted admiration of Grant?

CHAPTER SEVEN

On Tuesday evening, Grant didn't know what to do with himself. For the first time since *Song & Dance* made its debut with him apart of the charter cast over four years ago, the hours leading up to the premiere breezed by smooth and carefree. In every season past, Grant's partners were, for the most part, nervous, hyperventilating wrecks throughout major chunks of premiere day. Naturally, dealing with such volatile women made him pull his hair out and his tongue grew sore from biting back curse words as he tried over and over to soothe their fears of the performance, the cameras, the judges, the viewers' opinions, their status in the rankings, and any other random terrifying thought that popped into their brains and ruffled their feathers in the midst of what they considered a personal crisis.

But not this season. This season, he'd been given the most relaxed contestant on the show—who happened to, thankfully, be talented, too. After that rocky second day of rehearsals, they'd eased into a comfortable routine. With their days packed to the brim, Grant didn't have time to worry about feelings or infatuation or anything other than nailing their dance routine and song performance.

So far today, they'd breezed through an early morning practice, keeping them right on schedule with production. Evie nailed every step every time they ran through the number, so there were no worries in that department, and after rehearsals, they'd even had time to run the treadmills together before starting the long, tedious process of getting ready for the pre-show activities.

As long as he viewed her as his student, he was golden. As long as they didn't have any more moments like they'd had in the elevator . . . or in wardrobe . . . or every time they sang together . . . or . . . Grant's shoulders uncharacteristically slumped. When he thought about it, there was no getting away from the way she made him really feel. That's why he kept them both busy—leaving no time to think was a real good thing this season.

Laine finished fussing over his attire in the show's wardrobe department earlier than usual, giving Grant over an hour free before he and Evie were scheduled for pre-show interviews with the media. He straightened his bowtie that matched a certain blonde's high heels and lipstick, and double-checked the laces of his dance shoes before ducking out of the wild, frenzied wardrobe department, and darting through the crazed crew milling around to reach the hair and makeup trailer just outside their soundstage's back entrance. Grant always styled his own hair, but he had to suffer through having the required stage makeup applied no matter how much he despised it. That stuff was such a pain to scrub off every Tuesday night.

According to their show day schedule, Evie should've been finishing up in hair and makeup just then. As Grant turned the corner inside the large, sectioned off trailer filled with vanities, chairs, makeup mirrors and every member of the cast that wasn't currently in wardrobe, he heard her soft, sweet laughter before he caught his first glimpse of her. With her hair in rollers, wearing a silky black robe, her eyes were closed as a makeup artist worked on applying lash extensions.

He wondered what the final, decked out version of Evie would look like for the show tonight. She was easy on the eyes as it was—even in rehearsals, when they were both pouring sweat, her cheeks rosy and her mascara smeared. Then again, maybe he was biased. Knowing how big of a sweetheart she was—how in the infinitesimal bit of free time she'd had this past week, she'd had coffee with a friend, visited the children's hospital because a fan had written her a letter about their little sister having surgery and how much it would mean for her to meet Evie, and had went to prayer group at a local church. These things made her even more beautiful to him. How could anyone know those things about her and not find her beautiful?

There happened to be a makeup artist's station free beside Evie's, so he took a seat in the director's style chair. It wasn't like he really cared who applied that thick, pancake crap to his face—anyone could do it and it would still be gross. Some of the dancers preferred specific makeup people, but not him. He'd do it himself if he could dig around and find the right stuff, but the last time he tried, he frustrated quite a few people.

Evie opened her eyes when the makeup artist finished up, and noticed him sitting in the chair next to hers. "How much longer until we are due for interviews?" she asked, not commenting on his unexpected appearance at her side or the fact that she'd caught him staring at her.

A couple of stylists quickly plucked the rollers out of her hair. She winced as one of the stylists started teasing it with a comb.

"In about forty minutes. Are you nervous?"

"Yes, but only because my hair isn't finished and I'm not dressed yet. The interviews have me a little anxious. So, I'm not as worried about the actual performance as I am everything else surrounding it," she explained.

"Really?" He questioned, eyebrows raised in surprise.

"Yes, really. I feel super comfortable with the routine, which surprises me, I have to admit. But it's all thanks to you. We've been busting it at breakneck speed all week. With all the hard work and practice, you've made me feel confident that I'm doing a good job. I just hope everyone likes the dance as much as I do," she smiled.

Keke, a makeup artist who'd just finished up with Adam, came over and began applying Grant's required stage makeup. He closed his eyes, and by the time he reopened them when Keke finished with his face, Evie wasn't there. She'd probably hurried over to wardrobe.

"Nervous, man?" Jared asked as he walked by Grant's chair wearing a silky turquoise button up and matching pants with sequins down the sides.

"Nope. I'm surprisingly calm. Probably because I'm confident in Evie's abilities. I don't foresee her choking," he told Jared, jumping out of the chair intent on hunting down his partner. She would be dressed and ready by the time he retraced his steps back to wardrobe.

"That's good. I'm a little worried about Amelia. She nails every step perfectly in practice, but she's getting in her own head really bad right now, and I'm worried she'll draw a blank when we hit the dance floor," Jared said, popping his knuckles as he shared his concerns.

"You owe me ten bucks," Grant told him, gesturing to Jared's knuckles.

"Crap! You're right, I do," he exclaimed, "I only pop them when I'm stressed," he added in defense.

"Hey, it's not me that cares so much. You're the one that gave me strict instructions to take your money when you popped them," he reminded Jared.

Jared sighed, pulling out his wallet and handing Grant a ten dollar bill. Grant took the money from him, but promptly stuck it in a random makeup caddy. Who wouldn't like finding free money at Jared's expense?

"It's almost time." Grant told him, glancing at his watch. "I've got to catch up with Evie."

They parted ways—Grant to wardrobe, Jared to the sports therapist to check on a muscle spasm he'd had earlier.

Grant dashed out of the trailer and back into the main building again. Several female members of the dance troupe bolted past him in a blur of sequins, heels and hairspray flashing smiles at him as they scurried along. At the speed they traveled, they were probably running late for the final run through of tonight's opening number. Usually, they liked to stop and chat.

Right as he reached the door to the wardrobe department, out walked a dream. The white, 50s-style dress she wore showcased her tanned legs and the hot pink heels Laine insisted that she wear for the number. With a flirty veil pinned into her long, bouncy curls, white satin gloves that stopped just above her elbows, hot pink lips and long, dark lashes, she looked every bit of the character they'd created—mid-century bride meets modern girl. Laine's ability to nail costumes blew Grant's mind, and the girl sauntering towards him, breaking into a wide, excited smile as she drew close, took his breath away.

So there he stood in the studio hallway, brainless and breathless as Evie approached. She did an excited twirl, smoothing the ruffles of the dress beneath her fingertips. His heart did a strange flip flop in his chest—something it only did when Evie came around.

"Oh my goodness. Grant. I'm in love with this costume! This show is like playing dress up, but like, multiplied by ten thousand. I saw a girl in there wearing some sort of bird costume, but there wasn't much bird . . . well, there wasn't much of anything to it, honestly," she chatted away excitedly as she hurried to where Grant still stood in shock.

"You look stunning, Evie. Absolutely stunning," he finally managed to say, ignoring her wardrobe department fascination and babbling.

"Thanks, you look great, too," she said, sounding a little shy as she straightened her gloves and took in his rather boring apparel in comparison to the vision she portrayed.

"Come on, we need to get to the ballroom—we have three pre-show interviews," Grant reminded her, offering her his arm. She happily linked her arm through his as they walked.

When they entered the ballroom, the first reporter on the press line, Ann Fitzgibbon of Elite Magazine, met them at once, full of comments and questions.

"Well, well! Here comes the most beautiful bride and groom that I've ever seen!" Ann exclaimed, clasping her hands. "You two look ready for the altar!"

Oh great. Evie's biggest fear about their themed routine hit them square in the face the moment they stepped out in costume. The show didn't even start for another hour and a half. How many more comments or innuendos would they hear? Great. Just great.

"Why, thank you! We do look pretty striking in these get ups!" Evie responded enthusiastically, nudging Grant with her elbow as she smiled broadly. He glanced at her with eyebrows raised.

"What do you have to say about your beautiful bride, Grant?" Ann pressed. Those reporters and their tricks—they were always looking to stir up a story if they caught even a whiff of chemistry.

"I'd like to say that my partner, Evie, looks extremely beautiful tonight—wardrobe has outdone themselves as usual—they took our theme and vision for this week and created these costumes. We're really excited for everyone to see our dance tonight," he told Ann diplomatically.

"Evie, our readers want to know if there is a special someone in your life. Didn't you mention having a boyfriend during your time on *America Sings?*"

"Yes, I have a boyfriend back home in Alabama, and we've been together since we were fourteen," Evie told Ann automatically.

"That wasn't all that long ago was it?"

Evie laughed. "We're going on nine years together."

"Wow. Now, Grant, what about you? Still seeing Kacie Little?"

"Last I checked," he replied, being as noncommittal as possible while trying to not come off like a jerk. Kacie and he may be together today, but that could change tomorrow—such was the nature of their relationship, and the reason he hated commenting on it in interviews.

Evie shot him a look, and Grant shrugged his shoulders.

"How was your first week together coming into the competition?" Ann asked.

"We seem to work well together. The chemistry is definitely there, and Evie is a fast learner," Grant commented.

"Grant's an awesome teacher," Evie added.

Ann studied the two of them for a couple of seconds and scribbled a quick note with a decisive nod of her head. She asked a few more questions, and once satisfied with her interview questions and their answers, she dismissed them and they continued to the next reporter waiting patiently for his turn to question them.

"If I was your girlfriend, when I read whatever article Ann writes, I would be so pissed at you," Evie told him quietly as they made it to the local news reporter and his cameraman. Over the past week, Evie had asked about Kacie quite a few times, but Grant avoided the subject—he and Kacie had a complicated relationship, and he wanted to keep Evie's focus strictly on their partnership, not on dissecting the ins and outs of his love life. However, more of an explanation about their relationship proved necessary now.

"She may, or she may not. We aren't very serious. I care about her, but we've always been on and off again, never lasting more than a few months at a time," he told her after they'd finished with the reporter.

"Oh," was her only response. He wondered what she really thought about his casual approach to his relationship with Kacie in comparison to her long, loyal commitment to her boyfriend, who seemed to be a self-involved jerk from what Grant could surmise.

After finishing with their interviews, which were generally about what dance and what song they were performing, how they met, did they get along—all the typical, run-of-the-mill, first week questions—they posed for a few pictures.

"You know, these pics will look like they've been yanked right out of a wedding album. Tabloid City, here we come," Evie said through her teeth as the cameras clicked away.

"Just remember, it's not my fault—I just worked with the concept we were given," he defended. The photographer finished, and as Evie and Grant walked away, they put about a foot between one another. After all the questions and pics, distance seemed like a good idea. No need to add to the rumor mill.

"I'm not blaming you, Grant. I told you—I love the costumes and the dance. I just forgot about the rumors the look would spark," she explained.

"If it's any consolation, if people comment and speculate about our personal relationship, they are very likely going to vote for us. It's the intrigue of it all," he told her, his voice low.

"Just so you know, I'm pretty sure the media has pegged us for the showmance angle," he added, shrugging his shoulders. Much to his surprise, Evie nodded and stepped closer to him, hooking her arm back through his as they made their way backstage.

"We know the truth, and right now, that's all that matters and later, I will communicate that truth to my boyfriend," Evie said decisively as they snuck through the maze of spray tans and sequins. The troupe members trickled onto the dance floor, and the audience members settled into their seats as the final ten-minute countdown until the live show popped up on the huge screens overhead.

Grant glanced at Evie, gauging her reaction to the sudden energy rush tangible in the room. She didn't appear nervous and maintained her calm despite the whirl of last-minute activity part and parcel with a live show minutes from airing, but he noticed her free hand fidgeting with the satin trim of her skirt.

"You okay?" he asked.

"Yep, perfectly fine," she replied brightly.

"It's okay to be nervous," he allowed.

"I know, but I'm trying not to think about the butterflies in my stomach or how I would kind of like to pass out right now. Let me keep thinking I'm perfectly fine, okay?" she blurted out.

Grant's eyes widened at her confession. "Got it. You look completely together. I wouldn't have thought you nervous at all except for how you're fidgeting with your skirt. Don't worry, Evie. You've got this—we've got this. Everything will go smoothly. Just relax," he coached.

"Thanks," she said, taking a deep breath, never losing her composure. They took their places for the first group performance and introductions. Grant slipped his arm around her waist and held her hand, holding the dancer's pose they'd practice dozens of times over the last few days. She felt stiff.

"Just relax," he whispered.

"Keep reminding me to do that," she replied softly, closing her eyes as she took in calming breaths.

"Absolutely," he murmured, watching her closed eyelids flutter as she focused her energy.

Half an hour later, Kim, their assigned producer, came up to Grant and Evie and began preparing them for their upcoming turn on the dance floor. "You're due on the dance floor in five," she told them as she and Harper, her assistant, went to work on getting them ready.

Just after their first group number, Kim had fitted him with the tiny earpiece the pro dancers wore during most of the live show so that they could be instructed on where to go and what to do without interrupting the taping process. Grant adjusted the earpiece to fit comfortably as Kim fiddled with his mic cord, making sure it was secure and wouldn't show as he danced. Harper secured the mic box hidden in the back of Evie's dress, and Liz, one of Laine's wardrobe assistants, fluffed her veil so that it fell in perfect symmetry over Evie's curls while Keke touched up that hot pink lipstick. Once they were spiffed up to the team's satisfaction, Grant reached for Evie's hand and drew her away from the crowd backstage.

"It's officially time. Ready?" he asked softly, leading her to the edge of the dance floor. They watched as crew members broke down and carted away the previous couple's set. Shanda and her pro partner, Alonzo's set was an elaborate nod to the Grand

Ole Opry—where Shanda and all other country artists considered it one of the highest honors to perform on the Opry's stage. The producers played up Shanda's status as a country music legend the way they focused the theme of "up-and-coming star meets the-girl-next-door" with Evie.

When the show took a commercial break, the crew wheeled out his and Evie's set—white picket fencing, an arched trellis, and flower boxes—all covered in hot pink roses that matched Evie's lips and heels. They even hung garlands of hot pink roses and greenery from the ceiling and rolled out a hot pink carpet. Kim thrusted a hot pink bouquet into Evie's hands, which she would immediately toss back to her once the music started, then Kim would slip it back to her off-camera in time for her to throw it over her shoulder at the end of the routine. The props and set fit the theme of the song perfectly, especially the ever-referenced white picket fence of most old school, girly daydreams.

"Okay, Grant, get into starting position. We'll be live in two," Kim's voice came through on his earpiece.

Grant and Evie headed out to the center of the floor, and the crowd burst into cheers at the sight of them.

Production members motioned for the audience to quiet down as Grant situated Evie in her starting spot beneath the trellis, holding her bouquet. Once he had her in place, he hurried over to take his position back on the edge of the dance floor.

The signal flashed on the huge projector screens that hung on both sides of the studio, and the five second warning came from somewhere offstage. The lights raised and their host, Corey Morgan, welcomed viewers back, briefly panning to Evie under the trellis before cutting to their weekly, three-minute clip for the viewers at home. The small package featuring interviews and clips from practice played on the big screens in real-time. Grant was always interested to see what made the final cut for the glimpse the viewers would see of their hectic week. Usually, the pieces were so edited and spliced, it was hard to figure out when the crew had actually filmed the rehearsal footage that they showed. Although he may be interested in seeing it, he prayed Evie would follow his advice and tune the footage out. The last thing they needed was whatever showed on that screen to mess with her head just before their debut dance.

Evie's face lit up on the overhead screen. The first shots were innocent enough with Evie giving a bit of her backstory spliced with a little footage of her time on *America Sings*, followed by a short blurb about her family back in Alabama. He was glad to see that her Southern charm resonated throughout the tiny package —that would go over well for them with viewers. After her introduction, Grant appeared as he gave his own brief intro, followed by scenes of the two of them rehearsing and laughing together.

Grant appreciated production's emphasis on his and Evie's natural chemistry and how well they worked together, but toward the end of the clip, the producers added in a scene faintly hinting that the two of them might be more than just friends, just as he expected them to do. It was a scene shot from a long distance featuring the two of them unaware of the filming crew although they still wore mics. At that distance and angle, no one would be able to make out what they were saying exactly, so production had typed words out along the bottom of the screen to add drama. And unfortunately, the bits of conversation they'd edited were rather intriguing.

"Do you want to grab dinner later?" Grant heard his own voice fill the studio.

"I suppose I could pencil you in," Evie replied flirtatiously.

"Thanks, I appreciate it," he laughed.

Grant rolled his eyes at the voiceover that sounded like they'd just planned their first date, flirty laughs and all. Production took that blip of conversation and blew it way out of context. The tricky technique they used insinuated that Evie and Grant were secretly communicating, as if they thought they were out of sight from the camera guy. The actual truth of the matter was that they'd simply forgotten that they were filming—just like they were supposed to be doing, and they'd been planning a friendly "get to know one another" outing. Grant shook his head. He'd be hearing about this later.

When the footage ended, the band started up the song, and Grant blocked the screen images out of his head. Evie began the routine, tossing the bouquet and happily skipping to the white fence, before Grant jumped in on cue, and they jived around the dance floor for an entire two minutes. He caught her eyes and she beamed at him before he spun her around, the happy energy of the song invading the entire room.

He guided Evie into the final turn of their routine just after she picked up the bouquet of hot pink roses from Kim. When Grant dipped her backwards, she tossed the bouquet behind her while the cover band, for the final time, crooned, "Going to the chapel of love."

Breathless and still in hold, he smiled down at her, adrenaline coursing through his veins, her arm wrapped tightly around his leg where her body rested. Her starry eyes looked up at him as the music faded away and the dance ended. The live audience erupted into applause, but Grant only vaguely noticed it in the background as he took in the radiant expression illuminating Evie's face as they stayed in hold for a few more seconds.

Still leaning over her, he whispered, "You nailed it, Evie. Great job!" before scooping her up and kissing her forehead. She wrapped her arms tightly around his neck as he lifted her off of the ground. His heart pounded the way it did the first time he competed on the dance floor years ago.

Grant sat her down as the applause trickled off, and they waited for the judges to give their opinions on Evie's debut dance. Since they were in the middle of the lineup, Evie and Grant braced themselves for the harsh critique they'd witnessed the judges dish out to other couples so far that evening. Just before they had taken the floor, Grant warned Evie that no matter how awesome or smooth their routine ended up going, it was the judge's job to find something to point out and criticize, so she needed to be prepared for whatever they had to say. He'd seen a look of terror in her eyes at his words, but she'd quickly donned a brave face, squaring her shoulders as she nodded her agreement.

"Well, well, well, Evie, my dear. Your dance was . . . simply marvelous," Clarice, the first judge to speak, said with unexpected flair. As the head judge, he'd expected the worst of the brunt to be delivered by her. His eyes widened in surprise at her compliment. "Your jive was wonderful. The whole thing didn't have the feel of a first week routine whatsoever! Well done, Grant, with the choreography, and the little theme was divine. I hope to see you both back next week," she clipped, finishing with a smile directed at Evie and an elegant flick of her wrist.

"Oh my goodness, you're beautiful and lively, and so was your jive! Just charming!" Esme Romano, the next judge added, all happy little claps and smiles.

There was a pause as they waited for Paulo Cortez, the third and final judge, to deliver his verdict. "Honey, you are not just charming, you are smoking hot! That dance was a whole lot of flirty fun, and I hope we will see more of that from you. The only thing I have to say, so far, is maybe work on relaxing a bit more —you seemed just a hair nervous at the beginning of the routine," he said, his Spanish accent heavy.

Evie and Grant both smiled and nodded once more at the judges before Grant escorted Evie over to where Corey, the host, waited to interview them live post dance. Corey would also remind viewers to vote while the judges finished scoring their dance.

"So Evie, how do you feel after your first dance?" Corey asked, holding his mic out to her.

"I feel great! I think everything went smoothly?" She turned to get Grant's agreement, scrunching her nose as she waited for him to confirm her assessment.

"I'm so proud of her, she did amazing," Grant added, sliding his arm around her shoulders and giving her a friendly squeeze.

"I agree with Grant. Let's see what the judges had to say with their scores," Corey said, and they turned to face one of the screens to see what would pop up.

Clarice's score for them appeared first. Four out of five stars. Grant's eyes widened. Four stars on premiere night was virtually unheard of, and to further the shock, Esme and Paulo followed suit, each giving them four stars, as well! They would be top-ranked for week one, no doubt about it. The crowd erupted as the high score glowed brightly on the big screens. Grant pulled Evie into his arms for a quick hug before taking her hand and hurrying backstage as fast as her pink high heels could carry her.

They ran to the back hallway, and Grant rushed Evie to the ladies' makeshift quick change room so that she could hurry and get dressed and styled for their next act. Before she headed inside the curtained room, she turned back around and threw her arms around his neck. Caught off guard, his hands slowly raised to return the hug, even though he had to rush to change himself.

"Thank you for being the best partner ever!" she whispered emotionally, her smile against his ear.

"Right back at you," he replied. While still in his arms, she leaned back and gave him one of those dazzling smiles of hers. In the back of his mind, he knew somewhere there was a camera trained on the two of them, and this display of affection would definitely make it into their package next week. Speculations about their relationship would fly off the charts, and to add fuel to the fire, the producers would spin this into a story about their budding romance— despite their significant others, different lives, or the fact that they'd only known each other a week. But who cared about rational reasoning when you could spin a love story that would attract viewers?

Oh well. There was nothing that he could do about it. Besides, the show thrived on showmances. Grant's only real concern was how Evie would feel about it, and if she would have to deal with a jealous boyfriend's perception of the situation. She didn't need that extra stress on her during the intense upcoming weeks of performance and competition.

"Grant, professional ensemble in five. Be ready," a production assistant reminded him as he passed by the two of them still hugging in the crowded back hallway. Grant nodded and unwrapped himself from Evie to go get changed.

CHAPTER EIGHT

Evie floated across the shadowy side of the dance floor in her long, backless dress the color of a peach not quite ready to be picked. Grant sucked in his breath. In the dim light, she glowed. That night, in *that* dress, with her hair still curled but now piled into a loose bun, the warm glow of her skin accentuated by the pale peach of the gown, Evie was . . . nothing less than a work of art. From her oceanic eyes made up to appear even more striking than usual to every graceful step she took in her sparkling heels, as soon as their performance started, Evie would own the ballroom. The wardrobe team, hair stylists and makeup artists deserved awards for their work on her. They'd taken Evie and transformed her into a mysterious, ethereal creature. Grant couldn't stop staring at her, despite every attempt to do so, which meant viewers wouldn't be able to stop staring at her either. Views would turn into votes.

They were standing in the shadows at the edge of the floor again, waiting to take their places. Evie shifted nervously from one foot to another. Now that the moment for their song set had arrived, the calm was gone. Her cagey movements, the slight twitch of her fingers and the tense set of her shoulders displayed her anxiety. Grant understood better than anyone else could have—going from dancing a fun and cutesy jive to preparing to perform a deep and intense song wasn't easy. After those awesome scores from the judges, the burden of pressure to exceed everyone's expectations weighed heavily on them both, but especially her. With good reason, the bar had been set high for her, so she had a lot more to lose than others if things didn't go as smoothly as planned.

Grant placed a light hand on her cool, bare back as he guided her to the grand piano waiting in the center of the still darkened dance floor. They needed to use these few minutes to settle into place for their song performance—both physically and emotionally, but Evie was too fidgety—she was nervous and still riding the rush of adrenaline left over from the fast-paced jive they'd finished only twenty minutes earlier.

To help her calm down and find her center, Grant put his hands on her keyed up shoulders, gently massaging them with deft fingers as Evie sat still with her hands poised to play the first chords the second the spotlight illuminated her. He leaned down, close to her ear.

"Relax. Just breathe," he whispered softly. The set of Evie's shoulders relaxed as she began to ease into the right frame of mind for the performance. Her shoulders rose and fell as she took a deep breath and let it out slowly. He continued to lightly massage as she breathed in and out in a smooth rhythm.

With seconds to spare, Grant jogged to the edge of the floor again, and the spotlight trained down on Evie alone in the middle of the studio. Although he faced her lovely back—all squared shoulders and graceful posture—Grant knew how intensely she stared at the ivory keys as she played the first few haunting notes of their song. When she started singing in that clear, breathy voice of hers, the intensity of the piece transported the studio into an ethereal world as Evie gave herself over to the music. His heart thudded as he watched her captivate the entire room—himself included.

When Evie reached the second stanza, he walked toward her and joined in with the harmony, and like every other time they'd sung that song, Grant couldn't believe the way their voices blended together. He'd never felt this . . . deep connection singing a song with someone, and like a drug, he wanted more. He couldn't get enough.

While Evie softly played and their voices echoed throughout the room, the dreamy setting, the lyrics, and even the simple yet intimately styled wardrobe drove the image of longing they portrayed into something akin to reality. But when their deep connection Grant couldn't even fully comprehend himself fell into the mix, the performance hit another level entirely.

The moment that surpassed all other moments happened as soon as they passed the climax of the song, right when the haunting, lonely notes returned. As the song ended, Grant lifted his hand to her cheek and brushed his fingers softly down her neck and along her bare shoulder, lingering momentarily before walking back into the shadows at the edge of the spotlight—just like they'd practiced a dozen times. Grant understood the character—a self-tortured man in love with a forbidden songbird—more so than ever before as an intense, confusing emotion clouded his mind.

After Evie finished playing the last couple of trailing notes, Grant trained his eyes on her as she carefully placed her hands in her lap and hung her head in an act that could be interpreted as either sorrow or defeat. Evie held perfectly still, but the stillness radiated louder than any words ever could have. The pricking of tears in his own eyes startled him. He shook the wave of emotion off quickly before anyone else noticed.

Now that they'd finished their song, instead of applause filling the studio, the room fell utterly silent— a pin could have dropped and he'd have heard it. Although the stillness was odd, Grant understood it— the audience had fallen under the same spell Evie put him under every time they'd sang that particular song together. A few seconds passed before he stepped over to her, barely grazing her shoulder with his fingertips to let her know she was free to move. Only then did she lift her elegantly bowed head as if she'd just snapped out of a trance. Evie met his eyes as he extended his hand to help her stand. He reached for her, noticing that her own eyes were damp, and she willingly stepped into his embrace. With her arms around his neck, he swung her around, and the dress she wore, *that dress,* caught a slight breeze, swirling about her as if they were dancing a waltz. While they embraced, the room erupted into deafening applause. On and on it continued as they made their way over to the judges for the second time that night.

Evie slid her arm across Grant's shoulders and his hand encircled her waist while they waited for the audience to settle down a bit. Evie glowed, and her smile reached from ear to ear. His own smile mirrored hers just then—pride in Evie and their performance overwhelming all other thoughts and show schedules.

Finally, the cheers eased into a dull roar, and an emotional Esme started off the judges' thoughts on Evie and Grant's performance.

"I'm in tears, honey. Tears!" Esme exclaimed as she dabbed at her eyes with a tissue. "It's so hard to believe that you two have only been working together for a week. Your chemistry is undeniable! That performance was star caliber and this is only week one! Maybe my most favorite performance ever!" Esme was a pretty emotional person, so her tears weren't that big of a deal, but her comments were still influential and felt good to hear.

"I agree with Esme. There's no doubt that you two are going to be the couple to beat. The chemistry between you and Grant, Evie, well there simply isn't a way to describe it in words that would do it justice," Clarice said, shaking her head in literal disbelief. Clarice was the hardest judge to win over. Grant gave Evie a little squeeze to emphasize the importance of Clarice's compliments.

Paulo simply stood and dramatically bowed.

"But what do you have to say about the song?" Corey jested, prompting Paulo to say something.

"Perfection," Paulo declared as he took his seat, waving his hands like he just couldn't even handle it. Grant appreciated Paulo for that very reason. He may have been a little flamboyant for some, but Paulo always got his point across without having to say all that much.

"There you have it folks," Corey spoke into the camera, "let's see their scores."

Grant took Evie's hand in his as they watched and waited for their scores to pop up on the screen. Five out of five stars across the board. Dumbfounded, Grant stood there next to Evie with his mouth open as the crowd broke into crazed cheering. After taking a couple of seconds to adjust, he jumped up into the air before pulling Evie into his celebration.

"There's never been a perfect score given on a premiere night—ever!" he explained in Evie's ear, lifting her feet from the floor and kissing her cheek. Stunned and new to the show, she wasn't comprehending the magnitude of what she'd accomplished. Grant could hardly comprehend it himself.

The tears pooling in her green eyes escaped, but Evie brushed them away quickly. Grant took her by the hand and led her backstage as the crowd still continued to cheer. Out of sight, he promptly pulled her back into his arms again, hoping to offer comfort and reassurance in the overwhelming moment, even if he didn't fully understand why she was crying. He rubbed his hands up and down her arms as she shook from the adrenaline powering through her body.

"Evie, I don't know what happens when we sing that song, but it's amazing," he told her bluntly, and she shivered again.

"I know, it's crazy." Her voice was husky and barely above a whisper, and something in her words sounded different, stirring something deep within him in an uncomfortable way he couldn't pinpoint.

As the high of the performance started to ebb away, Grant became awkwardly aware that the moment, her body curved into his and his face nuzzled into her hair, was entirely too intimate. Every fiber of his being was alert, singing with want for her. The embrace had started out innocently enough, he'd only wanted to calm her rattled nerves, bring her down easy after the strong emotions the song awakened without relent.

Evie quickly untwisted herself from his embrace. "I'd really like to watch the other performances," she cleared her throat and announced, lifting the hem of her dress and practically running towards the steps leading to the contestants' viewing balcony.

"Okay, sure. You're wish is my command. At least for the next half hour anyway. Then, we have to line up for the final contestant shot and do an hour's worth of press." Grant laughed as he followed her up the staircase, attempting to shake off the awkwardness. He couldn't believe he'd let himself get carried away in the moment like that. At the taping. In plain view of any random passerby. Thankfully, Evie pulled away, stopping him from making a fool of himself. He still felt horrible, though. He should have known better.

Six other couples were poised at the edge of the balcony, watching the crew set up for Nell and Adam's upcoming number. In dress rehearsal earlier, Grant had watched a bit of their practice, and even though Nell had talent, the whole routine and her choice of costume screamed seduction. Honestly, Nell herself screamed seduction. He shuddered, thinking about how uncomfortable she made things by constantly coming on to him whenever he was around her. She'd already propositioned him twice, but she wasn't—and wouldn't ever be—his cup of tea. Even if he'd been single, Grant still wouldn't have been interested. Not to mention, he'd lost a lot of respect for Nell when she'd acted so rudely toward Evie the other night at dinner.

"I wonder what they have planned," Evie quietly commented, nodding towards the floor where Adam and Nell stood.

"Nell has a big say, just like you and all the other singers, in the musical portion of the competition. Adam's usually known for intense, sexy routines, but from what I've seen, this performance is on a whole new level. I guess he couldn't talk her down. Remember what I said in wardrobe about being pigeonholed?" Grant gestured towards the dance floor where Nell posed proudly in a costume that was little more than skimpy black lingerie.

Evie stared at the racy singer, her eyebrows furrowed. He wondered what thoughts were in her head right then. When the performance started, Grant kept his eyes on Evie as she watched the show, her lips slightly parted in shock, her eyes wide. Throughout the song, Nell gyrated her hips and ran her hands down her own and Adam's body whenever she had the chance.

"I feel like I need to put my hands over your eyes," Grant joked after Adam ripped open his shirt, buttons flying wildly.

"I'm innocent, but not that innocent," she laughed. Grant raised an eyebrow at her. His mind worked against him as he digested her comment. What was that supposed to mean? To his frustration, he stood there beside her, spending way too much time inappropriately contemplating what she meant. Not that it was really any of his business. He stretched his arms and popped his knuckles—desperately trying to stop thinking about the girl beside him.

They watched the rest of the couples perform—some were really good, some were mediocre, and there were a couple of pairings that were just . . . off. Maybe it was their song choice, or it had been too long since the last time they'd performed live, but a few particular pairings didn't go over all that well with the audience.

"Alright, time to go down to the stage and finish out the night," Grant said as he took Evie by the hand again. They made their way to the raised stage erected on the edge of the ballroom floor, and situated themselves in their designated places. Grant stood behind Evie, his hand firm around her waist, doing his best to symbolize the solidarity of their partnership, while the other couples settled into their places around them.

Once everyone was in formation, Corey went through his little spiel for the at-home viewers about voting for their favorite couple to keep them in the competition while the cameras panned over all of the couples, focusing in on each pairing as their voting number displayed across the screen. When Corey wrapped up with a reminder to tune in next week to see what inspired the singers, Evie turned to Grant with her eyes raised in question.

"Next week's theme is inspiration," he explained. The dancers had been told the day before in a brief meeting. She only nodded her acknowledgement since they were technically still on camera as the credits rolled, but he could sense a million questions rolling around in her head.

* * * *

"Your partner this season is . . ." Kacie trailed off before taking a sip from her beer bottle. Seated in a booth at a little Mexican restaurant off of the beaten West Hollywood path, he stared at her, waiting for her to finish her thought. She hadn't made it to the show that night since her studio session had ran over, but he was cool with that. He didn't expect her to be able to come to all of the tapings anyway.

"I guess you caught some of the show?" he asked her, treading cautiously, uncertain as to where this conversation might be heading, especially since she never finished her sentence. Kacie's frown and lack of eating her favorite, chicken chimichangas, didn't bode well. Something was on her mind.

She nodded. "Your partner . . ." she trailed off again.

"Is Evie Michaelson," Grant finally finished for her. "And?" he waved his fork, wishing she'd just spit it out already.

"Well, she's very pretty." Even Kacie's matter of fact tone sounded troubled. She pushed rice around with her fork before leaning back against the booth and tossing her dark hair over her shoulder with a disgruntled sigh.

"All of my partners have been nice looking." Grant tried to brush off his girlfriend's unwarranted jealousy. Okay, maybe it really wasn't unwarranted, but it should have been. For all she knew anyway.

"Yeah, but this particular one is ridiculously hot. And somehow elegant and poised and . . . her voice. Good grief, her voice. If she'd been singing and dancing with anyone other than my boyfriend tonight, I would be her biggest fan," Kacie explained before leaning up and taking a bite of her food at last.

Grant's face drained of color. Clearly, Kacie needed to know where things stood between Evie and him. "Wait. What are you saying? You don't like her? That's not very fair, and besides, she's not from here and she has a boyfriend. You have nothing to worry about when it comes to Evie and me."

"The fact that you feel the need to explain all of that in one rambling thought to me means I definitely have something to worry about, Grant."

"Kacie, I'm not going to lie to you because I never have and I don't want to start—Evie and I have amazing chemistry, but it's only in regards to performing. We're partners and friends, that's all." He took a big gulp of his beer.

"Didn't you mention last week that you were taking your new partner out to dinner?"

"Yes, so? It's not like I hid it from you, and it was only to get to know her better and to show her around the area."

"Why didn't you invite me?" Kacie asked, sounding a little hurt. This was all coming from so far out of left field, Grant couldn't keep up with it. She never got like this about his partners on the show, and he hung out with them without her all of the time.

"Because we met up with people from the show. I guess I viewed it as more of a work thing." He shrugged, staring at his plate.

"Grant, I wish I believed you. I'm going to try really hard to believe you, but I think there's something going on between you two—whether you realize it yet or not. That song with her at the piano—the way you looked at her, Grant . . ." Kacie started to cry a little in the middle of the restaurant. Grant wanted to crawl under the table. She used her cloth napkin to dab at her running mascara. Although the place wasn't all that crowded, a couple eyed them warily. "You've never looked at me like that," she sniffled.

"I was just emoting for the performance, Kacie. It's my job," Grant defended, feeling like a deer in headlights. He wasn't sure why he felt so guilty all of a sudden. He hadn't done anything wrong, other than having a handful of involuntary feelings that he pushed down whenever they tried to surface. That was natural, wasn't it? They had good chemistry, and with that, random feelings were prone to pop up. It didn't mean anything. If anything, Kacie should be thrilled to have such a faithful boyfriend.

"Tell yourself whatever you want, Grant, but you aren't that great of an actor."

CHAPTER NINE

"Did you decide on your inspiration?" Grant asked Evie, getting right to business as soon as she sat down at the table outside of a small cafe in West Hollywood the next morning. Still fuzzy from rising so early after the *Song & Dance* premiere, she desperately needed a humongous dose of caffeine. Maybe even an IV drip if she was supposed to get through another day at the breakneck pace they were required to keep.

To add to the exhaustion, she'd stayed up way too late after leaving the live taping the night before. Spending most of the night on the phone with a worried Davis, she'd had to explain over and over that there wasn't anything going on between her and Grant outside of friendship and dancing.

But, alas, there was no rest for the weary—just a breakfast meeting at seven in the morning with Grant, who, of course, looked like he'd just stepped off the cover of *GQ* in his fitted gray t-shirt and designer jeans, complemented by his freshly shaven, chiseled jaw and perfectly mussed hair. Meanwhile, she'd plopped into the wicker chair fifteen minutes late wearing sunglasses and gym clothes with her hair, stiff and full of dry shampoo, piled into a messy bun—and it wasn't cute, it was straight up ratty.

"Coffee," she said, too tired and cranky to say anything else.

"Coffee is your inspiration? I've never had a partner choose that before," Grant said, much too chipper as he pretended to mull it over. Evie rolled her eyes behind her sunglasses, tempted to throw the phone she held in her hand at his head. Instead, she picked up the cup sitting in front of him and took a big sip, hoping a little caffeine would offer the immediate pick-me-up she needed so badly. As the warm drink touched her tongue, she tried not to spit it out, choke or gag as she swallowed the infinitesimal amount that had made it into her mouth.

"What the heck is in this?" she asked him, peering into the white porcelain cup, wondering why the innocent looking brew tasted so terrible.

"It's a double espresso with soy milk," he explained as she sat his cup back down in front of him.

"My taste buds have just been murdered."

"I take it you're not an early morning person?"

"What gives you that idea?" she asked sarcastically as she waved down the waitress.

"For the most part, I'd say your general snarkiness gives it away, but the way you're slouching in your chair and looking murderous really drives it home," he told her, eyebrow arched.

"You don't seem like a real ball of sunshine yourself this morning, Grant," she countered, taking in the dark edge starting to seep around his cheerful facade. Crinkle-free smiles had abounded at the table now that she thought about it.

"Rough night," he said, but didn't elaborate.

After she flagged down their server and ordered a nice, normal cup of Colombian coffee with cream and sugar on the side, she turned her attention fully to Grant.

"I'll be a morning person after I have a cup or three of coffee," she told him, smiling brightly as their server promptly returned with a steaming cup and sat the aromatic brew in front of her. The waitress must have picked up on her desperation for a caffeine hit.

After a few sips, she started feeling less like a zombie and more like herself. Still not a morning person, but at least she didn't want to dump soy-ruined coffee on anyone's head anymore.

"I'd like to focus inspiration week around my parents. They are coming to see the show, so I think it would be nice to dedicate our performances to them. Is that okay with you?" she asked Grant after their food arrived and she'd had a moment to think about it. The scent of cinnamon apples rose from her steaming bowl of oatmeal.

"That sounds perfect. We're dancing a Viennese waltz, and there are a few songs that I've already screened and cleared—they'll work for anything or anyone inspiring if you don't have a specific song for the dance in mind." When she shook her head that she didn't, he continued, "We can listen to them after breakfast and you can pick which one you like best. As far as song performance, do you have something in mind for that?"

"Actually, I do. It's called 'Be Alright.'"

"Does it have duet possibilities? Or would you want me to just play?"

"There are a few spots where a nice harmony would work really well, and I think it's important that you sing as much as possible in our performances. It shows our versatility and strength, you know?" she waited a beat before adding, "There's something else about the song—I don't want to put the focus on my boyfriend, but the song is sort of love song. I still think it applies well to any relationship, but in a way, it can kind of be a tribute to Davis, too. What do you think about that spin on it?"

"Yeah, that's cool," Grant replied, looking down at his phone. It didn't seem all that cool with him, whether he admitted it or not. Strangely enough, an odd tug of guilt yanked at her as she talked about singing a song indirectly for Davis with Grant.

"He's going to try to make it to the taping next week, but it just depends on his schedule," she informed him.

"Great, I'd love to meet him," Grant clipped, shutting down, smiling the smile she didn't like, "As soon as we are done here, we can head over to the studio so that you can listen to those songs and we can start practicing our Viennese waltz."

"Okay, sounds good." Evie hurried to eat her oatmeal and sliced apples as Grant waved down the waitress to pay.

An hour later, they were settled into a small room at the dance studio listening to Grant's song selections for their dance. In the dimly lit room, cozied up in a comfortable leather desk chair, holding a warm to go cup of coffee in her hands, as she listened to the lilting, rhythmical melodies, her eyes drooped. She longed to curl up and take a morning nap. Instead, she forced her eyes to widen as she paid closer attention to the songs.

"What are your thoughts so far?" Grant asked her after she'd listened to two of the four options.

"They're nice." The songs had pretty melodies and sounded soft and romantic. They would both work just fine.

"Listen to the next one. I think you're going to love it," he said, tapping the playlist.

And of course, she did. Still romantic, but a little edgy, the song was kind of folksy, kind of bluesy. Plus, she generally loved anything by Ray Lamontagne.

"Do we have a winner?" he asked, staring down at her with a triumphant grin.

"Yes, and I think you knew I would like this one the best. Why didn't you just go ahead and choose it for us?"

"I wanted you to at least have options," Grant shrugged, standing up from his perch on the edge of an armchair and stretching before he extended his hand to help her up from her seat.

They headed out of the small room, down a long hallway and up a flight of steps. She could hear the muffled sounds of other couples practicing behind closed doors as they walked down the corridor. All the teams were hard at work and already preparing for the next round of competition. Grant pulled her along—his swift gait giving her no choice but to run-walk to match his hurried pace. They couldn't waste precious rehearsal time.

* * * *

Two days later, Grant called out, "That's a wrap for today!" After four solid hours of grueling practice, Evie collapsed into a heap of sore limbs on the floor.

"Thank God!" she exclaimed, breathing hard. The waltz was no joke. Who would've imagined that a traditional, slow dance would be so hard to learn? The technical movements twisted her brain like a pretzel and left her body aching and sore.

Grant walked over to the wooden bench, retrieved her steel water bottle and brought it to where she'd turned over to lie prostrate on the dance floor, zapped of all will or strength to move any further. She'd never been so tired before.

"I can assure you, Evie, that you are, in fact, not dying, nor am I torturing you, despite your insistence of both at least ten times today in practice," Grant remarked as she slowly sat up to take a swig from her bottle, wincing the whole time.

"You could've fooled me," she muttered, stretching her ridiculously sore arms. When she first woke up that morning, they'd hurt so bad she'd barely been able to slide her tank top over her shoulders. At one point, with her arms stuck halfway in the holes, she'd whimpered and briefly considered feigning an illness to get out of another long practice. It was only the second week of competition, but her body wasn't used to the constant physical exercise and the rubber had met the road, hitting hard.

"Go home, take a long, hot bath and relax for the rest of the night," he instructed her.

"Ha. I wish, but I have a show lined up tonight. It's with a few other performers, and the vibe is really low key, which means that I can thankfully sit at the piano for most of my set," she told him, already tired just thinking about the long night ahead of her. Moira booked the gig for her without really talking to her about the pace of the *Song & Dance* schedule—she'd just seen the opening in Evie's schedule and jumped at the last-minute opportunity when another band had canceled. If Moira had any idea how rough their practices were, she wouldn't have done that to her— even if she was trying to capitalize on Evie's presence in LA.

"I'm surprised you didn't mention it to me. Where's the show?"

"The El Rey."

"Impressive, Evie. The El Rey is small, but it's one of those places that hosts serious stars on the rise. What time is your show?"

"It was a last-minute thing. I'm going on at nine, and I'm supposed to have a forty-five-minute set."

"They gave you a great time. I might have to swing by and check it out. I'd love to see you live and in action."

Evie rolled her eyes. "You hear me sing all the time. This thing tonight isn't all that big of a deal, but it would be nice to have a friend in the crowd. The one person I'm semi-close to in LA outside of this show is working tonight and can't come," she confessed, attempting to get up, but flopping immediately back to the floor as her abs screamed in protest.

Maybe it was her crazy schedule over the past few days, the recent, little bout of homesickness she'd suffered, or a combination of both of those factors, but going to her set tonight all alone stressed her out. Moira said she would try and stop by between two other events, but their relationship was strictly businesslike in nature and that wasn't a guarantee, so Grant wanting to come hear her set lifted her spirits more than she cared to admit.

"I'll definitely be there, but I have an even better idea. What if I just went with you?" he offered.

Evie hesitated. Under normal circumstances, she would immediately turn down such a generous offer outright. Going with her would take over his whole night. Between practices, show-required press appearances and the tapings, the show and consequentially, she, monopolized almost all of his time. Adding something else to his plate involving her seemed selfish. However, she wasn't feeling like her normal, hospitable self.

"Yes, I would really like it if you came to the show with me. I'm a little overwhelmed coming off of the premiere, and practicing all day yesterday and today, and now having to rush home, get dressed and perform this evening. I have to stay for an after party, too, so it's going to be really late . . ."

"Wait. Were you planning to go do all of this by yourself?"

"Well, yeah. Who else would be going with me? Besides, I know a couple of people from *America Sings* that were already on the line up. Acquaintances, at least, and my agent said she was going to stop by, too."

"It's not that I don't think you're entirely capable of doing this on your own—because you are—but I'm happy to go with you. You do seem a little overwhelmed today. I think you need my support tonight, and that's what I'm here for . . . as your partner. Plus, I can make sure you get home as early as feasibly possible and into bed. I'll give you a pass and we won't start rehearsals until ten tomorrow," he said with a wink, holding out his hands to help her off the floor.

"I knew there would be a really good reason for you to come along! You won't want to get up in the morning either," Evie pointed out.

"What time do you have to be there?"

"An hour before my set starts."

"I'll pick you up at seven then."

Evie managed, with great effort, to put her body into motion and hobble across the gym floor, gather her stuff together and scoot out the door. There was no time to waste. Traffic was a beast everywhere in LA, and it took time and effort to get full-on stage ready. At least she already knew what she was going to wear—a flowing emerald maxi dress and strappy, gold sandals. That was one less thing she'd have to stress over this evening.

The rest of the afternoon and early evening passed in a blur of traffic, makeup and hot rollers, and as she was putting in a pair of nice-sized diamond studs, Grant knocked at the door.

"Coming!" she called from the bedroom, hurrying through the little studio, her emerald dress flapping behind her. She grabbed her clutch purse before swinging the door open. Standing there, in a black t-shirt and jeans, which she sort of thought of as his uniform at this point, Grant waited in all of his smoldering glory. His admiring gaze washed over her and butterflies filled her stomach. As someone else's girlfriend, the warmth creeping up her neck and her excited, fluttering heart teetered dangerously over the line of inappropriate, but it was involuntary. There was no helping it.

"You look spectacular, Evie," he complimented, leaning in to give her a brief hug and a quick kiss on the cheek in familiar greeting. Catching a whiff of his subtle, spicy cologne, she fought the urge to bury her nose in the hollow of his neck.

"You don't look so bad yourself," she replied. It took great effort not to linger too close to him as she stepped into the hallway and locked the door behind them. Maybe it wasn't such a good idea for him to go with her, now that she thought about it. Oh well, too late to turn him away. She would just have to be on guard against herself.

On the ride over to the venue, she relaxed as their conversation focused solely on music. After Evie had explained in detail the attributes of what she classified as a good, classic rock guitar riff, out of nowhere, Grant asked her about Davis.

"Did your boyfriend watch the show the other night?" he asked, drumming his fingers on the steering wheel while staring a hole through the light they were waiting on to turn green. Neither of them had mentioned their significant others since the show aired.

"Yep," she said after a moment, hesitant to delve further into the touchy subject. He glanced at her.

"Hmm, I see."

"What do you see?" she questioned, turning in her seat to face him.

"I see that you're dealing with a jealous boyfriend who doesn't understand performance chemistry," he explained, hitting the nail on the head. He heard the things she said when she didn't say much of anything at all.

"Do you ever have that problem with Kacie?" Evie questioned, watching Grant's jaw flex.

"From time to time. She usually understands since she is a performer herself."

"That makes sense. Hopefully, when Davis comes to the show next week, he can meet you and he'll understand a little better."

"So, he is coming?"

"He says that he is."

"I can't promise that it will help all that much, Evie," Grant warned as they pulled into a parking lot.

"What do you mean?" Evie asked when he'd parked. He pulled the keys from the ignition and got out of the car. She hopped out after him.

"What do you mean?" She repeated her question.

"Our chemistry—it's of the variety that makes significant others feel threatened," he explained, across the top of his car.

"Does Kacie feel threatened . . . by me?" Evie ventured. She couldn't imagine that someone as edgy, hot and hip as Grant's indie-artist, LA-native girlfriend could ever see her—still fresh from the sticks of rural Alabama—as a threat.

Grant didn't answer right away. But when he did, it took all within her power to keep her jaw from dropping to the pavement as they headed towards the theater.

"Yes, unfortunately. We actually had a bit of an argument about it after the show the other night," he confided as he held the backstage door open for her.

"Oh no, I'm sorry, Grant," she apologized, but before she could say anything else, he stopped her in the backstage hallway and grabbed hold of her arms, startling her, as he stared straight into her eyes. Growing uncomfortable under his intense gaze, she glanced away.

"You have nothing to apologize for," he said, each word fierce and deliberate. "You haven't done anything wrong. Don't say you're sorry."

She couldn't avoid those eyes of his any longer, nor his defiant proclamation and admonishment. In that intense moment as his piercing gaze cut straight into her soul, she admitted to herself that she wasn't innocent. Her eyes darted down again, guilty. She did have wayward feelings for Grant—something his astute girlfriend had probably picked up on when she watched them together. There was a spark between the two of them. Why else would his girlfriend be so worried?

From that point forward, Evie resolved to keep the spark between them just that—a harmless spark. The spark could not be allowed to ignite into untamed, raging brushfire flames.

He'd yet to let her go. Grant wouldn't allow her to escape his gaze or grasp until she acknowledged her innocence and agreed to stop apologizing.

"Okay," she whispered, forcing herself to meet Grant's smoldering gaze once more. Sparks flew. Her heart thudded. The goal changed. Keep the fire contained, and don't fan flames, she thought. As they stood stone still, his hands still holding her arms, whatever was going on between them was no longer just a spark.

* * * *

Grant's eyes were fixated on Evie as she performed onstage. He took a sip of his drink, whiskey neat. Nothing fruity or syrupy ever made its way into his drink if he could help it. He watched as Evie sang her heart out, currently belting out one of her originals, the words poignant, the music mysterious.

From his spot near the stage, he had a perfect view of her at the keyboard. Man, she could play. He could listen to her playing all night, but when she sang in that breathy voice of hers, chills would shoot down his spine. She would one day be selling out arenas, no doubt about it.

"Hey, y'all," Evie said, her Southern twang evident, after she'd finished her song. "I have a special friend in the audience tonight, and I was wondering if it'd be okay if he came up and sang this next song with me?"

The audience hooted and hollered, calling out their approval.

"Grant, would you join me up here, please?" She asked, peering into the darkened theater, seeking him out among the crowd. When she spotted him, she grew bright, a fresh smile spread across her face, and his heart did that thing he didn't quite understand when he was around her. He hopped onto the stage, following her directions, trying his hardest not to put too much thought into it.

"Mr. Grant Merritt, y'all, my partner on a little show called *Song & Dance!*" She said with a flourish and the crowd broke into cheers and applause. He leaned over to Evie where she sat at the keyboard. "What song are we singing?" He asked, praying he would know it.

"'Let It Go,' James Bay?" She suggested. He nodded—he knew her first suggestion, thank God. She started playing the chords and the melody filled the theater. She sang the first verse, captivating everyone in a way he didn't understand, but was just as drawn in as everyone else. Grant watched her closely.

When she started in on the chorus, he joined her with a harmony. Being with her on stage—he loved every second. Just being with her period was something he enjoyed way too much. What was going on between them was unstoppable, even though neither had yet to admit it, nor would they. Too much was at stake.

"I hope it was okay that I surprised you like that," she confided, leaning in close to be heard over the loud music of the after-party. They'd settled in a cozy booth in the VIP Lounge.

"Of course, it was okay. Thanks for letting me sing with you—it was an honor," he replied, slipping his arm around her and giving her a squeeze.

"I love singing with you," she said, leaning even closer, and he didn't stop her, nor did he move his arm away. He eyed her second glass of wine. "You smell so good," she whispered. "Like Christmas and happiness and a walk in the woods," she rambled, leaning her head on his shoulder.

"Thanks, I think," he responded, raising an eyebrow.

"It was a compliment, for sure."

"You smell good, too, Evie," he said, sniffing her hair, which smelled like coconuts and vanilla, lingering longer than he should have.

"I like spending time with you," she said happily. He froze. As much as he felt the same way, saying certain things out loud would change everything.

"And I like spending time with you, but you're a little tipsy, Evie, and I should probably get you home. We're swimming into dangerous waters."

She stared at him. "Why would they be dangerous?"

"You know why. I don't think I need to, nor should I, spell it out. It's best if neither of us say it out loud, so please, for both of our sakes, let me take you home and let you sleep off whatever it is you drank tonight."

"Okay," she pouted as he moved his arm and stood up. He helped her out and they headed out of the party and across the dark parking lot without saying a word to one another. The tension between them weighed heavy.

Once he had her safely tucked into his car, he hopped in, cranked it up and pulled away. "This was fun," he ventured, attempting to break the awkward silence as he pulled onto the highway. She'd grown strangely quiet.

"Yes, as always, although, according to you, I shouldn't admit that," she replied snidely. He sighed.

"Evie, there's a line we really shouldn't cross and you and I have both been dancing really close to it tonight."

"What are you saying without really saying it?" She asked in exasperation.

"I'm saying there's a reason we're the showmance, a reason our significant others are jealous, and a reason I can't keep my eyes off of you."

She touched his arm where it lay resting on the console in the dark interior of his car. "I can't keep mine off of you either." She surprised him by saying not another word the rest of the way back to her apartment.

CHAPTER TEN

"Mom, Dad, I'd like y'all to meet Grant, my dance partner." Evie announced the following Tuesday night, pulling Grant into her infinitesimal trailer and presenting him proudly to her parents. Her parents stood from their cramped seats on the trailer's tiny navy sofa and smiled stiffly when Grant entered. Their awkward reaction was hard to understand. Decked out in her sequin and feather-trimmed mint ball gown beside Grant in his tuxedo with tails and matching mint tie, she and Grant made quite the dashing pair for Inspirations Week. Her parents were supposed to be impressed, not stressed and strained.

"Nice to meet you, Grant. I'm Evie's mother, Sue Anne Michaelson, and this is my husband, Jim." Her mother forced her sugary, sweet "company" smile across her face as she extended her tan, perfectly manicured hand to Grant in greeting.

"It's an honor to meet the two of you. It's been a pleasure to work with Evie these past couple of weeks —she's a true gem and the hardest worker I've ever met. You guys have a wonderful daughter," Grant gushed, shaking both of their hands warmly.

"We think so. Now, tell me Grant, has my Evie been using her good Southern manners and being real sweet to you?" her mother asked, an eyebrow arched. Evie knew she was only half kidding.

"Evie is the most graceful example of a lady that I have ever had the pleasure of being around," Grant replied frankly and her mother finally broke into a sincere smile.

"That's sweet of you to say, Grant," Evie told him, feeling her cheeks growing red.

"Aww, Evie, you're blushing!" her mother exclaimed.

"Hush, Mom! Don't make it worse," Evie added, confused at the mixture of emotions whirling inside of her. Undeniable attraction to Grant, trying to stop the feels for Grant, happiness at her parents' presence even if she couldn't pinpoint the source of their wariness— all topped off with anxiety over her and Grant's impending live performance. The wild range of emotions waged war for dominance within her. Plus, Davis' absence added a touch of melancholy to the evening. She missed him, of course, but she was guiltily a little relieved that he wasn't meeting Grant in person yet.

She stared down at her folded hands, encased in white satin gloves. Distracted by her inner struggles, how would she ever calm down enough to remember all the subtle nuances that really made their Viennese waltz special?

"Don't worry, Evie. I'd be blushing, too, if such a handsome man paid me such a wonderful compliment," her mother added flirtatiously. Evie wanted to crawl under the vanity table as Grant coughed and edged toward the doorway.

"Mr. and Mrs. Michaelson, it was lovely to meet you both. Now if you'll excuse me, I have to attend to a few more details before we're due to meet with the press," he said before ducking out of the trailer.

"Well, what do you think of him?" Evie asked as she checked her lipstick in the mirror after Grant fled the trailer.

Her parents exchanged knowing looks. Evie stood up straight, turning to face her parents directly and discern the meaning of their silent conversation.

"Grant seems like a wonderful man, Evie—he really does—but I have to ask . . . is something going on there between you two?" her mother questioned, eying her intently.

"Mom, good grief! No, I'm with Davis and besides, Grant has a girlfriend named Kacie that he's been with for a long time, too," Evie rushed to explain, feeling the spread of a blush *again*—this time at her mother's unexpected and all-too-intuitive questioning.

Her mom studied her for a moment before replying, choosing her words carefully. "It just seems like . . . well, never mind. If you say nothing is going on, I believe you," her mother replied with a determined nod of her head.

"Too bad Davis wasn't able to come tonight. I miss him so much," Evie added, attempting to distract her parents from thoughts of her and Grant's partnership. She swallowed hard, feeling like a child that had misbehaved at the dinner table. She vividly remembered one instance when she'd given a similarly weak excuse as she was caught spooning lima beans from her plate into a nearby potted plant.

"We haven't seen him at church in a while—he's been at school every weekend since his finals are coming up," her dad pitched in, helping to lighten the conversation.

"I talk to him almost every day. This semester has been really tough for him," Evie supplied, checking her makeup once more in the trailer's mirror.

"He has to be missing you so much," her mother added, placing a warm hand on Evie's shoulder. While she knew her mother was her biggest fan, Davis could claim her as his biggest fan, too. Davis' mother and her mother had been the best of friends since their own glory days in high school and subsequently as roommates and sorority sisters at Auburn. They'd started preliminary plans for Davis and Evie's wedding, to both of the latter's dismay, the second they'd graduated high school.

"I miss him, too, Mom."

"Really? You might be saying that, sugar, but you're not acting like it."

"My life is crazy right now, Mom. This competition is fierce and it's taking a lot of my focus. Plus, I had a gig this past weekend, too."

"I'm glad you are having a good time, sweetie. Just don't forget what's most important," her mother admonished, catching Evie's eyes in the mirror knowingly before giving her a light kiss on the cheek. Evie swallowed the lump forming in her throat. Her mother's guilt trip had been subtle, yet effective, and while Evie usually valued and appreciated her mother's soft reminders, tonight her hackles raised. What exactly *was* most important?

She watched her parents silently exit the trailer, tension still hanging in the air.

* * * *

"Your mother is a sweetheart," Grant remarked when Evie sidled up beside him backstage twenty minutes later.

"I'm glad you think so," Evie replied brightly. Grant looked at her oddly.

"Don't try and read me like a book right now, I don't think I could take it," Evie hissed under her breath, shaking her head.

"Got it." Grant gently squeezed her shoulder before walking over to where Jared and Adam stood talking several feet away. Evie didn't blame him for leaving her alone—she needed to get herself together. How could she dance a light and airy Viennese waltz when she felt like stomping up and down and crossing her arms like a five year old whose favorite toy had been taken away?

She walked over to the refreshment cart, picked up a bottle of water and tried to twist the top off, but her satin gloves prevented success, much to her frustration. She thought about smacking the bottle against the table, but then decided against doing something so dumb in front of all these people. Before she peeled off one of her gloves so she could twist the cap, Grant appeared out of nowhere, took the bottle from her hand, opened it and wordlessly handed it back to her.

"Thanks." She offered a begrudging smile.

"No problem. The show is starting soon," he reminded her softly before walking off again, still respecting the space she needed.

Of course, she knew that the show was starting soon. In less than half an hour, she would dance a romantic and tender routine with him—in honor of her parents of all people—but before that happened, the heavy chains of guilt that they'd tossed across her shoulders had to go.

Some things were easier said than done.

* * * *

"See? That wasn't so bad," Grant whispered as they walked backstage right after they'd performed their waltz and received their scores.

Evie nodded. She'd somehow managed to put aside her issues and finish the dance with only a slight misstep during a particularly difficult turn. The judges pointed out the mistake, but enjoyed the dance, so their scores were good. Not perfect, but good.

"Just means we still have to work towards a perfect dance score," Grant pointed out.

"That perfect song score last week has me super nervous right now. There's a lot of pressure for this week to be just as good," Evie confided.

"Don't worry, it is just as good, if not better. You sound amazing, and the song is great for your voice."

"Thank you. I'm sorry I was in a bit of a funk earlier. My mom just has a way of getting under my skin, but even when we disagree, I still love her," she replied.

"Moms are good at getting under skin," he said, winking. "Sometimes, as performers, we have to compartmentalize. The show must go on...even when we feel like crap," he added, his voice serious.

"You're right, and I'm pushing through it."

"I know you are, and you're doing great," he encouraged, smiling. She could always count on Grant to say what she needed to her. Not always what she wanted to hear, but definitely what she needed. His coaching skills were on point.

She parted ways with him to go change into the gold, strapless, mermaid gown they'd selected for the song set. She'd be lying if she said she didn't enjoy the beautiful costumes and professional hair and makeup team that managed to transform her so efficiently for the past two weeks in a row.

"What do you think?" she asked Grant, twirling around to show off her new look when she met back up with him on the viewing balcony. With her hair in a low, loose bun, ruby red lips and tons of gold sequins sparkling and reflecting the light as she moved in her couture gown, she felt like a glamorous starlet.

"Beautiful, as always," he said, his voice tender, yet resigned.

"Thank you, you look great, too . . . as always," she told him, mimicking his strange tone for delivering a sentiment. He gestured for her to stand with him before turning back to watch Jared and Amelia singing below them. Amelia sounded great, but her nerves were evident.

"How do you feel about being last to perform tonight?" Grant asked.

She shrugged. "It is what it is. Don't get me wrong—I'd rather get it over with and relax during everyone else's performances, but someone has to be first and someone has to be last. We all can't be in the comfortable middle."

"Good point." They watched the others perform until they had to go down and prepare for their own turn to take the stage.

For the performance, Evie took center stage singing into a vintage-style microphone as the spotlights caught the sparkle of her dress and Grant stood back a bit with the rest of the band, playing his guitar and only singing backup vocals during the chorus. "Be Alright" was an emotional choice for her, and she caught both her mother's and father's eye as much as she could throughout the song, letting go of any differences they may have had earlier in the evening. She briefly thought about Davis as she sung, wondering if he was watching from his dorm room.

Grant's baritone came in with the low harmony during the chorus, and she sensed his strong presence behind her. As much as she loved this song, she missed him having a bigger part in the performance. She'd keep that in mind if they made it through to the next round of competition.

"Is this what you call love? This is what I'm thinking of…" she crooned as the song came to an end and the room filled with hearty applause. She dipped the tiniest of curtsies in her snug gown.

After a few, encouraging sentiments from the judges, their scores were revealed once more. They weren't perfect, but she wasn't going to complain about the four out of five stars they received. It kind of took the pressure off maintaining a perfect record. Immediately after their scoring, Grant and Evie rushed to get into the lineup with all the other couples for the show's first elimination of the season.

Evie held her breath as couple after couple were pronounced safe. When the stage occupants narrowed down to just her and Grant and another couple—the older, doo-wop singer, Melvin, and his pro partner, Katia—her hands started shaking. She pressed them tightly together as Grant rubbed his hand up and down her arm in a soothing motion.

"The couple with the lowest votes who'll be heading home tonight is . . ." Corey dramatically tapered off. Several seconds passed as Evie's heart pounded so loudly she heard each pulsing beat in her ears.

"Melvin and Katia," he finally announced before she fainted. "Grant and Evie, you're safe and we'll see you next week," he added.

A whoosh of relief flooded her trembling body, but she didn't celebrate too openly—that would've been mean. She just gave Grant a quick hug and walked over to offer a kind word to Melvin and Katia. This wasn't her first experience on a reality competition show—no one liked a smug or thoughtless winner. Besides, she really liked Melvin and felt bad for his early exit.

Once the credits started rolling, Grant quickly escorted Evie backstage.

He stopped short, taking hold of her arm when they reached the curtained hallway. "Are you alright?" he asked, eyeing her closely.

"Yes, yeah, I mean, I guess," she chattered. Keyed up nerves were coming into play now that it was all over.

"It really sucks when they do that. I knew we weren't going home over Melvin and Katia, but it doesn't make it any less nerve wracking. They waited to call us safe until the very end for dramatic effect, you know that right? It has nothing to do with the number of votes we received," he explained, studying her closely.

"I figured as much, but it doesn't make it any easier. That was hard!"

Grant pulled Evie into a big bear hug. "I know. It's no fun to have your emotions played with like that," he said against her hair.

Behind her, someone cleared their throat. Evie pulled away from Grant and turned around to see her parents standing there, looking like they'd caught a cat eating a canary.

"Mom, Dad," she acknowledged, unable to stifle the guilty feelings rolling in like a thunderstorm.

"Evie, we just wanted to tell you how beautiful you looked and how wonderful your performance was tonight. You too, Grant," Evie's mother said, her hands folded primly in front of her.

"Thanks, Mom," she said softly. Her mother stepped closer to her.

"That song you sang was breathtaking, Evie. I love you so much, sweet girl." Her voice broke as she let down her guard and wrapped her arms around Evie.

"I love you, too, Mom," Evie said, tears welling as she returned her mother's hug.

"Did you guys want to go to dinner now?" Evie asked them after she'd stepped back from her mother's embrace.

"Our flight leaves at six tomorrow morning, Evie, so I think we're just going to call it a night. We'll pick up some takeout and see you back at your apartment once you've finish with the press," her mother told her with a yawn.

Evie nodded, a little disappointed as she watched them walk away after saying goodnight to the two of them.

"I don't think your parents like me," Grant commented when her parents were out of ear shot.

She turned to him. "It's not what you think," she assured him, "I'm sure they'd like you very much if they got the chance to know you." *And if they didn't feel like you were a threat to my relationship with Davis,* she silently added.

* * * *

"Hey, Evie. Sorry I missed the show last night," Davis said into the phone the next morning once she'd dropped her parents off at the airport.

"It's okay—I understand. How's school going?" she asked.

"Brutal. These last few classes are intense. It's not like high school where senior year is a breeze, that's for sure."

"Take it easy, okay? You don't want to overstress," Evie warned as she pulled back onto the interstate, heading to meet Grant for practice.

"Thanks, Mom. I will," Davis said, his voice dripping with sarcasm.

"No need to get touchy, Davis. I care about you, that's all."

"How's old Grant?" Davis asked, abruptly changing the subject.

"He's fine. Disappointed he didn't get to meet you," Evie offered as she darted through traffic in the direction of the studio.

"I'm sure he is." Davis' sarcasm game was strong that morning.

"You don't have anything to worry about there." Evie cut straight to the point.

"That's what you keep telling me, and I keep telling myself that I wish I believed you."

"I wish you did, too," Evie said sadly. Although, she couldn't expect him to believe her if she wasn't sure she even believed herself.

"Maybe I'll try to make it out there for the show next week," he offered.

"That would be great, Davis. I would love to see you. I've been missing you." She prayed he would really come this time. Seeing him would remind her of why they were together, how much he meant to her, and squash the infatuation she had brewing for Grant.

CHAPTER ELEVEN

"What's wrong, Evs?" Grant asked Evie that Saturday at practice. She stared out the window as she sipped water between run throughs of their cha cha.

"Nothing," she replied, her eyes darting toward Steve. Grant nodded, dropping it. Over the past few weeks they'd developed a sort of code in front of the camera and crew. Something was wrong, but a quick glance at the camera guy meant she absolutely did not want to talk about it in front of the cameras. They could take filming breaks, and he considered taking one so they could talk through her melancholy mood, but she'd already sat her water bottle down and was waiting for him in the middle of the studio to start practicing again.

"Talk later?" he mouthed. She infinitesimally nodded as the music filled the room. As the beat started, he came up behind her, pulled her into his arms and started moving to the rhythm. They moved around the floor in synchronicity before separating and she danced towards him before he took her back into his arms again.

"Remember, only the hips go back, keep your frame forward," he reminder her as they danced. She nodded, saying nothing, which wasn't surprising. She'd said only a handful of things to him all morning.

Once they'd practiced the routine several more times, their studio time ran out and they gathered their stuff up to leave. Steve packed up his camera and headed out.

"I'll see you guys tomorrow at three," he told them with a small wave on his way out the door.

"Bye, Steve," Evie called out as she and Grant waved goodbye to him.

"Will you tell me what's the matter now?" Grant asked as soon as the door shut behind Steve. Their mics were safely packed up and headed for a night of charging along with Steve's camera and they had about a five-minute window before the next group in line for the room would bustle in.

"Davis isn't coming to LA this week either." Evie stared out the window again, not meeting his eyes.

"Are you all that surprised?" Grant asked, actually trying not to sound insensitive, but tired of Evie's boyfriend disappointing her.

"Yes, I am, Grant," she replied angrily. "We haven't seen each other in almost a month."

Grant stared at her, confused. "I didn't think that was all that strange...I thought you guys had pretty conflicting schedules."

Evie tossed her hands in the air and turned to leave. "Yeah, well, I just really needed him to come out here, okay? And I'm frustrated. I'll talk to you later." She left the room without looking back.

What was her deal? Ever since her parents had visited, she'd been acting strangely. And very distant.

Later that afternoon, he tried calling her, but she didn't answer, and her replies to his texts were only one word. They didn't speak until the next morning at their meeting over coffee. They met at the same café, "their café" they'd started calling it, where they met three times a week for Grant to go over coaching tips, for Evie to give her feedback, and where they brainstormed for their performances before Grant approached production. These weekly meetings were vital to their success in Grant's opinion. Especially this one. Communication between them was at a standstill and that had to be fixed immediately.

"Evie, spill it," Grant said as soon as she took a seat across from him. He'd already ordered her coffee and it was waiting in front of her. She took a sip before responding to his direct command.

"Grant, I'm just working through some stuff on my own, okay? You don't need to know everything that goes through my head every second of the day."

"You're right, Evie, I don't. But whatever is going on with you is affecting our partnership. I can't help solve a problem if I don't have a clue as to what's going on."

She rolled her eyes. "I get that you want to fix it, and I appreciate your concern, I really do. But, you can't solve this. I'm struggling with my relationships outside of the show. My parents and Davis and honestly, I miss my friends, too. And all of this isn't the show's fault—I kind of stopped reaching out when I competed on *America Sings* last year. Don't get me wrong, I have plenty of acquaintances and I get tons of well-wishing texts, and I've even gone to lunch, you know, with Amelia and Shanda, and then there's you, of course, so I'm not missing out on companionship.

"It's something I can't really explain. My college roommates are getting ready to graduate and you're not going to believe this—all three of them are getting married before the end of the year. It's not weird, I promise. It's just a different culture. They're finished with school, they love their boyfriends and they're ready to be wives and moms. They've waited their whole lives for that, and where we're from, that's just how it is. It's what's expected and it's…nice.

I'm living a completely different life now, which Davis resents. I think he was going to propose at Christmas, but I hinted that there was still a lot of career things I wanted to do before I got married, and so I feel like he resents me because Mark and Sarah Beth, Jake and Lindsey, and Connor and Katie are all in this stage of life together and because of me, he's, I mean, we're not."

Grant processed what she'd just unloaded. He was pushing thirty and hadn't even remotely thought about marriage, and the girl in front of him was struggling with it in a way he couldn't fathom. He tried putting himself into the narrative.

"Do you think it's that you're not ready for marriage or that you're not sure Davis is the one you want to marry?" He asked her.

She sipped her coffee thoughtfully. "I don't say much about marriage because I feel like it's something that I've felt so much pressure from that I almost rebel against it. But that isn't how I really feel. I love the idea of marriage—the commitment, the partner through thick and thin. I'm realistic and I've been in a relationship that's lasted longer than many couples' marriages, so I get that "feelings" are not the basis of love. My struggle with Davis is that our goals and ideals aren't really lining up, and it's almost like he wants me to "hurry up and be done" with music so that we can get on with our lives. He doesn't want long distance. The NFL draft is next weekend in Denver. If he gets drafted, I don't know what that means for us. If he doesn't, he might try to walk on with the Saints, or he may just settle down and work at his dad's insurance company."

"It sounds like no matter what, he wants you to come to him, not he come to you," Grant pointed out, stirring the granola and fruit the server had just placed in front of him.

Evie sighed, picking at a muffin. "Pretty much. Which makes me feel like I have to choose between a career I love and the man I love."

"That's an unfair decision. A man that really loves you wouldn't want to hold you back from living the life God has given you to live. You have too much talent and charisma to sit it on a shelf, Evie," Grant told her. How could her boyfriend not see that? "I have another question for you to consider," he continued, "if Davis was willing to compromise and figure out something that worked for both of you, if he asked you to marry him would you say yes?"

She didn't answer right away. Finally, in a soft voice, she admitted to him the answer he already knew.

"No."

"Why not?"

"I'm not sure, and I don't know how I feel about that. You don't understand the amount of people I will disappoint if I don't marry Davis one day. And maybe, that's it. I'm just not ready yet. Maybe one day I'll be ready."

"You just said that you love the idea of being married. If you love Davis, and he compromised on the career aspect, or was even willing to completely support you, why wouldn't you?"

She turned the tables on him. "How do you feel about marriage? Why haven't you asked Kacie?"

"That's a completely different set of circumstances, Evie, and you know it. I don't ever see myself marrying Kacie. I'm not sure if I'll ever get married at all. I've never even thought about it."

"Then you need to quit wasting her time. She loves you, Grant, and she sees a future with you. If you're not willing to give her that, you need to let her go and leave her alone."

"I think the pot is calling the kettle black right now," he replied, tugging at the collar of his shirt.

"I'm only telling you the truth. At this point, we're pretty good friends and I feel comfortable saying that to you, just like you feel comfortable telling me how Davis doesn't deserve me on the regular."

"He doesn't," Grant immediately replied. "I think you've outgrown him and he's jealous of you and the attention you get. You need someone that celebrates you and pushes you to be more, not someone that you need to dim your light around, so they aren't intimidated by the way you shine."

"You're getting on a soapbox and we're way off of the subject at hand, Grant. The bottom line is, I feel out of sorts, like I'm straddling a fence. Half of me misses my old, uncomplicated life—even the expectations that I thought I hated so much, but the other half is dying to let go and live this amazing life opportunity I've been handed—see the world, sing and play, and just see what happens without having it all figured out." Evie sighed wistfully.

"Does it have to be one or the other? Are you afraid of being all alone if you give up your old life?"

Tears welled in Evie's eyes. She nodded. "Yes, of course, I am. Who do I have? I thought my mom was supportive, but over the past week, she's pretty much told me she sees this the same way Davis sees it, and my dad goes along with whatever she says. Sarah Beth, Lindsey and Katie—well, I've been pretty MIA this last year and they're all about to marry Davis' buddies, so of course, if things don't go well for Davis and me, they'll be on his side. I'm friends with a few *America Sings* alumni, but I wouldn't call those close relationships, and well, you know, the situation with Davis."

Grant reached across the table and took her hand. He gave it a squeeze. "You forgot someone. You have me."

A tear spilled down her cheek. "What are you talking about? You're my dance partner. I consider you a wonderful friend, but once this show is over, it won't be the same."

"Why do you say that? Have I given you a reason to think that? I'll let you in on a little secret—I've liked and appreciated all my partners, and I'm still friends with them, but I haven't cared about any of them as much as I care about you. We click in a way I didn't expect, and you have a real, true friend and supporter for life sitting right across from you." His eyes never left hers.

"Grant, I don't…you don't…" She pulled her hand from his and grabbed her napkin to dab at her eyes.

"Just stop it. We've developed a strong, genuine friendship in a short amount of time. I'm a huge Evie fan and I always will be. You have someone in your corner no matter what. Now, let go of whatever is holding you back and follow your heart. Don't make your decisions based on other people's expectations. If they really love you, they love all of you—smart, beautiful and successful you. You just said love isn't only about feelings. It's unconditional. It isn't supposed to be transactional, and I'm not just talking about romantic love—I'm talking about in all of your relationships."

Evie took a deep breath and fanned her face. "You're right. I have a lot to process. Thanks for listening to me and offering such honest advice. I didn't realize how much I've been bottling up until it finally poured out of me."

He looked at her across the table—messy ponytail, blotchy face from crying. She wasn't wearing anything special—just a plain tank top and jeans. The only makeup she wore was a bit of smudged mascara. Passersby didn't recognize her as the girl gracing their television screen every week and receiving millions of votes. Kim hinted to him (even though she wasn't supposed to) that the amounts of votes Evie was receiving was breaking show records. But the girl sitting across from him was just a regular girl dealing with regular life issues and feeling lost and lonely. The Evie everyone saw on television and adored was authentically wonderful, but the real-life Evie in front of him was his favorite. She was honest and imperfect and genuine to her core. He meant what he said—he would be her friend for life.

CHAPTER TWELVE

A week and a half later, as he took in her costume and makeup, there was no doubt about it— Evie could pull off any look. Grant had been skeptical about the hip hop costume, but in her ripped black leggings and off-the-shoulder shirt, she could have passed for one of J. Lo's backup dancers. As was par for the course at this point, he struggled to drag his eyes off of her, but it was crunch time and he had to focus. He stretched and did a little running in place to get his blood pumping as Cindy, one of the hair stylists, worked hard to make sure not even one inch of Evie's honey-blonde curls would go awry during their high energy, hip hop routine for the fourth week of competition. He took a few steps to close the distance and stood right beside her makeup chair.

"You ready?" Grant asked her.

"This dance is hard. I'm more nervous about this dance than I've been about any of the others," she said, biting her lip but immediately letting it go when Cindy gave her a stern look. Couldn't mess with the makeup so close to show time. For Grant, it was another reminder of why he was glad he wasn't a girl. A quick change, a little hair gel and stage makeup, and he was pretty much ready to perform. No sitting in makeup and hair for hours on end.

"You're nailing it every time. Just stay out of your own head when we go live. The second you stop having fun and start worrying about your every move is when you're vulnerable to make mistakes. If you miss a step, you know what to do."

"Just keep going," she replied. He'd been drilling her with that mantra all week because of the routine's fast and specific choreography. Interrupting his impromptu coaching session, Kim's voice in his earpiece reminded him of the time. They were on in ten.

"Is she good to go?" Grant asked Cindy, who gave him a confident nod, proud of her work. Evie did her customary little spin and he took a couple of seconds, all in the name of being a good partner, of course, to appreciate the way she wore everything way too well.

"Evie, you . . . look . . ." he trailed off. Why did she do this to him? It wasn't even a fancy or mind-blowing ensemble.

"Are you speechless, Grant?" she teased, hooking her arm through his. "I'm guessing it's about that time?" she queried.

"Yep. Time to take our places. You look good. I can't think of the right word for it—pretty is too soft, but fierce isn't right either."

She laughed. "Well, perfectly ordinary sounds like what you're trying to say!" she teased.

"You know that's not what I meant. This look fits this dance," he explained.

Once they were in place, they waited for their cues after the music and the troupe dancers started. This was their first dance with half a dozen troupe members. On cue, Evie popped into the middle and began dancing at the front of the troupe as they all went through an intricate routine that involved a few new styles, including isolations, a little street style animation and some neck rolls for good measure. When they got to the song's hook, Grant and Evie stepped into a tight ballroom hold, and when he locked eyes with her, their connection intensified as they never lost eye contact while performing the complicated steps, finishing their partnered portion of the dance with a spin and a deep dip. They hurried into formation with the rest of their troupe to finish out the performance.

The audience burst into wild applause as the dancers stayed stone still after darkness covered the dance floor at the song's abrupt ending. The energy in the ballroom flew off the charts. At Grant's cue, they all broke hold and Evie jumped towards him, throwing her arms around his neck in her excitement. He knew how she felt—his own adrenaline pumped swiftly through his veins. Grant put his arms around her, picking her up and swinging her around.

"You did awesome, babe," he said, kissing her cheek. She looked radiant. In his whole time on the show, he'd never been prouder and more invested in a partner before. He didn't even care what the judges said at this point—she deserved a perfect score in his eyes, and if the roar of the crowd was any indication, in their eyes, too. That's all that mattered.

All three of the judges gushed about how great her form and musicality were, she didn't have a single misstep, and Clarice, who wasn't generally a fan of hip hop dances, pointed out that it was her favorite dance of the night so far.

The only comment that irked Grant came from Paulo. The older man jumped up and exclaimed to Evie, "Sweetheart, with those moves and your beauty, you are downright sex on a stick!" and leered at her, which was a little too much for Grant. Evie's eyes grew wide and her cheeks burned red.

Grant gave Paulo a disapproving look and wagged a finger at him in jest, but he seriously couldn't believe Paulo had called her that. It felt a little out of line in Grant's opinion. Evie wasn't the "sexy" competitor. She was the "sweetheart/girl-next-door."

They hurried backstage after getting their scores, which were all fives this week, of course. Grant expected no less.

"I'm mortified right now!" Evie whispered loudly as they maneuvered through the chaos of makeup and wardrobe.

"Just shake his comment off," he told her still bristling at it himself.

"I'm going to try," she said, peering into the nearby mirror, twisting back and forth.

"You aren't what he said, Evie. Trust me, you look beautiful and modest, which is hard to pull off in a hip-hop routine, and we made sure the moves weren't suggestive. Paulo's comment was a little out of line, but that's just him," Grant explained.

Seemingly satisfied, Evie hurried off to change for their next performance, as did he. Ready to move on to their song, Grant changed into a comfortable black tee and dark jeans. His uniform, as Evie called it.

He liked the theme this week— Anthems. They'd just performed to "You Can't Stop Me" by Andy Mineo and now they were going to sing, "Break" by Rebecca Roubion. The theme allowed for a lot of artistic and varied performances. Last week, Eighties Week, had been a little difficult, but that could've been partially due to Evie's mini-crisis of identity. She seemed a lot better this week—even when she'd gotten the call from Davis that he'd been drafted by the The Browns.

"One day at a time, Grant. I'm taking this one day at a time," she'd told him.

"Yeah, but there isn't going to be any day where you're going to enjoy life as a housewife in Cleveland."

She'd arched an eyebrow at him and bit her lip. Maybe he shouldn't have said it, but someone needed to tell her.

* * * *

Three hours later, Grant knocked on Kacie's apartment door. He sucked in a sharp breath when he saw her red-rimmed eyes and the troubled look lurking within their depths. The look did not bode well.

"Hey, I got your message and came as soon as I could. What's going on?" Grant stepped inside her Bohemian-style studio and took her in his arms, leaning down to kiss her. She froze at his touch.

"Come in and sit down. We need to talk." Kacie broke away from his embrace and led him to the sofa. She didn't take a seat beside him, but instead sat in the easy chair positioned beside the plum velvet couch. His heart sank. He knew what was coming and wasn't sure how he felt now that the moment had arrived.

"I've done a lot of thinking, Grant. A lot. We both know that this relationship is over," she said with a sob.

Grant took a deep breath, feeling terrible. He didn't want her to be sad—he really did care about her. Although she spoke the truth, it still didn't make the actual breaking up part any easier. They'd been comfortable for a long time.

"I know, Kacie, and I'm so sorry," he replied glumly, leaning over and rubbing her arm.

She glanced up from where she'd been crying into her hands. "Is that all you have to say?" She sniffled.

"What do you want me to say?" He shrugged, holding both hands out. He had nothing helpful to offer.

That's when Kacie exploded.

"ARE YOU AN IDIOT?? WHAT DO YOU THINK I WANT?!?! I want you to fight for me! I want you to say that you love me—that you can't live without me! And for once, *just once*, I'd like for you to

194

look at me the way you look at *HER*." She spat out the last word.

"Her?" Grant asked in confusion.

"Do NOT play dumb with me, Grant Merritt. After the two years of my life that you've wasted, I deserve much more than what you're giving me right now."

"Kacie, you just said that we both know that this relationship is over. Come on, we break up every two months or so. People in healthy relationships don't do that," he defended.

"I love how you're avoiding talking about the *real* issue here."

"I'm not avoiding anything. I've been feeling like it was time to end whatever it is we attempt to keep alive, and you just confirmed it. I'm sorry that I've hurt you—it was wrong of me to not end things before now." He thought back to breakfast a couple of weeks ago and Evie telling him how unfair he was being to Kacie.

"Grant, admit to me that you have feelings for Evie. Admit to me that you want to end things because you are falling for her." Kacie burst into tears again. He rubbed his temples, at a loss as to what to do or what to say.

How could she tell he had feelings for Evie? He never said anything out loud to anyone, and he'd tried so hard to keep it hidden, to not think or say anything ever, to keep things 100 percent friendly with Evie—only allowing for feelings of friendship. That was it. They were just friends. Nothing more.

What was he supposed to say to Kacie? Yes, he had feelings for someone he shouldn't? He wasn't going to act on them, and he hadn't nor would he cheat on her. But, the truth was that the way Evie made him feel made him want something more than what he had with Kacie.

"I can't say that, Kacie," he said, his voice low.

"What you won't say right now, says *everything!* Grant, I love you! I put up with your nonchalant attitude about us, you're fickleness—all because I hoped you would eventually see how much I really cared. But now I know, it's me. It's me! You are more than capable of loving someone with your whole heart and every bit of your being—I'm watching you fall in that kind of love with someone every week from the comfort of my living room sofa!" Kacie jumped up from her seat and grabbed a cardboard box from the kitchen table. She shoved the box at Grant.

"Here's the tiny handful of stuff you've left here randomly and never on purpose over the years. Get out." Her voice was cold, but her eyes were clear.

Grant stood wordlessly and walked out of her apartment with a box containing a couple of t-shirts, a toothbrush and a copy of *Men's Health*. As he heard the door slam loudly behind him, it was official. He and Kacie were through for good. There was no coming back from this—the door was shut in every sense of the word. Right then, he felt lower than pond scum. She deserved someone that would love her fully, the way she'd obviously loved him and he hadn't even cared enough to realize it.

He didn't want to feel relieved after their breakup, but he did. Now that things were over, a weight had lifted, and he could breathe once again. It didn't, however, take anything away from the "I've-hurt-someone" guilt weighing heavily on his shoulders. Grant drove home and spent the night watching reruns of *That 70s Show* until the early morning hours when he finally fell asleep still dressed with his keys in his pocket on the sofa.

CHAPTER THIRTEEN

"What's up with you today?"

Grant just shook his head at her before glancing at Steve, wanting her to drop it, but with the way he was acting, that wasn't happening today.

"You're here, but you're not. What's going on?" She asked him, nudging gently on his shoulder as they still stood in hold.

"Let's just practice, Evie. I really don't want to talk about it," he said in exasperation, putting his arm around her waist and starting to twirl her around the room again. They ran through the foxtrot another time before she stopped him again with the intent to draw out whatever was bothering him. She couldn't stand watching him try to practice while carrying the weight of the world around on his shoulders. It wasn't a pleasant sight.

"How did you do this when I was in a funk?" she asked him.

"I'm a man, and I can compartmentalize, which I wish you could do right now," he said shortly.

"Um, yeah. No, I can't. I can literally feel your bad mood."

"I'm fine. For real. Not girl fine, but really fine."

"That's it. I'm sitting down right here, right now on this floor, and I'm not budging until you tell me what's wrong with you and why you're being so difficult," she challenged. Plopping down onto the glossy maple planks, she stretched out comfortably to drive home her point. Grant rolled his eyes and shook his head at her obstinance, but knowing he was defeated, he sighed and sat down cross-legged beside her, surrendering to his fate.

Steve still had the camera rolling, but Grant caught his attention and signaled for him to cut. Thankfully, they were able to request three 20 minute film-free breaks if they needed it each day. Steve nodded and headed out of the room as Grant and Evie cut off their microphones.

"Kacie and I broke up last night," he told her after a moment or so of silence passed. After the words tumbled out of his mouth, Grant waited for her to respond, but she was shocked speechless.

Oh my. The breakup was a lot for her to take in, but it explained why he'd been so mopey. Ending a two-year relationship, even if it was constantly on and off and really needed to end, was still a pretty big deal.

"I'm sorry, Grant. That's awful. Do you think it's for good this time?" she questioned sincerely, resting a hand lightly on his arm. Their breakup and makeup pattern was common knowledge, so she found herself wondering if this was just a part of their normal routine.

"We are officially over." He confirmed with a nod, staring at the floor.

"That sucks. What happened?" She squeezed his arm to encourage him to talk, even though his face bore the strangest expression.

"I don't want to talk about it," he said. Evie lifted her hand and sat it back in her lap, her feelings a little hurt.

"I thought we were pretty good friends, and I like, completely bore my soul to you a couple of weeks ago, but if you really don't want to talk about it, that's fine," she told him.

"Way to guilt trip me, Evie. It's just not something I want to talk about with you, okay?"

"Okay? I guess?" She studied him, confused.

"Kacie thought that we were getting too close," he revealed, still staring at the floor as he spoke. This was the first time she'd seen suave, confident Grant so uncomfortable and out of sorts.

"Like, she didn't want to be committed to you?" Evie ventured, trying to flesh out the details. Kacie must have been crazy if she didn't want to commit to Grant. Who wouldn't want to commit to him? Grant was, like, the perfect guy—even if she was attached to someone else, she still found him wonderful and breathtaking and for someone not to think so confused the heck out of her.

"No, not me and her getting too close . . . me . . . and . . . you . . . getting too close." He cut his eyes at Evie when he finally admitted the truth, and now she really struggled to find a response. Why on earth would such a gorgeous, cultured musician/model like Kacie feel even the slightest bit threatened by her?

She and Grant were just really good friends who happened to have undeniable chemistry. Sure, maybe she had a little crush on him, but she would *never* admit that to anyone and she certainly wouldn't act on it. But, seriously, who wouldn't have a crush if they were in her same situation? Despite trying to keep her feelings battened down, it seemed like someone was always questioning the relationship they shared—Davis, the media, her parents, other pros, now Kacie, too. No one wanted to believe that there wasn't anything going on between them.

"I-I don't know what to say. You told her that there was nothing going on, right?" Evie queried, her voice strained. When she'd plopped onto the floor moments earlier, she'd had no idea that this was what she'd bargained for in getting Grant to open up to her.

"Of course I did! There isn't anything going on, but it doesn't matter. Kacie insisted that there was."

"Well, I guess she knows something that we don't. You told her I had a boyfriend, didn't you?"

"She knows that, Evie. I can only guess she felt threatened by the chemistry we share."

Evie nodded her head slowly. She could see where Kacie might possibly have a problem with that, even though Grant insisted since she was a performer, she understood the importance of connection. However, she'd had her own relationship drama with Davis about the very same issue. Their chemistry may have been giving them quite the edge in the competition, but it was wreaking serious havoc in their personal lives.

And if Evie was completely honest with herself, it wasn't just a little crush she felt for Grant—it was growing harder and harder not to completely fall in lose-her-mind-and-follow-him-to-the-ends-of-the-earth love with the guy. If she could've selected the perfect man for herself from a catalog, he fit into every custom option she'd choose. Every. Single. One.

"Are you happy now? You know my deal. Can we get back to work?" Grant griped as he hopped back onto his feet and held his hands out to help up Evie.

"Yes, let's get back to work," she said with a little too much enthusiasm. Eager for the conversation to be finished, Grant cued the music and Evie practiced her frame on her own for a few minutes.

But once she was back in his arms, things felt different. The music swirled around the studio and every move sizzled with underlying tension. When he pulled her in close and they swayed back and forth, she closed her eyes, just for a second to savor the moment. She relished his cheek against hers, his arm strong around her waist, his hand intertwined with hers. Why had things changed all of a sudden? She needed to go back to believing he was attached and unavailable.

"Evie, your frame is atrocious right now," Grant murmured, snapping her out of her reverie.

"Oops. I guess I'm tired," she lied as he swung her back out, pausing the music to straighten her arm, push her shoulders down and lift her chin.

"That's better," he smiled as they swirled around the room. She concentrated solely on the steps—putting no focus on how good it felt to whirl around the room with him.

"What are you doing later?" she asked him without thinking.

"I was going to see if you were up for an extra rehearsal and a late dinner."

"That's fine with me. I don't want you to go home and mope."

"I don't mope, Evie."

"Yes, in fact, you do."

Grant stopped short, eying her down.

"What?" she asked.

"Do you think I'll be sorrowful and depressed, walking the moors with my hounds when I'm not here with you? Is that how you view me right now?"

She burst out laughing. "Of course not! This isn't a gothic romance novel, but your reference is surprising and hilarious. I don't care who you are, breakups are no fun for anyone with a beating heart, and I don't want you to dwell on it and get down and out," she admitted.

He took her chin in his hand and smiled down at her. "You're a little ray of sunshine, Evie. How could I ever be down and out when I'm with you?"

She swallowed hard and looked down at her dancing shoes. She couldn't bring herself to look into his eyes—she knew what she would find there, and she wasn't sure she was ready to see it.

CHAPTER FOURTEEN

It was over. All over. Evie had his heart. She could ask him to fly to the moon and back and he'd do it. He had it bad— like he wasn't ever going to come back from this kind of bad.

He'd put it off as long as possible. In the beginning, Grant didn't want to think of her in that light and he'd made every effort within his power not to have those types of feelings for her. Neither of them had been available, *and* she was a good bit younger than the women he typically dated, *and* she came from an entirely different culture, unfamiliar with the LA scene.

Evie regularly attended Sunday church services and her squeaky-clean persona wasn't just for the cameras. She was . . . pure. Plain and simple. Her version of edgy was Converse sneakers and an ironic tee. Whereas, he'd grown up in northern Cali, but moved to LA just after college. He'd been in and around the Hollywood scene ever since and *nothing* surprised or shocked him anymore. He wouldn't necessarily call himself jaded, but he was close. Besides, in addition to all their differences, once the show was over, she'd be moving back to the other side of the country.

But none of that mattered to him anymore. He loved everything that made her different. It didn't matter what others said. He'd heard other pros comment when they thought he wasn't listening about how she was too "sugary" for them, and how no one was *that* good—that her Southern sweetheart schtick got on their nerves. He paid them no mind. America loved her, and so did he. He knew jealousy when he saw it.

And the more he got to know her—flaws and all, his feelings only grew stronger. So, a week and three days after talking through his breakup with Kacie on the dance floor, here he was, closing his eyes and holding Evie against him, as he'd done so many times before—and not just with her. He'd held other contestants in seasons past the same way. But it was different with Evie—he had no interest in ever letting her go.

This girl moved him like no one ever had before, and he was finally *really* admitting the bittersweet truth to himself. Not like admitting it changed anything. He wouldn't, no, he *couldn't* tell her.

Did he think she belonged with that knucklehead, Davis? No.

Would he be the one to tell her outright she should break up with him? Nope.

She needed to figure that out on her own, and he wasn't going to try and make that decision for her or have his feelings for her hold any sway in the matter. Whether she had feelings for him or she headed back to Alabama and lived happily ever after with her boyfriend, it wouldn't change the heart-thudding intensity he felt for her.

Looking back, he knew the moment she'd officially stolen his heart, even though he never would have admitted it at that point. Back on the very first evening they'd spent together, she'd fallen asleep in his car on the ride back to her apartment. He'd glanced over just as her lips curved into a dreamy smile and his heart grew tight and an overwhelming sense of longing washed over him. With that simple glance, he'd found himself wanting to know everything about her—how she took her coffee, what she dreamed about as she slept, how old she was when she lost her first tooth— everything about her fascinated him from that point forward—although he told her and himself, too, that it was just because she was his partner. That he needed to know her story to be a better coach and partner. It may've been true, but there was so much more to it than that.

"Hey, earth to Grant, earth to Grant," Evie joked, waving her hand in front of his face to get his attention.

"Are we going to run through this routine again or what?" she asked impatiently, sweat trickling down her adorable, flushed face.

"Yeah, yes, from the top," he cleared his throat and cued the music to start again. They danced, moving around the room to the rhythm of the sultry song. The Argentine Tango he'd choreographed for them had turned into an intense mix of unfulfilled desire and longing. He'd combined difficult steps requiring enormous amounts of precision with technical, tricky lifts. His initial vision had been a moving piece filled with the heat the Argentine Tango was known for, yes, but still on the sweet, romantic side. However, somewhere between choreographing and practicing the routine, their tango morphed into a much more angsty piece.

As Grant ran his fingertips down the side of Evie's waist and then pulled her close, he reveled in the way her hands lingered intentionally around his neck. He'd had flashes of desire for other partners before—it was common in his line of work to occasionally develop feelings for a co-star or dance partner from time to time since he worked so closely with them—but what he felt for Evie far surpassed being a simple and only physical attraction.

He wanted to be with her all the time—talk to her, sing with her, hang out with her. Grant had it bad, and sadly, he knew it, too. He certainly didn't blame Kacie for breaking up with him. She'd recognized it before he had. Now, his number one goal was to keep Evie from knowing it, which was no easy task.

Sliding an arm around Evie and lifting her over his head, he spun three times before slowly lowering her back down until they were nose to nose. A few more lifts, synchronized moves and intricate embraces and they finished the dance with Evie in his arms lying on the dance floor, their cheeks pressed together. Grant jumped up and away from her the second the music cut, desperate for air. They needed serious space between them.

After running through the entire routine a few more times, they broke for lunch, with Grant instructing Evie to meet him afterward in Studio 4A to practice their song set.

"Do you want to grab lunch together?" Evie casually asked as she pulled her damp hair back into a smooth bun.

"You know I'd love to, but I have a meeting with the producers in a few minutes," Grant replied. He wondered if she caught the disappointment in his voice.

"No worries, do you want me to bring you anything?"

"Nah, I'm good. I've got a sandwich in the break room."

"Okay, then. See ya in a bit," she said with a happy little wave as she headed through the swinging double doors.

When the doors shut behind her with a loud clang, Grant threw his empty water bottle in frustration. It hit a metal folding chair and noisily fell to the floor. He'd never been in this particular situation before, and it had more than its fair share of difficult moments. What was he supposed to do? He was a professional for crying out loud, and she had a boyfriend! However, those two facts did nothing to stray his thoughts from her or help all that much in keeping them contained.

Grabbing his stuff, Grant hurried out of the room. It was crucial that he arrived on time for the last-minute production meeting Kim informed him that he needed to attend. The powers-that-be didn't care that he'd only found out about it less than an hour ago.

When he reached the glass-walled conference room in the network's executive offices across the lot from the studios, to his surprise almost every member of the show's production staff, including the executive producer, filled each chair but one at the large, polished table. He picked up on an ominous atmosphere in the room. What was happening? Something big, whatever it was.

"Have a seat, Grant," Dan Dean, the executive producer, the main man in charge himself, instructed him with a brief, but polite, smile as he gestured to the only vacant chair. As Grant sunk into the plush leather seat, he started worrying. What had he done to garner reproof? Racking his brain, nothing immediately came to mind.

"We have a problem, Grant," Dan began, folding his hands in front of him and getting right to the point. "The chemistry between you and Evie is jaw-dropping, and you two are clearly the fan favorites."

"Thanks, I'm glad to hear it, but that doesn't sound like much of a problem," Grant replied, confused by Dan's meaning.

"Technically, it's not. But, as the producers of this show we know there could be a huge backlash if anything really happened because of the chemistry between you two. Do you follow me? It's widespread knowledge that she's in a committed relationship, Grant."

"I know that." He wasn't in the mood for the lecture, and with his own personal struggle with this very issue, he wasn't interested in talking about it with a bunch of suits either.

"Well, this is just a friendly reminder of how important it is that you don't let anything . . . happen that could garner a bunch of bad press," Kim piped into the conversation. She knew better than anyone in the room what was going on between Evie and him.

"Got it. I'm hearing you loud and clear. Can I go now? We have a lot to do to get ready for Tuesday night's show."

"Just one more thing, we may not want anything official between the two of you, but don't shut her out either. The viewers want the chemistry, the tease—the will they/won't they is what sells—but under no circumstances should you let it go any further than that," Dan Dean added dismissively.

Great. They wanted him to continue to fall in love with her, but didn't want anyone, including her, to know. Basically, he just needed to keep on doing what he was already doing anyway. It wasn't easy though when production usually assigned them the more romantic songs each week, solidifying the showmance the producers craved for ratings. Grant felt sick to his stomach at the amount of control these people wielded. They asked him a few, too personal questions, outlined a couple more requirements, and then, finally allowed him to leave.

As he headed to the break room, he wondered if maybe he shouldn't have let Kacie break things off so easily after all. When she ended their long, on-again/ off-again relationship, he'd thought that he was doing them both a favor by agreeing, knowing that it really was over for good. She may have initiated the break up, but he had sealed the deal, and he'd left her upset and angry at him. But now that he was aware that he was helplessly falling for Evie, it wouldn't have been fair to keep things going with Kacie—even if it would've kept the rumor mill at bay and made his job easier.

He ate lunch in a daze, dreading his return to rehearsing with Evie. It was torture enough to deal with his feelings, but to know production could tell something was up? He was in for a long afternoon.

* * * *

"Hey, what is with you?" Evie asked later that afternoon, pausing her playing, hands still lingering above the keys as she eyed Grant. He held his guitar loosely as he stared into space, frowning. In studio 4A, they were working on their duet—both playing instruments this time. The theme for week five, Latin Week, required them to sing two songs rather than the typical one, and they really needed to focus. She had been under the impression that their smoky rendition of "I Could Fall in Love" sounded awesome, but Grant was sitting there, frowning at the wall, lost in his thoughts.

"Nothing, Evie, nothing. Let's just start again from the top," he said, shaking his head and strumming the first few chords and she jumped back in

211

with the keys. She started singing the words, and the frustration seemed to melt away from Grant as he sang the chorus with her. As he started to sing the second verse, she took the chance to admire Grant—he sung with emotion, eyes closed, the muscles in his forearm flexing as he changed keys. She quickly glanced away, realizing what a bad idea staring at him had been, and desperately tried not to pay attention to the way he affected her as he crooned, *"I should keep this to myself and never let you know."*

It was a given that he was an exceptional dancer, and she danced in his arms often, loving every minute of it, but she could listen to him play his guitar and sing for hours upon end. His playing and singing was her absolute favorite, even if it added to her own stress. Although she didn't dwell on it, there was a lot of pressure on her simply because she was *his* partner. Grant had won the competition three out of the five seasons it had been on air. He had a huge fan following of his own right and a solid place as a favorite among the cast and crew.

To add an extra layer of complicated, she had to constantly remind herself of the reasons why she shouldn't be into him. It was exhausting. He didn't make it easy for her being everything she ever wanted in a man—kind, competitive but fun, incredibly handsome but didn't let it go to his head, and he had the ability to keep her laughing constantly. Most of all, she loved that she could just be herself with him and he accepted her—whatever that looked like. She didn't doubt that he cared about her, and she cared about him. The vein of friendship ran deep with them.

Well, except for today. Today was different and she couldn't put her finger on why.

"Dude, you've got to snap out of it," she told him when they'd finished another run through of the song, but he just looked away, still acting strange. His aloofness reminded her of last week when he had told her about breaking up with Kacie, but his mood today was even more sullen.

"Let's just call it a day, okay?" he retorted, putting his guitar back in its case.

Evie's mouth popped open in shock. They still had forty minutes of studio time, and he usually made her stay and squeeze out every last second. But today, Grant was being a total grumpy pants, which was completely out of character for him.

"Fine, but you aren't leaving until you tell me what the heck is going on with you," she said hotly, crossing her arms in front of her.

"I'm not discussing this with you, and I won't let you strong-arm it out of me the way you did last week."

His brush off sank her heart. She stood right in front of him, but he wouldn't look her straight in the eyes. His words were like a knife, twisting hard and deep, and his cold demeanor affected her far worse than she would ever dare admit to anyone.

Swallowing the lump rapidly forming in her throat, she gathered what was left of her pride and stalked away from him, snatching up her bag by the door and leaving without a single glance back at him. As she heard the finality of the heavy metal door slamming back into place, tears welled in her eyes, fueling her anger. At what point had she given him the power to make her cry? She *thought* they were close friends—she'd believed him when he had promised he was her friend for life. Obviously, if he could dismiss her like she was nothing, he didn't mean that. They were just partners in this competition, nothing more, and if he wanted to be a jerk, so be it. She wouldn't let it bother her. Maybe if she kept telling herself that, she'd believe it eventually.

Seeking comfort and a familiar voice, she called Davis as soon as she'd shut the car door and buckled her seatbelt. Maybe he'd have some words of wisdom, or at least he could shed some light on what was behind Grant's out-of-nowhere personality switch. She needed a guy's perspective, and besides, he'd probably be happy to hear she and Grant weren't getting along.

"Hey, Evie," Davis answered flatly.

"Hey, honey," Evie sweetly replied.

"What's wrong?" he asked. He knew her well. All was not sunshine and roses in LA.

"Grant is acting weird."

Davis let out an exasperated sigh in response. "Do we really have to waste time talking about him? We haven't seen each other in weeks and every time you call, all you ever want to talk about is your dang dance partner. You know, I have stuff going on, too, around here."

"Davis, I'm sorry—Grant's just a huge part of my life right now, so of course I tend to want to talk about what's going on with him. That's all it is. He's a jerk."

"To be honest, Evie, I've been picking up that you have a thing for him."

"Whatever. That couldn't be further from the truth. You're just jealous," she teased, attempting to lighten the mood and sound playful, even as the realization hit her that calling Davis had backfired. Now, she was dealing with yet another frustrating guy. One frustrating man was more than enough for her at that moment.

"Rightfully so, Evie! I've been watching the show—all everyone talks about is wanting you two to hook up! Imagine how it feels to be your boyfriend right about now."

"Come on. You're kidding me right? There's no way anyone really sees us together like that—they just enjoy watching us perform together. Plus, everyone knows that I have boyfriend," she defended. The words came out by rote since she said them multiple times a day to whoever asked. Without fail, someone somewhere asked her every single day about her and Grant's relationship—the press, the crew, random strangers on the street.

She wasn't stupid. In all fairness, sure, the thought of being with Grant had crossed her mind—more than once or ten times. But, she had her defensive mental blocks in place. She'd just repeat her mantra—*I'm not single, we're very different, and we live on opposite sides of the country*—until the fuzzy feelings eventually fizzled away. However, her boyfriend didn't need to know that's what it took for her not to dream about Grant.

"If you Google y'all's names together, you'll see what pops up. I'm not making this stuff up," he added tersely. Evie rolled her eyes and sighed. She couldn't deal.

"Look, I don't have time for this. I've got to go." She hung up before Davis said anything else. She was being rude, but she couldn't take the jealousy on top of fighting with Grant, and she didn't have time to invest in soothing Davis' fragile ego.

When she'd initially signed on to do the show, she'd told Davis that she was going to have to focus on the experience and fully commit to it if she wanted to do well. Now, every time she called him, she dealt with jealous boyfriend drama on top of the issues they were already struggling to overcome. Sometimes, she wondered if she should just bite the bullet and break up with him, but she had a loyal streak that bordered on unhealthy, and he'd been a part of her life since before she could remember. It didn't seem right to throw such a long relationship away. Her parents would freak. Davis was as much a part of her life as any member of her family.

Evie pulled into the parking garage, glad to finally be back at her place. A nice, long soak in the tub, a sappy movie, and some ice cream after the day she'd just had called her name, but as soon as she was inside the small apartment, she tossed her stuff in a careless heap by the front door, kicked off her shoes and threw herself dejectedly onto the sofa. She hated how she felt —guilty for hanging up on Davis and worried about Grant despite telling herself that he was a jerk and he didn't mean anything to her. Her stomach ached. All this stress couldn't be good for her.

What was she supposed to do now? Everything was out of sorts. She was angry with Grant for being so short with her, of course, but she was also worried about what caused him to be that way. It wasn't like him at all.

Still languishing on the sofa in the sweatpants and tank top she'd worn to practice, insistent knocking at her door startled Evie from her melancholy musings. Curious with a dash of fear for good measure, she jumped up to see who was there. Occasionally, Amelia or Grant stopped by for this or that, but they usually called first. Evie peeped through the little hole and, lo and behold, it was Grant standing on her doorstep looking no less frustrated or pissed off than he had earlier at the studio.

Evie yanked the door open, her temper flaring. In her own territory now, she stewed for a fight. "You'd better be here to explain yourself because the way you're acting is not okay," she spat out as he waltzed— more like stomped—past her and into the apartment.

"I know. That's why I'm here." He brooded.

Grant paced around the tiny living area, raking his hands through his hair from time to time. She motioned for him to take a seat on the sofa, but he shook his head and continued to pace, so she sat down in a huff, crossed her arms and waited for him to start talking.

"I've went over how to handle this in my head at least a dozen times, and after weighing all of my options, I've decided to go with the truth."

"Okay, let's hear it then," she prompted.

"I had a meeting with production during lunch today and it went horrible. I was told that we are doing awesome, that everyone loves us together, and we are the fan favorites. But with the producer's very next breath, I was also reminded not to get too close to you —just close enough for the fans to be happy," he confessed.

"Wait. What? I'm confused. They want you fake caring about me to please fans?" That seemed shallow and heartless on so many levels, not to mention it made no sense. Why did the producers care so much?

Bewildered, she implored him with her eyes to explain, but Grant wore a funny look on his face, avoiding her gaze. She'd never seen him act like this before—he was the calm and collected one of their duo. The sophisticated one. She was the dramatic mess, not him. To see him this keyed up and off his game was a totally new shade of strange.

"Basically—yes, I mean, no. There's more to it," he stammered. What was going on that had him so flustered?

"I don't get it, Grant. What are you trying to say? It really sucks that production wants to interfere in our personal relationship. It doesn't make any sense at all."

"Evie, they don't care if we're friends or not—it doesn't matter to them one way or another. They just wanted me to assure them that we are not, um . . . more than friends, nor would we ever be. Well, at least for the duration of the season. You know, because you're in a relationship and all of that. They think it would cause bad press and it wouldn't work well for ratings." Grant coughed awkwardly and looked away.

She swallowed hard and willed herself to pretend that this wasn't a cause for concern. That production had it all wrong. Evie repeated her mantra in her head at least ten times, adding to it that this wasn't an issue before she spoke.

"You told them that there is nothing to worry about, right? We're just friends. Geez. Sorry, Grant. No wonder you've been so frustrated—that sucks that you had to deal with all of this at lunch today by yourself."

"Of course, I told them that we're just friends, but then I was told that it was important to make it at least seem like there was *maybe* a possibility of us eventually being . . . something. That's when it got really frustrating for me.

"They want it to appear that I've fallen for you, but make sure I don't do anything about it or make it seem too serious at any point. I've always hated showmances, and it makes me mad that we are smack in the middle of one and I let them get in my head about what's going on between the two of us.

"The fact is, I love spending time with you, Evie, and just in the past few weeks, you've quickly became one of my closest friends. As far as performing goes, you inspire me in so many different ways, I couldn't really narrow it down to just one. I can't believe I let them get to me this afternoon to the point it affected how I treated you."

After he finished what he had to say, Grant sat down on the sofa beside Evie and put his head in his hands. She sensed his relief in getting all of that off his chest. Now, he would be able to relax. However, his sweet confession made Evie feel something that the producers certainly wouldn't like.

Of course, the feelings had been there all along, but so far, she'd been able to deny them, to keep them under control, and think of them as a part of a simple crush. She'd pushed them down to the deepest, hidden part of her heart, only allowing herself to admire him because she had no intention of it ever being more than just that. But with his confession about the meeting and knowing that everyone already saw what they continually tried to deny, a shift in the atmosphere around them had changed. The only hope they had of keeping things on the straight and narrow lied in neither of them saying anything further about it to one another.

"I'm glad you told me what was going on. I didn't like feeling as if you were keeping something from me because I feel the same way that you do. In a short amount of time, you've come to mean a lot to me too, Grant," she said quietly, tentatively taking his hand in hers and leaning her head against his shoulder, carefully watching her words. Even though slipping her hand into his was mostly an innocent gesture on her part, she shouldn't be holding hands with him on the sofa alone in her apartment. She knew better. They were dangerously close to crossing that line the stupid show people didn't want them to cross.

Although they'd just told one another that the idea of them having feelings for each other was ridiculous, that wasn't the truth. Not for her anyway. Studying his profile, Evie wondered if his feelings for her had slipped past friendship. It was his job to appear interested in her, and she wasn't sure where "show Grant" ended and "real Grant" started sometimes. Only a handful of looks and words solidly hinted to him seeing her as something more, and even though she shouldn't, she secretly wished that she could know for certain that he really felt the same way that she did.

* * * *

Evie didn't have a clue what she was doing to him—what she'd been doing to him since the first day they'd met. As her head snuggled against his shoulder, Grant caught the scent of her coconut and vanilla shampoo—so very her—and clenched his fist to keep from running his hands through her hair and planting kisses on her temple. Evie tempted him past his limits without even trying. His gaze fell to her lips, and he wondered if it would feel like fireworks and summer breezes to kiss her. That's what he imagined it would be like, and it was all that he could think about doing right then. Of course, over their past few weeks together, there'd been several other moments when he'd thought about it, too. Starting with the first day they had laid eyes on each other.

Grant rested his head against the back of the sofa and stared at the ceiling, distracting himself from the close, intimate predicament that he'd gone and put himself in that evening. When he'd initially decided to stop by Evie's apartment and explain his abrupt and cold attitude at the studio earlier, he hadn't grasped the level of temptation in which he would be placing himself. Sort of tempting, yeah, naturally, he'd expected that, but her so close and cozy? No, he hadn't expected that at all.

Not stopping by her apartment hadn't been an option. He'd jumped into his car, and sped as fast as the clogged traffic on Wilshire would allow. Sitting in a sea of cars, he'd drummed the steering wheel with nervous energy. He'd ran on pure adrenaline as he parked beneath her building and raced to the elevator doors. He'd lost every bit of patience he prided himself on owning during the painstakingly slow elevator ride to her floor. That ride had unfortunately given him too much time to think about what he was doing. What if she wasn't there? What if she was, but she was on the phone with her meathead of a boyfriend? What was he going to actually say? A million questions and pangs of doubt filled Grant's heart and mind, but not seeing Evie and explaining his behavior simply wasn't an option.

He couldn't be at odds with her. He couldn't think or work or go about his business knowing that she was upset with him, and with good reason at that.

She wasn't to blame for their explosive chemistry, or that production exasperated him with their ridiculous expectations. He'd needed to see her, to apologize for his actions earlier and to explain the reasons behind them so she would understand and hopefully forgive him. Grant planned to only stay a few minutes—just long enough to make sure that all was well between them once more.

But, no. This visit wouldn't be quick. She wanted him to stay, and how could he tell her no, he needed to go? How could he admit that he didn't trust himself with her? She trusted herself completely with him.

As she curled closer to him, her leg pressed against his, a soft sigh escaped from her lips, a sound of relief that signaled all was right in the world now that they were good again.

"You always make me feel better, Grant. I'm glad that we're okay. You have no idea how upset I was. You're one of my closest friends and I couldn't figure out why you were suddenly acting so strange. Do you want to hang out tonight? I can order pizza and we can watch movies." She looked up at him from her spot on the couch beside him, those gorgeous eyes of hers imploring him to stay, her face mere inches from him as she waited for his answer.

He deliberated. He really did. He'd planned on catching his good friend, Rowan's band at a show downtown later. On one hand, staying could be dangerous, and more temptation than he could handle. On the other hand, he couldn't imagine saying no to this girl even if he did have prior plans. As she waited, he studied her, this time unable to break his eyes away from hers.

Rowan would understand why Grant didn't make it to his show.

"Yes, sure. Sounds like a plan," Grant smiled down at Evie, picking up a tendril of her hair and playing with it. Evie's mouth curved upward in response, and in that moment, with their lips mere inches away from one another's, everything else faded away and for the first time, he realized what he felt wasn't only one-sided. No doubt about it—Evie felt it, too. He'd never been so certain of anything in his life. Evie sucked in her breath sharply and pushed herself from her cozy spot. She jumped off of the sofa and grabbed her cell phone. Still a bit dazed at what he'd seen, what they'd shared, Grant didn't move. If Evie hadn't bolted away so quickly, they would've kissed. He'd been seconds away from leaning into her, closing the deal.

"Evie? Maybe I should go. I forgot I told Rowan I'd catch his band's show tonight." Grant's voice sounded hoarse as he stood and ran his hands through his hair, unnerved.

"Oh? I guess you should go then." Her voice trembled as she bit her lip. He couldn't tell if she truly wanted him to stay or go, but it was for the best that he left before something happened that couldn't be undone. He didn't trust himself, and he couldn't risk ruining their partnership.

She walked him out, and before he turned and headed to the elevator, Grant reached out and took her hand in his, lifting it to his lips and pressing a kiss against her warm skin.

"See you tomorrow, Evie," he said before letting her hand go and reluctantly telling her goodnight.

CHAPTER FIFTEEN

"Latin week is no joke and we have to be at the top of our game," Grant explained as Evie sat cross-legged on the dance room floor the next morning.

"You know I'm all in. What other dance do we have?" she asked.

"The salsa. It's a hot dance. You ready?" he teased her. She swallowed. Things were about to get completely out of her comfort zone. Two dances, two songs and extra spice. Whew.

"I suppose so. They're really pushing this showmance stuff, huh?"

"Yes, it's ridiculous."

"Do you have the choreo ready to go?"

"Yep." He reached down and took her hands, pulling her to her feet.

Grant started showing her the routine, slowly at first, as they always did, making sure she could easily handle the basic steps before adding in the more complicated techniques. It started out easy enough, even with the hip swivels, dips and lots of shaking, but when he smacked her on the bottom, she looked up, stopping mid-step to stare up at him.

"A little warning would've been nice," she admonished, still a little stunned.

"I barely tapped you. It's part of the dance. The song literally says, 'I gave Susie a little pat up on the booty.' If the move wasn't important in the song, you know I wouldn't put it in the dance, and besides, we've been far more up close and personal in other dances."

"I don't know, Grant . . ."

"Evie, it's Latin week. Everyone ups the spiciness big time, and I've kept this pretty tame. This is the only week I will ever push you a little out of your comfort zone when it comes to this kind of stuff, I promise. It's still staying true to who you are, and honestly, I'd rather keep things as squeaky clean as possible to help keep the rumors down. But, the salsa requires a certain level of steam. Besides, we'll make this dance playful, not sleazy, okay?"

What he didn't understand was how all of their recent dances already pushed her completely out of her comfort zone. She was free-falling and dancing a spicy salsa wasn't going to help the rush of attraction overtaking her whenever he stepped into a room.

"I'm going to trust you, but don't forget—my parents watch this show . . . and my boyfriend."

"I promise, I don't ever forget that, Evie." He reached his hand out to her again, leading her through the steps a little faster this time.

A few minutes later, he placed his hands on each side of her hips. "Okay, I'm going to move your hips with the timing. Follow along." Grant started his quick count and Evie struggled to keep up—he was taking names and kicking butt today—no messing around.

"Evie, seriously. Focus. Your hips need to sway in continuous movement at this part. It should look and feel fluid. Your costume will be covered in fringe, so it will look more pronounced, but I need you to give 110 percent in this move. If it feels comfortable to you, you're probably not doing it right."

Evie pushed the hair that had fallen out of her bun out of her face and huffed in frustration. Not only were they doing a more difficult dance utterly out of her element, he was teaching her at a breakneck speed and tolerating nothing.

"You need to chill out on me just a little," she hissed, her teeth clenched.

"I can't. I know I'm being rough on you right now, but you only have four more days to learn two dances and make this look like it comes naturally to you, which it very much does not."

"Thanks for the vote of confidence," she pouted. The remark rubbed her the wrong way.

"I didn't mean that the way you took it, Evie. You're kind and glowing and genuine and all that good stuff, which I've told you I personally find seriously attractive, for the record. But there's an innocent sweetness about you, and Latin week isn't going to be your friend. We have to fight dirty and bring out an unexpected side of you if we don't want harsh criticism from the judges. Can you trust me and my methods?"

"Yeah, I can. Just don't be so mean. I'll practice extra, whenever you want, but that extra Spanish song we're singing is whipping my tail, too. This week is hard!" She meant what she said—her body ached, every muscle was sore and she would have liked to spend at least three days straight doing nothing but sleeping, but she hadn't made it this far to slack off now.

"I won't be mean, but I will be tough."

"Oh! And give me a heads up the next time you decide to smack me as part of the choreography."

"Sorry, I will next time, Evie," he laughed. "But in my defense, I barely touched you. I didn't think to warn you."

* * * *

On Tuesday night, the fast, Latin guitar notes were Evie's cue to saucily walk to her place in the center of the dance floor as cameras zoomed in on her. Flanked on either side by two shirtless male members of the dance troupe, she stopped and shimmied out of the coat she wore, revealing her ruby-red sequined and fringed dress as she pushed the guys away. She balanced the line between sweet and saucy as she shook her hips, tossed her bouncy curls over her shoulder and turned to face Grant's direction, beckoning with elegant lines for him to join her on the floor. He hopped in on cue and started the fast salsa he'd choreographed with her in mind.

The sultry dances for Latin week were the only time he would use the tension and passion they shared to their advantage. Their natural chemistry, the undercurrent of feelings, all of that ignited in every dance and song they'd performed so far, but the tension? He'd kept that played down as much as possible until this week, and everyone in the audience watched as a fiery connection charged between the two of them, first in the intense Argentine Tango and now in their salsa. Every move sung with electricity, each touch with liquid fire. She sucked in a breath as he pulled her tight, his jaw clenching with intensity.

In her eyes that never left his, he saw more than what he'd planned to bargain. They were playing with fire. He might get in trouble with production after this performance, even though they did approve the concept, but he enjoyed every second of it.

The dance ended as Grant dipped Evie low and held her in his arms mere inches from the ground. Hovering over her, they both struggled to catch their breaths as they stayed locked in hold for a few more seconds.

"Whoa," Evie whispered.

He echoed the sentiment.

* * * *

With both dances and the slow ballad behind them, for the first time this season, Grant was nervous. Maybe choosing a Spanish hip hop song for their encore performance wasn't necessarily the best idea he'd ever had. Evie sounded hypnotic singing the fast verses, but she'd only gotten through the whole thing once without missing a word or stumbling over a line or two.

"If we can pull this off, I'm buying a bottle of champagne to celebrate," he whispered to her as they stood waiting for the cameras and lights to train in on them. Evie nodded distractedly as she tugged on the black lace of her dress. Grant could barely look at her after that salsa earlier. He was having a hard time keeping himself in check.

Unfortunately for him, wardrobe had worked wonders again. From about mid-thigh and down to the floor, her dress trailed in waves of transparent, embroidered black lace. Her legs, one of her best assets, especially in the black heels she wore, were on display, but only through the veil of lace. The gown's neckline grazed her collarbone, but the back dipped low in a lacy V shape. Tasteful, but sensual—Laine had a gift.

"Keyword is 'if,' Grant, and after we get through this song, you better be buying the good stuff! I'm so nervous I could throw up. My four years of high school Spanish isn't serving me as well as I thought it would when I first agreed to do this."

"If you mess up, just keep going. You sound great and you'll have the audience under your spell once again when they hear you sing this," he reassured her. She nodded nervously as he reached his hand out to take hers.

CHAPTER SIXTEEN

"What in the world was that!?!" Evie winced as Davis screeched into the phone as she sat straight up in bed the next morning. It may have been nine in Alabama, but it was barely six in LA, and she had to hold the phone away from her ear as he ranted. Her sleep-fogged brain had yet to figure out what was happening.

"What are you talking about?" she asked.

"Last night, Evie. What do you think I'm talking about???"

"What you saw on television last night was a performance by two professional entertainers, Davis."

"You're not really a professional, Evie."

"Harsh, dude. Way too harsh."

"Tell me the truth, Evie, I need to know. Are you sleeping with him?"

"WHAT? NO! Why would you think that I would do that? You know my feelings about that. *We haven't even done that.*"

"People change, Evie. That's why I ask, and because I have eyes in my head! You two basically make out every time you're onscreen."

"You're being a jerk!"

"And you're being a whore!"

"THAT IS WAY OUT OF LINE!" she shouted, indignation taking over, no longer allowing for a cool head. How dare he call her that!

"Is it, Evie? You know, we both have a lot going on right now. If you haven't given yourself to Grant yet, it's only because of your intent on beating this old horse we call a relationship to its death. It's time we move on like we should've done a long time ago. We're too different now, and we don't bring out very good parts of each other," Davis said, calming down a little.

She did not like how easy those words came from his mouth, even if he spoke the truth. "This has nothing to do with Grant, but for the record, you're right. We're over. We've been over for a long time," she finally agreed, still steaming from his rude comment.

The line fell silent. Without saying goodbye or much of an attempt to fight, they'd put an end to a lifelong friendship and an eight-year relationship in a matter of minutes . . . over the phone. She sat her phone on the bedside table and stared at it offensively—still in shock at how fast it had all unfolded.

Evie put her head in her hands. Maybe, this was what she really wanted, but at the moment, it hurt. Real bad. No matter the circumstances, she'd just lost someone that had been her world for a long time. She sank back against the headboard. Hugging her knees up to her chest, the tears flowed. Sure, she was mad at how Davis had spoken to her, and maybe she had feelings for someone else, but it didn't stop her from mourning the loss. They'd been so happy once.

Two hours later, she pulled into the studio parking lot and checked her reflection in the rearview mirror. Puffy, red-rimmed eyes stared back at her. Her skin was splotchy and she hadn't done much with her hair or makeup to make the situation any better. But she didn't care. Today she needed to just make it through. Tomorrow, her focus would return. She'd be able to bring her A-game once more after this first, painful day was over.

She threw on a pair of aviators and a ball cap. The last thing she wanted was press photos showing her visibly upset. Hopping out of the car, she dashed to the door, not looking to the left or right. Normally, she smiled and waved to the paparazzi and signed autographs. But not today. She couldn't do it today.

"Hey!" Grant called out cheerfully, but his expression immediately turned from excitement to concern when he took in Evie's appearance. "What's wrong?" He signaled for Steve and Kim to give them some privacy, and they immediately packed up and left the room. She must look even worse than she thought.

She took off of the glasses and Grant opened his arms to her. She immediately rushed to him, sobbing into his shoulder. "Davis . . . and I . . . br-oke . . . u-p!" The last word was a sob in and of itself. Evie hated herself for being unable to keep it together, for bringing her problems to work, to Grant. This wasn't his fault. This was all on her.

"Shhh," he soothed, rubbing her back in a circular motion as he cradled her close. "Everything is going to be fine." He didn't push her to be okay or tell her to get it together despite his probable relief that she'd ended things with Davis. Grant was no fan of his. But, he just held her—saying and expecting nothing. He was simply there for her. When she could finally speak intelligibly again, they took seats on the floor facing one another.

"I knew it was coming, and I know it's for the best—we're just in two different places now. But, it didn't stop it from being painful. My heart feels ripped to shreds right now. He was such a huge part of my life for so long, you know?"

Grant nodded, taking her hand. "Someone recently told me that breakups hurt—no matter what the circumstances are. I'm so sorry, Evie. Is there anything I can do?" She caught a glimpse of their reflections in the mirror. He was leaning toward her, eyes overflowing with genuine concern and she was red-faced and sniffling.

"I hate that you had to deal with me ugly crying, and I'm sorry it's cutting so deeply into our practice time."

Grant laughed lightly. "You weren't ugly crying, whatever that is, and don't worry about practice."

"Ugly crying is what I just did—scrunched up face, puffy eyes, with a lot of sniffles and snot involved."

"Okay, maybe you've been ugly crying, but you didn't look ugly doing it."

She rolled her eyes at his compliment to her hot-mess self. "Well, either way, we have to practice. I don't want my personal life to get in the way of our goals."

Grant glanced at the clock. "We only have about an hour of studio time left. What if we head over to the music studio and just work on our song today? I don't think you're up for learning a jazz routine right now."

"You are, unfortunately, right. I'll rally and get myself together before tomorrow, I promise," she assured him. He hopped up and held his hands out to help her from the floor.

"You have no need to keep explaining yourself, Evie. I know you're hurt, and it takes a minute to feel better."

"But after you and Kacie broke up, you were in the studio the next day—"

Grant interrupted her, "And I was in a crappy mood. Remember?"

"Yeah, okay. You were," she sighed.

They walked to the music studio. Once they were set up in a practice room, Grant handed Evie the sheet music. She studied the papers.

"500 Miles?"

"Yeah, but not like you're thinking," he said with a wink, beginning to slowly play the melody of the cover for her.

Later, when they parted ways, despite Grant's multiple attempts to get her to do something—hang out, go to the movies—anything, she headed straight back to her apartment.

After a quick shower, she threw on a pair of ruffled pajama shorts and a tank top. Screw dinner. The bottle of chardonnay in the fridge had her name on it.

She docked her phone and cranked up the country music. She might have been living in LA, singing soulful, indie ballads and having magazines praise her chic style, but in her heart of hearts, she was still an Alabama girl and always would be. She needed wine—lots of wine—and some good country breakup songs to process and mourn her loss. She'd been called something terrible and completely untrue by a man who she'd loved and respected for a very long time. She was no longer someone's girlfriend, and that alone was a foreign feeling. The reasons to throw a pity party were piling up.

Two glasses later, in the middle of a pint of blackberry crumble frozen yogurt, as the sound of classic country starlets crooning about cheating hearts and lonesome feelings filled her apartment, she wondered what had happened to the scrawny little girl running through her Memama's sheets as they hung on the clotheslines to dry in rural southern Alabama—the kid that never doubted life was simple and carefree. Summer after summer, she'd drank glass-bottled Dr. Peppers on her grandparent's screened in back porch and helped them shell peas into a big tin pan—all the while thinking it the most glorious way to spend a random Tuesday in June. Boys and music and television shows and production and dance steps and friends getting married and not finishing college—none of that was of any concern. Angling for quarters when the ice cream truck came through town and surviving nights when the air conditioning quit working were her biggest struggles.

"Who am I?" she asked the empty room, sticking a spoonful of yogurt into her mouth. Sometimes, she believed herself to be pretty dang awesome—not just because she was a little bit famous either, but simply because she liked who God had made her to be and what she was able to accomplish using the talents He'd given her. Other times, she felt like a complete failure and a disappointment to everyone—all of mankind and God included. That night, she definitely fell into the latter category.

As she was pouring her third glass of Chardonnay, studying how empty the bottle looked, the doorbell rang. Great, just great. Someone had arrived to witness her utter fall from grace. Maybe, if she didn't answer, they would just go away.

"I'm not home!" She called out, her lips feeling a little tingly, her mind a little fuzzy.

"Yes, you are," Grant's voice called back in a sing song tune. She rolled her eyes. Just what she needed. Grant wouldn't go away, so she might as well go ahead and open the door.

"What do you want?" she asked, a smidge on the surly side.

Grant's eyes grew wide in surprise. "Where's my sweet little Evie?" he asked as he stepped inside.

"We lost her about a half a bottle of wine ago," Evie called over her shoulder as she went to retrieve her wine glass from the kitchen counter. "Let me pour you a glass, I have another bottle."

"If it will keep you from drinking *another* bottle entirely by yourself, I'll take a glass."

She nodded and pulled a glass for him from the cabinet.

"What are you listening to?" he asked, walking over and leaning against the counter as she poured him a glass.

"The best sappy, sad breakup music that exists—classic country."

"While I appreciate music of all genres, including the musical stylings of Johnny, Waylon, and Willie, what you're currently listening to is . . ."

"Hush your face, Grant. I'm wallowing in my misery," she said, the Southern twang growing stronger the more she drank. Grant took a big sip of his wine.

"Evie, I'm here to talk some sense into you."

"I don't need any sense talked into me," she said defensively.

"Davis was a total jerk. You outgrew him a long time ago and you know it. I've told you this before, but I felt the need to repeat it tonight after giving you some time to process today. Why are you throwing yourself a big pity party?"

She saw red. She poked a finger into her chest. "You, sir, have no right to say that or judge how long I'm allowed to wallow. What do you know about relationships? You strung poor Kacie along forever! I'm sorry if it bothers me a little that I broke up with my boyfriend of *eight years* today, even if it was for the best. Sorry if it annoys you that I'm not all sunshine and roses for you right now. Everyone can't be 'up' all the time, you know."

Grant sat his glass back down and lifted his hands in surrender. "Whoa, sorry if I offended you. It just seems like you are going off the deep end a little over someone who did not treat you all that well and definitely doesn't deserve the homage."

"You never even met him."

"I didn't need to meet him, I know his type, and for the record, I didn't come here to pick a fight with your feisty self. I'm here to be your friend," he said gently.

Her own expression softened. "I'm sorry if I went a little psycho on you."

"Don't be. I had no right to pry like that. You have every right to feel how you feel. But Evie?"

"Hmm?"

"Maybe it's time to chill out on the wine and country? We have rehearsals tomorrow," he reminded her.

"Coffee?" she asked, sitting her empty wine glass in the sink. Grant poured the contents of his half empty glass in the sink, too.

"Yes, perfect," he smiled at her.

"It's not fair." She poured water in her coffee maker.

"What's not fair?"

"You coming in here, taking charge and making me feel better. I was in the middle of a real good pity party. Stirring up childhood memories and everything."

"So sorry to ruin such a perfect party," he laughed.

"You should be," she said way too seriously before laughing at herself. "Thanks for coming," she added. "How about we watch a few episodes of that show you were telling me about?" She sidled up next to him, two mugs for coffee in her hands. "I just have the plain stuff, no fancy espresso with soy milk."

"I think I'll manage, and binge-watching *Two and a Half Detectives* with you—there's seriously no other way I'd want to spend my evening."

"You wouldn't believe what Davis called me," she said over her shoulder from the fridge.

"What's that?"

"He called me a whore! Me! A whore!" She laughed. "I'm the farthest thing from a whore, Grant." She found the creamer and shut the fridge, turning to see Grant standing frozen…and livid.

"He shouldn't have called you that. It isn't okay," he said.

"It hurt so bad because he was the one that said it," Evie admitted, "but it isn't true, so it doesn't matter. He knows my vow."

"What vow?" Grant asked her as the coffee maker beeped.

"My vow not to have sex until I get married," Evie said bluntly, the wine lowering her inhibitions about sharing personal information with him.

"You—you're not?"

"Don't sound so shocked, Grant."

"It's not something you hear every day."

She poured them each a cup of coffee. "I know— it's uncommon, but I made a vow a long time ago—

eighth grade to be exact—that I wouldn't 'awaken love until it so desires.'"

"What does that mean?"

"It means that I'm not having sex until I get married. Davis and I both agreed to it. Why do you think he was so resentful and frustrated about me not being ready to get married?"

"Well, yeah. I can understand that a little better now."

"You're surprised, aren't you?" Evie asked him, taking a sip of her coffee. Most people thought she was crazy when she told them about her personal wait, which was why she told very few people about it and never, ever brought it up.

"Yes and no. So many things make sense now." Grant took the cup of coffee she'd poured for him from her hand.

"Like what?"

"Your modesty, how easy it is to make you blush, your aversion to sexier dances, how uncomfortable you get when someone brings up sex…I could keep going," he told her.

"Please don't!"

"So, what made you decide something like this?"

Evie shrugged. "A combination of things. My faith was part of it. I made this decision right around the time Davis and I started noticing each other as more than just pals. Sex is such a huge thing and we were really young. I didn't want to make a big mistake and neither did he. But after we graduated, he started applying the pressure. 'We're going to get married one day, Evie, why should we wait?' 'Evie, we've been together for six years, that's longer than some people's marriages last.' I've heard it all, but the more he argued, the firmer I held to my convictions, and now that we've broken up, I'm so, so, so glad I did."

"Do you think you'll still stick with it, or give it up now that Davis is out of the picture? It sounds like you were just being stubborn."

She shook her head. "Nope, I'm sticking with it. My relationship with Davis was complicated without sex—I couldn't imagine how much more complicated it would've been if we had been together like that. Besides, it's easier to wait for something you haven't experienced yet. That's what I hear over and over—once you've done it, it's harder to keep from doing it."

"There's truth in that. Wow, Evie. Your willpower is pretty impressive."

"Yeah, well, I'm not married yet and I don't have plans to be on the horizon. Davis was a safe-haven for me. I knew how to handle him, and for all his pressuring, he respected my decision and never pushed past my boundaries. I knew I could trust him."

"So, you're going to stay a virgin until you get married?"

"Yes, Grant. To be very clear, I am not going to have sex until my wedding night."

"Wow."

"You keep saying that."

"It's just hard to believe. Admirable, don't get me wrong, but hard to believe."

"True love waits," she repeated the age old saying. She even had a ring with the words printed on it in her jewelry box back home. "If something… or someone…is worth waiting for, you wait. And when you finally get it, how much more amazing could it be?"

"I get that. Some people are definitely worth waiting for," Grant smiled at her.

CHAPTER SEVENTEEN

Evie moaned as her alarm clock chirped. Her head pounded, and her throat was scratchy. Just as she reached over to fumble for her phone on the table, someone other than herself shifted their weight . . . in her bed. Her eyes flew open, but immediately squeezed back shut in protest. The tiny sliver of light cutting into the room hurt her eyes, sensitive and raw from crying so much the day before.

She didn't have to look to know who was in her bed. She patted her arms, legs, stomach—she breathed a sigh of relief to note that she was still fully clothed, wearing the pjs she'd thrown on prior to popping open the wine the night before. Cracking one eye open, in the dim light she made out Grant's sleeping…and shirtless…form.

What had happened? She remembered telling him about her vow, to her utter mortification in the still, sober morning, and settling on the sofa with their coffees, but after that everything was a blur. And now he was in her bed! Surely, they hadn't…surely, she would know if they had…

Grant stirred. She nudged his arm with her hand and he turned on his side, yawning as he woke up.

"Good morning," he said, his voice low and gravelly.

"Good morning to you," she replied, her voice oddly chipper. "What happened last night?" she asked.

"You don't remember, do you?"

She shook her head. "No, I don't. I didn't think I drank that much."

"You poured yourself another glass."

"Oh. Did we...?"

Grant's eyes widened. "Of course not, Evie! I stayed the night because we were still talking at three this morning and you were a little sloppy. I didn't want you to throw up in your sleep or anything. Honestly, after you told me all of that stuff last night, do you really think for one second that I would take advantage of you while you're drunk?"

"No! Not at all...I didn't mean that. I know you wouldn't do that. I put two and two together this morning and figured *that* didn't happen. I actually meant...did we kiss?"

"No, we didn't. You would have let me if I tried, but where's the fun in kissing you when you're drunk and I'm sober?"

Her cheeks reddened. "So, you want to kiss me?"

"Maybe," he replied.

She was waiting for him to add an addendum to his answer—*but* she'd just gotten out of relationship, *but* she was too old-fashioned in her beliefs to bother, *but* they were partners and it would screw everything up. However, he said none of those things.

The air hung thick between them.

"I'm not sure how to take that."

"Maybe, your kisses are worth waiting for, and if or when I kiss you, it will mean more than just something we wanted in the moment."

"I never said I was waiting to kiss," she reminded him.

"I know, but you gave me a lot to think about."

"I'd love for you to elaborate," she said, propping her head up with one arm.

"I'm sure you would, but if we don't get going, we're going to be late for practice."

"You're the coach. You can change our practice time," she reminded him.

He hopped up from the bed, tossing his shirt back on. "Yeah, but I gave you a lot of slack yesterday and we have to work double time to make up for it today, Sunshine."

She flopped back over, moaning dramatically as he drew back the curtains, filling the room with light.

CHAPTER EIGHTEEN

"This contemporary is going to be amazing," Grant told Evie as soon as she stepped into the studio.

Evie yawned.

"I'm so tired!" She stretched before tossing her bag against the wall and shrugging out of her windbreaker.

"Look at those guns!" he teased. Her arms had gotten way more defined since the competition began.

Evie flexed her arm. "You like that, don't you?" She laughed. Looking around the empty room, she stared back at him. "Where's the crew?"

"Production meeting. Besides, they have two days' worth of footage of us working on this exact dance already. I don't think they'll be missing anything groundbreaking or newsworthy."

She shrugged. "I'll take the break in filming. It'll be much easier to relax and focus on practice."

"Ready to get started? I'm turning the song on repeat."

She stretched and rolled her shoulders. "Let's do this," she said with an enthusiastic clap. Grant stared at her, sure his adoration for her was starting to shine through. He'd been trying his hardest to keep a little distance between them, but it never worked out.

They'd somehow spent every evening together, after being together all day, for the past week and a half since her breakup with Davis. Multiple practices, her small West Hollywood gig, a night at the movies—they'd done it all as a team. All that time together, and he still felt like a kid on Christmas morning when she burst into the studio.

He took her into his arms as the dance started, and they began the difficult routine as he lifted her above his head before bringing her swiftly down and tossing her forward. She landed and took several steps away as they worked the floor and he reached out for her throughout the choreo. Just as he "gave up" and turned around, she grabbed his arm and he scooped her up with his other arm. She tucked her knees and pointed her toes as he turned in rapid succession. Stopping, she slid down his body and their faces touched for just a brief second before she arched her back and straightened her legs as he spun with her. Just as he was about to throw her in the air again, she stumbled.

"Crap! Sorry, Grant!"

He shook his head and turned from her. He wasn't frustrated with her—he was frustrated with himself. He'd really pushed the limits with the choreography—even for someone on a professional level.

"Are you mad?" she asked.

"No, not at all. Let's start again." He ran over and hit the button to start the song once more.

They made it to the same spot in the routine and she stumbled again. And then again. On the fifth attempt, after messing up again, she hit the floor in frustration. "I am going to pull my hair out if I don't get it this time!"

"Maybe we should take a break?" Grant ventured.

Evie shook her head. "No, I'll get it this time. For you," she smiled.

And the very next time, she did get it. They finished the rest of the routine's lyrical choreography complete with a couple more intricate lifts before he laid her on the ground and took his place beside her, pulling her close as the music trailed away.

"Yes!" Grant said, shooting a fist into the air while they still lay in hold, breathing heavily. He jumped up and helped her up, too.

We did it!" Evie squealed, reaching out for him. He pulled her into a huge hug, so happy they'd managed to make it through the whole routine without a mistake. Why had he ever doubted her?

Overwhelmed by the darling girl in his arms, the words came out of his mouth before he had a chance to think about what he was saying.

"I'm in love with you, Evie," Grant said, still catching his breath. She pulled back and stared at him, those green eyes of hers registering shock. Surely, what he'd just told her was the last thing she'd expected to hear today. But the secret was now out and there was no going back.

"You're in love with me? How can you be in love with me?" she finally asked, her brow furrowed. He stood and captured her hands in his.

"For so many reasons, Evie, and I know it's crazy to just come out and say it like that, but I couldn't *not* say it any longer."

"Any longer? How long . . ." she swallowed, "have you loved me?"

"Truthfully? Since the moment I met you. But I didn't fully realize it to be actual love until about two weeks ago when we were practicing that song and I watched you close your eyes as your hand went to your heart in the practice room. Something about the rawness of that moment—you poured every drop of feeling within you into that song and it sealed the deal for me. I was a goner. There's no one on earth that could possibly have more passion and heart and kindness and beauty than you. God, Evie. To tell the truth, there's nothing about you that I don't love."

"I—I don't know what to say, Grant. I could say, I mean I want to say . . . so, so much, please believe me," she said, searching his face. "But I just broke up with Davis not even two weeks ago! I need some time," she said, looking away. He took her chin in his fingertips and gently tilted it up, causing her to meet his gaze.

"Hey, I'm not telling you that I'm hopelessly in love with you just because I want you to say it back to me, nor do I expect you to feel the exact same way that I do. Yeah, that'd be great, but it's not why I told you. Truth is, I want you to be happy more than I want anything else. I want you to have everything you've ever wanted and for your heart to soak in all it can hold, and then some, of love and happiness each and every day. If I'm right, if you feel even a little of what I'm feeling, then that's what we'll have together, but there's no rush. I'm not going anywhere. I'll wait for you to be ready forever if that's what it takes because," he stroked her cheek gently, "whatever is going on between us is worth that wait." He smiled at her.

"Grant," she whispered. Her eyes were soft and hazy—they looked the way he felt every time he was around her. Happy and mesmerized and a little tortured. "I promise you won't have to wait long," she added wistfully, stepping a little closer.

He wanted to kiss her, and from the way she stood, leaning in, eyes hopeful, lips tilted toward him, she wanted it, too. But he'd just promised to give her time, to wait for her. He wanted a kiss to really mean something between them. "I think it's time to call practice for the day," he said, his voice strained. He went to let go of her hands, but she held them tight.

She pulled on his hands, catching him off-guard and causing him to step forward—until they were but a breath apart. "Who am I kidding? What's the point in waiting to tell you what we both already know to be true? You know I'm just as much in love with you as you are with me," she admitted.

Their lips were nearly touching. He smiled down at her confession, tilting his head as she leaned up.

This was their moment.

His eyes closed as his lips brushed against hers. Softly at first, whispers of the happiest of smiles on both of their faces. It wasn't a typical first kiss. Maybe it wasn't the most romantic of settings, but this kiss was a promise, a surrender, a life-changing event. Perfection is what came to Grant's mind. He would never forget that moment—it didn't matter that they were in the studio in gym clothes, sweaty and tired, the song for their contemporary playing on repeat in the background.

> *Whenever you're ready.*
> *Can we, can we . . .*
> *Surrender?*

There couldn't have been a more perfect song, Grant thought as the breathy words and strong beat surrounded them in the studio. He took his hands out of hers and wrapped his arms around her waist, hugging her close and lifting her slightly off of the ground as they kissed, her arms around his neck.

A moment later as they were catching their breath after their epic first kiss, Evie caressed his cheek. "Everything is different now," she said, smiling up at him.

He beamed at her. "Yes, it most certainly is." Grant kissed her once more before adding, "Maybe we should have dinner tonight? Talk about this a little more?"

She nodded. "Sounds like a date," she said with a wink.

"Good. Because that's exactly what I was angling for."

* * * *

When Evie made it back to her apartment after her life-altering afternoon at the dance studio, she floated on air. Sinking back against the front door, she pressed her fingers against her smiling lips, almost in tears as the purest, most euphoric happiness overwhelmed her senses. The only way to think, the only way to be for her just then, was in extreme descriptions. Her heart overflowed—bursting with love and joy and excitement and all things hearts, flowers, sunshine and rainbows. This was love—true and crazy and terrifying and magical and . . .

She let out a happy little sigh of contentment and a tiny giggle escaped her lips. Waltzing to her bedroom, Evie thought long and hard about what she would wear on her first "official" date with Grant. At that thought, her laugh filled the small room. She and Grant had already proclaimed their undying love for one another and had yet to go on their first, real date. Everything about the two of them being together was unexpected and different. They were from two different worlds, they'd been attached to other people when they had first met, and they never would have even crossed paths had it not been for the show. But all that didn't matter now . . .

Evie pulled out a dress from the closet that was the faintest whisper of pink. She'd been saving the dress for a special occasion. The short, sleeveless dress with its flounces and flare was the perfect blend of romantic, flirty and sophisticated. She quickly showered and rolled her hair. She applied her makeup, sticking with a more natural look, thankful for the lash extensions she'd been rocking as of late. After applying a pink gloss, she pulled her hair out of the rollers and swept her curls over one shoulder in a sleek wave. Checking the time, she threw on the dress, popped in her pearl earrings and was sliding on a pair of strappy gold heels when she heard Grant's knock at the door.

She ran to answer it, almost tripping over her own feet in her hurry, swinging it wide open, and beaming broadly.

"Hello, again," she greeted.

He stepped just inside the door and scooped her up, kissing her soundly. "Hello," he whispered against her cheek.

"You must be as happy as I am right now," she said, closing her eyes and inhaling his clean, spicy scent and relishing the feel of his cheek against hers and his strong arms around her waist.

"Let me get this straight—I just kissed you, right?" He leaned back and asked her.

She planted a soft kiss on his lips. "Yes," she said with a wink.

"Then I'm the happiest man alive," he replied.

CHAPTER NINETEEN

"Mmm . . . so good." Evie closed her eyes. Grant couldn't peel his eyes off his date seated across from him. With the candlelight flickering in the dimly lit French restaurant, her creamy skin glowed and the highlights in her hair reminded him of liquid gold. The place, the moment, the two of them—everything about the evening felt cozy and romantic.

As they were finishing up dessert, he reached across the table and took her hand in his, but he thought better of it and pulled it back immediately.

"Evie, we need to talk." Alarm flashed in her eyes, but he shook his head.

"It's nothing bad, I promise!" He reassured her before continuing, "I've been thinking about everything that has happened today, and we need to decide if we want to make this public. Since the competition is getting serious and the season wraps in just four weeks, the press will be picking up intense interest for all of the remaining contestants."

"Oh, I didn't even think about that. Sometimes, I still forget about press and stories and how to spin them and blah, blah, blah," she rolled her eyes as she placed another forkful of cheesecake to her lips.

"I know it can be frustrating, but we still need to decide what, if anything, we're saying so that we're on the same page."

"What do you think about keeping it just between the two of us for a little while?" she suggested.

"I was hoping you would want to do that. People can speculate, but we don't have to confirm anything until we're ready, and besides, the producers were initially against us having any sort of real relationship, but now that you're single, I don't think it will be as big of a deal. I think staying quiet will have people guessing, and we'll avoid a lot of extra stress if we don't actually confirm our relationship."

Evie nodded. "Then keeping this between the two of us sounds like the best plan of action." She yawned.

"Tired?" he asked.

"Always, as of late," she replied, stretching her sore arms.

"Did you want to call it a night? Or would you like to come over to my place?"

Her eyes widened. "Grant . . ."

"You can trust me, Evie. Always."

Her expression softened. "I know that. I'd love to come over."

He itched to take her hand again, but knew better. Public displays of affection were off limits for the time being.

Less than an hour later, Grant led Evie up the stairs to his third-floor loft located not all that far from her apartment building. As he pulled out his key, he fumbled with the lock, uncharacteristically nervous. The girl holding his hand in the hallway meant the world to him, and he didn't want to mess this up. He finally got the door open and held it for Evie to enter.

"Wow, Grant. This is a really nice place you have," she remarked as she looked around the open space. Her eyes darted to the bedroom enclosed by glass-paneled black doors. "Why do we always hang out at my place? Yours is way nicer!"

"I guess it just didn't feel right to me before now," he told her. "But I want you to be here—I want you everywhere that I am."

"Well, this place beats my tiny little corporate apartment hands down, so it wins as our new place to hang out," she joked as she took in the space, walking over to one of the floor-to-ceiling windows, gazing out at the traffic moving on the street below. He came up behind her and wrapped his arms around her waist, nuzzling her neck as she rested her head against his shoulder.

"And all is right in the world," she whispered. She turned around in his arms so that she faced him. Reaching up, she ran her fingertips along the five o'clock shadow framing his jawline. He leaned down, hovering his lips over hers until he couldn't stand not kissing her for even one more second.

"I love you, Evie," he whispered against her lips.

"You . . . love me," she repeated slowly, leaning back a little, studying him as she reached up and brushed a wayward lock of hair from his forehead. She bit her lip as she took in his expression and eyed him closely, almost as if she didn't believe the words he'd just spoken, even as his hand tenderly grazed her cheek. If she needed to hear specifics, he would give her specifics.

"Of course, I love you. You really couldn't tell before now? Evie, you bring out a side of me that I didn't even know existed. I know what it means now when people say that something makes their heart smile because that's how I feel when I'm with you. I never thought I would be this sappy, but if I could be near you every minute of every day until the end of forever, I'd still wish for more time. You're pure sunshine—and you've brightened every dark place inside of me. I honestly didn't know that those type of feelings existed before I met you, or that I would ever be caught dead saying something like this. There are no words that really capture what you mean to me, so just know that when I tell you that I'm in love with you, it means that I adore you, and I'd do anything for you. It means that you're my world, and I had to tell you because there's no way I could go on denying it any longer."

"Oh, Grant," she whispered, leaning close. "I love you, too. So much it scares me," she added, baring her soul as she gazed at him with those starry eyes of hers. Her whisper, those eyes—that moment would be permanently etched in his memory.

He leaned down until their lips were nearly touching once more. Taking a few seconds to breathe her in—her flushed cheeks, warm skin, tousled hair—

he paused just a little longer to revel in the beauty of those sparkling eyes of hers. Windows to her soul, full of secrets and excitement, love brightly shone in their sea green depths, and he knew, right then, he didn't stand a chance. There was no way he could ever do life without Evie in it. She was his forever, seared in his soul.

The subtle scent of her soft, sweet perfume filled his senses, reminding him of early summer nights back home when wildflowers bloomed in abandon. Breathing her in, he closed his eyes as his lips gently met hers. Sparks sizzled down his spine. They stood there, locked in each other's arms, kissing and swaying, slow dancing in his living room to nonexistent music. He never wanted this moment to end. Placing his cheek against hers, he sang softly into her ear. She sighed happily and leaned into him, recognizing the song from a few weeks ago.

When I wake up, well I hope I'm gonna be, I'm gonna be the man whose waking up with you, and when I'm dreamin' I know I'm gonna dream, I'm gonna dream about the time I had with you . . .

His cheek grew damp, and startled, he pulled back to make sure she was alright.

"What's wrong? Please don't cry," he said, his heart growing uncomfortably tight at the sight of her tears.

"Nothing is wrong, Grant. This moment—it's overwhelming. I love you so much, and to be able to finally be here with you and say those words—I can't believe it. This feels surreal. Too good. These are just happy tears, I swear," she smiled at him, causing a tear to fall from her eye and trickle down her cheek. Grant caught it with his thumb and wiped it away with a featherlight touch. He caressed her face in his hands before leaning down to kiss her again. He would never grow tired of kissing her. Or holding her. Or singing to her. Or hearing her sweet voice sing. Or dancing with her. The list was endless.

Capturing her lips, his kiss was soft, gentle.

* * * *

"Grant!" Evie whispered the next afternoon, stifling a giggle as he snuck a kiss in the music room. "You have to stop that!"

"Being in here alone with you is too tempting," he murmured, pulling her onto his lap and snuggling her. She briefly threw her arms around his neck and gave him a quick kiss before hopping up.

"Be that as it may, someone could come in here any second. We can't take that risk," she reminded him.

"I think you're worth the risk," he said, taking her hand in his, intertwining their fingers. She melted.

"Right back at you. But, there's a lot at stake here, and we decided to keep this a secret for now," she reminded him, gesturing between the two of them.

"Well, Sunshine, I guess we better get back to practice then," he sighed in resignation.

"What a fitting nickname," she teased. "By the way, I never thought I'd be the one coercing *you* to practice."

He picked up his guitar and strummed the classic song they'd been assigned. "Oh, what do you think about dinner at my place tonight? I want to cook for you."

"You cook?" she questioned, eyebrows raised.

"Don't look so surprised or anything, but yes, I cook. I usually don't have the time, but I guess you're worth the effort."

"Ha ha. I *guess* I'll come over then, since you *guess* that I'm worth the trouble," she deadpanned, rolling her eyes. "Are we going to start this song or what?"

"I'd rather find out about this 'or what' to which you could be referring, but I guess we'd better practice."

"You're just full of the jokes today."

"What can I say? I'm in a good mood," he shrugged.

She arched an eyebrow at him, smirking. "Hmm, I wonder why . . ."

"I was kissing you a couple of minutes ago, that might have something to do with it, but if you let me kiss you right now, it would definitely be the reason."

"Grant!" She shushed him.

"You asked."

"It was rhetorical! Discretion, dude! Discretion," she repeated, staring at her sheet music and trying her hardest to focus at the task at hand and not the hot guy holding his guitar and making eyes at her a few feet away.

CHAPTER TWENTY

Grant drizzled a little olive oil into a sauté pan before turning back, towel over his shoulder, to finish chopping the red peppers. He hoped Evie liked his Tuscan pasta. He'd picked a recipe that was simple enough but used all fresh ingredients to make it special. He'd stopped by the Grove's farmer's market on his way home to purchase everything—even homemade, organic angel hair pasta.

As he turned and added the chopped peppers to the sizzling oil, the intercom buzzed and he ran over and pressed the button to let Evie up, a little surprised that she was so early, but he had to rush back to the stove to make sure the peppers didn't burn.

A minute later, there was a knock at his door. "It's open!" he called out, busy managing the pasta and peppers.

"Hello there, Grant."

His hand stilled on the spatula. He slowly turned to see not Evie, but Kacie, standing inside his apartment.

"Kacie . . . I wasn't expecting you," he said coolly, lowering the range's heat and placing the utensil he held onto the spoon rest.

"Clearly, you're expecting someone," she replied, gesturing to the kitchen island where he was prepping most of his and Evie's upcoming dinner.

He cleared his throat. "That's not really any of your business, is it?"

Her eyes widened. "Whoa, Grant. Geez. I didn't mean to push a button. I just came over to talk."

"Now's not really a good time."

"I'll be quick. Is Evie coming over?" she ventured, peering around the loft, probably trying to find evidence of Evie.

Grant thought fast on his feet. He and Evie were keeping their relationship under wraps. "No, not Evie," he lied.

"Oh, hmm. That's surprising."

"I am expecting someone, though, so if you have something to say, please hurry and say it."

"I miss you. I think we should get back together," she said bluntly, crossing the room and coming to stand within inches from him.

"What?" His brow wrinkled in confusion, sure that he'd heard her wrong.

"I think we should get back together," she repeated, coming even closer. "That's what we do, Grant."

"We both know that isn't a good idea."

"Why not?" she asked, looking up at him with a pouty expression.

"Because we just broke up a month ago for like the fifth time."

"And your point is?" she prompted.

"We both know that isn't healthy. The relationship wasn't working."

"But Grant," she purred, running a hand up his arm as he attempted to shrug her off, "I'm sorry if I blew things out of proportion, I just got so ridiculously jealous. I miss you so much."

"Kacie, I really don't want to hurt you anymore than I have. Nothing is ever going to happen between us again," he said firmly.

"Oh, yeah?" She asked hotly. Before he could stop her, she'd pulled his head down and kissed him wildly. Stunned, he didn't kiss her back, but it took him a second to realize what was happening.

A shriek from the living room stopped Kacie's aggressive kisses and he took the opportunity to push her away. But it was too late. Evie stood in the open doorway, a horrified expression on her face, the big bag she carried slipping off her shoulder and landing on the hardwood with an echoing thud.

"Evie!" He exclaimed in surprise. "It's not what you think," he started, but she interrupted him.

"Grant, how could you?" She cried, her voice breaking as she turned and left, her bag still laying in the open doorway. He brushed past a smug Kacie and ran to catch up with Evie, but she was already headed down the elevator. He took the stairs two at a time down three flights, but, by the time he reached the lobby, she'd already scooted out the door. Why did his building have to update their elevators last year??

"Is there anything I can help you with, Mr. Merritt?" Rico, the doorman, asked.

"Did you let Kacie upstairs? Then Evie?"

Rico looked guilty. "You buzzed someone up while I was attending another resident, and when your dance partner came in, I let her up, thinking you'd be happy to see her. I thought you said last night that she was always welcome."

"She is always welcome, Rico. You didn't do anything wrong. It was my bad for thinking Kacie was Evie. Not yours."

"She just left, Mr. Merritt."

"I know—I'm going to run upstairs and turn off my stove and then I'm going after her."

"Good plan, sir. Good plan," Rico nodded enthusiastically. Evie must've looked pretty upset when she'd ran through the small lobby moments earlier.

Grant took the elevator back up to his loft to find Kacie stirring the pot on the stove.

"I think you should leave," he declared, clenching his teeth.

"So, something is going on between you two," She accused, turning and folding her arms across her chest and narrowing her eyes.

He rolled his eyes. "I can't deal with this right now, Kacie. I have a very upset partner, and you and I are over. We've been over—you had no right to be here tonight."

"Well, that upset partner of yours, who you won't admit that you're sleeping with, left her overnight bag," Kacie added snidely, gesturing to the chambray bag with leather straps—complete with Evie's monogram—just inside his front door.

"Kacie, mind your own business and go home," he said mindlessly as he pulled out his phone and called Evie. Of course, it went straight to voicemail.

"You're playing with fire, Grant. Mark my words, this is going to blow up in your face," Kacie warned before saucily walking out of the apartment. Grant paid her no attention. She had no concrete facts, other than Evie's telltale bag—and she'd never believe it if Grant told her that they weren't going to be doing anything physical. Besides, to protect her own reputation, Kacie wouldn't say anything to the media. That wouldn't mesh well with the low-key, Bohemian chic vibe she'd carefully cultivated over the years.

Grant turned off the range top, grabbed his keys and hurried out to find Evie. She couldn't have gone too far—she'd probably just headed home. Within twenty minutes, after numerous unanswered calls and texts, he repeatedly knocked on her door. She didn't answer that either.

* * * *

Evie played with the straw in her gin and tonic, so sad she wanted to throw her head on the bar and cry like a baby. Why had she been so stupid? She'd believed Grant when he told her that he loved her! But clearly, he was still spending plenty of time up close and personal with Kacie. She'd just caught him red-handed.

"Chin up, buttercup. Why's such a pretty thing like yourself looking so down?" the bartender asked.

Evie eyed the edgy, handsome guy in his mid-thirties. A tattoo sleeve covered his right arm and his nails were painted black.

"I'm having a bad day," she replied shortly, finishing her drink and promptly gesturing for him to pour her another. She thought about texting Lex to meet her but thought better of it. No one knew about her and Grant, and as much as she enjoyed randomly hanging out with Lex from time to time, they definitely weren't close enough for Evie to consider her a confidante.

"The two shots and the gin and tonic you've downed in less than an hour says as much," he replied, sitting a fresh drink beside her empty glass.

"I'm giving up on love. It's just a waste of time," she complained. She winced at how cliché and slurry she sounded.

"I hear that at least ten times a night, sweetie, but that doesn't mean it's true," he said, collecting a few empty glasses nearby.

"In my case, it is," she sniffled. She felt so betrayed, and because she loved Grant more than she could even comprehend, utterly heartbroken.

"What happened?" the bartender gently inquired.

"The typical story—I fell for him, then I found him making out with his ex-girlfriend when I got to his apartment for our dinner date."

He grimaced. "Ooh, that is harsh."

"You're telling me," she lamented before taking a long sip from her drink.

"Maybe he has an excuse?"

"An excuse for his ex-girlfriend's tongue being down his throat? I don't think so."

"You have a point. I'm sorry, sweetie. The next one's on me, and I'll call you an Uber when you're ready to leave," he said sympathetically, patting her hand.

Evie groaned. This was terrible. Even the bartender, who heard his fair share of sob stories every night, felt bad for her. As her thoughts grew fuzzy and the sharp, stabbing pain slowly ebbed away, it occurred to her that she was going to have to face Grant. They were scheduled to practice in the morning. There was no avoiding him forever.

Why had she done this? If she'd never agreed to do *Song & Dance,* she would be back in Alabama, gearing up for the *America Sings* tour next month and still with safe, reliable Davis. She wouldn't have fallen head over heels for a guy that took her heart and stomped all over it.

CHAPTER TWENTY-ONE

Evie trudged into the dance studio, eyeing Kim and Steve warily. Grant was running through a bit of choreography with one of the troupe members. She'd texted him earlier that she was running an hour late, but at least she'd managed to get there in one piece. Holy hangover. Her head pounded and she felt like death warmed over.

When Kim, Steve, and Grant caught sight of her, they all froze what they were doing and stared at her.

"What?" she cried snarkily. "Do I have horns growing out of my head?"

"Evie, can we talk?" Grant asked, making an immediate beeline for her.

"I think we should get to practicing. I'm sorry I'm late," she replied, refusing to meet his eyes as she sat her stuff on the small bench, acutely aware of every pair of eyes in the room trained on her.

"I really think we should talk," he stressed, his voice quiet.

"And I," she cut her eyes to where Kim and Steve watched them curiously, "think we should start practicing."

He sighed. "Fine. Whatever you want."

She marched over to Kim to have her mic attached.

The music, so moving and full of happiness just two days ago, began, but the moment Grant took Evie in her arms, she froze. Stumbling through the song, every move seemed labored and just not right.

Starting the song over, they began the routine again, only marginally improving.

"Until we clear the air, it's going to affect our dancing," Grant whispered. She whipped her head in the opposite direction.

"You can't ignore me forever. Please, talk to me. Or at least, look at me," he tried again. She refused to do either, biting her lip to keep quiet.

She somehow made it through the worst, most uncomfortable two hours of her life. Not only was she dancing with the enemy, it was also being filmed. Any of this tense practice session could be used as footage, and could really damage their fan-favorite relationship.

"Okay, we're done," Grant announced, glancing up at the big clock on the wall.

Handing over the mic to Kim, and grabbing her stuff, Evie turned on her heels, about to make a swift break for it, when a strong hand took hold of her arm. She whirled around to face him, shooting daggers from her eyes.

"Let go of me," she seethed quietly.

"Please, Evie, please talk to me," he begged.

"What is there to say? I saw what happened with my own eyes!"

"There's a lot to say. Please, have lunch with me so we can talk privately," he said, glancing around the room.

"Fine. Only because of the show though. Otherwise, there is no way I would eat lunch with you ever again. You understand that right?"

"I do, Evie. Just hear me out. That's all I ask."

She sighed and followed him out of the studio. He led her to his car and opened the door for her.

"Where are we going?" she asked.

"Grub. I know you really enjoyed it that time we ate lunch there a few weeks ago," he told her.

"Whatever's fine," she said, sighing as she stared out the window listlessly. What did it matter where they went? What mattered at all anymore?

He pulled out of the parking lot. Just as they were reaching the café, he broke the silence. "Evie, I can't take this. I'm going crazy with you being upset with me. I am so sorry that I've hurt you, but in my defense, I did not want Kacie to kiss me. I didn't even want her in my home. She took me by complete surprise."

"You weren't *not* kissing her," Evie pointed out.

"I was stunned. She basically attacked me. I didn't even know she was coming over. I thought it was you in the lobby and I just buzzed her up on the assumption that it was you. She came in and I denied you were the one coming over because we'd just agreed to keep what's going on between us a secret. I swear, I tried to get her to leave, but she wasn't budging."

"So, she decided to start making out with you? That sounds a little far-fetched," Evie doubted.

"Well, it's the truth, I swear."

Evie turned to face him in the car. He *did* appear torn up about the whole thing, and she *did* think it completely out of left field—especially since he knew she was coming over. Her resolve faltered.

"I don't know, Grant. We admit our feelings, start dating, and then the next day, this happens—it's just a lot to take in."

"I get that, Evie, but I meant what I said—I'm in love with you. I wouldn't purposefully hurt someone I love. I've never felt like this about anyone else. Ever. Please tell me you believe me."

She knew the truth before he finished speaking, and reached out to gently touch his cheek. "Grant, I believe you, and I shouldn't have doubted you." Even as she said it, she felt guilty for thinking the worst before finding out the details.

"Well, seeing what you saw, I don't take offense. I'm still so sorry—I should've kicked her out immediately."

"You handled it the best way you knew how, I'm just sorry the whole debacle ruined last night and this morning. Let's not give her another second's thought," she said resolutely.

"That sounds good to me. Lunch?" he asked.

She slipped her hand in his. "Yes, I'm starving, and I have a hangover like nobody's business."

"What did you end up doing last night?"

"Something so stupid—a cliche straight out of a romance movie. I'll tell you about it over lunch," she said, shaking her head at the memory of her night spent getting sloshed at a bar down the street from her apartment. What a dumb decision that was in the bright noon sun of the following day—she could've gotten herself into serious danger going out alone like that.

Thank God she'd had sense enough to stay within walking distance of her building and the bartender was kind enough to start plying her with water after water an hour before the last call. She had a hunch he might've followed her to make sure she got home okay, too. She shook her head. One thing was for sure—nothing was bad enough to warrant a night like that again.

CHAPTER TWENTY-TWO

Three days later, Grant played a hypnotic, bluesy riff on his electric guitar, and Evie watched fascinated, unable to keep the smile from creeping onto her lips as she swayed to the music. He gave her the slightest of nods and she winked at his cue. She had no intentions of taking her eyes off him for the entire duration of their performance—she hoped he knew that. And as the guitar twanged and she leaned into the mic, she also hoped they would do the Stapleton's sultry version of this song the justice it deserved.

"You are my sunshine," she sang, staring a hole through that man of hers on the guitar as she continued, "my only sunshine."

She flipped the wavy curls Max, her favorite hair stylist on the show, had made sure fell in tousled perfection, over her shoulder, feeling warm—maybe from the stage lights or maybe from the way Grant met her eyes as she sang to him. Or both—she wasn't sure.

She glanced at the way his forearm flexed as he strummed just as the bass in the background picked up a solid beat that reverberated through her chest. Some of the folks out in the live audience hooted and hollered.

She sang the first verse, the poignant lyrics so much more powerful since she was singing them to her own personal sunshine, imagining how awful it would be were he to no longer be in her life, especially after their little tiff this past week. Heat continued to build within her and her cheeks flushed as the song moved along, her heart swelling with love and emotion.

Since their performances in song and dance were the only opportunities she had to show her feelings for Grant without any worries of real detection, she poured her heart and soul into all of them.

"You'll never know, dear, how much I love you," she smiled as Grant's voice harmonized so perfectly with her own.

He winked at her and she beamed from ear to ear. The song was all love and longing, and the tangible vibe from the audience so great, she never wanted their time on stage to end that night.

But when it finally did, the crowd broke into a louder and wilder applause than she had ever heard in the ballroom before. Grant, still wearing his guitar, came over and stood beside her, giving her a quick and "friendly" kiss on the cheek as they waited for the judges to comment and score them.

"Doesn't matter what they say," he whispered in her ear. "That was hands down my favorite duet of all time."

"Same for me," she replied, closing her eyes and smiling, the moment already branded within her memory. When she dared to open them again, she glanced over at the judges table and her jaw dropped.

All three of the judges were giving them a standing ovation.

"Just get married already!" Esme cried gleefully, teasing them when the crowd had settled a bit. Grant squeezed Evie's hand.

"You two remind me of the greats—Johnny and June. The energy and chemistry between the two of you is downright mesmerizing," Clarice added.

Paulo, once again, had a lot to say with the little he spoke. "It's too much—too much to take in all at once, but I'm left wanting more and more!"

"The judges have spoken. Do you guys have anything to add?" Corey asked Evie and Grant just before their song scores were announced.

"I just love singing with this girl right here," Grant said, his eyes shining on her.

"We make a good team," Evie blushed, acutely aware she probably appeared a lovesick, besotted fool on national television.

* * * *

"We can't keep this a secret forever." Snuggled up against him on his sofa later that night, Grant's low voice startled her awake. Evie positioned herself upright and stared sleepily at him.

"I know you're right, but it's barely been a week since it started, Grant. I kind of wanted to give it at least a couple of weeks before I tell my parents about us, and I don't want them finding out from an article online or anything."

"I get it. What's happened between us wasn't something expected—we've only known each other for a couple of months."

"It's going to be surprising—especially considering that up until about three weeks ago, I had a pretty serious boyfriend."

"So, if Davis was a 'pretty serious boyfriend,' what would you call me?"

Somewhat surprised at his question, she snuggled close again as she thought about how to answer. The truth won out. "I would certainly call what's going on between us serious." She searched his eyes, a little nervous about her admission despite all that had passed between them.

"I would, too, Evie." He kissed her softly. "I love you, you know."

"Everything between us is happening so fast, but I love you, too, and I don't care what anyone else thinks about it." As she said the words, she knew them to be true . . . but telling her mother and father about her new love wouldn't be easy. They were still torn up about her breakup with Davis and hoping they'd get back together. A day hadn't gone by since their breakup that her mother didn't call or text, asking if they'd made up yet.

"What's on your mind, babe?" Grant asked as he played with her hair.

She shook her head. "Nothing, really. I just don't know what my parents will think about the two of us."

"Yeah, I don't think they like me very much."

"It's not that they don't like you—they don't really know you. What worries me is that they are huuuge Davis fans. Mom is best friends with Davis' mom and no joke—the two of them have a scrapbook labeled 'Evie and Davis' Big Day' that they started after we graduated high school. They've clipped things they thought we would like to eat at the reception, dresses that would look good on me, color schemes—it's really ridiculous how big the book is."

"Not much to occupy one's time down in Alabama, huh?"

"You'll see one day." She smiled at him, playfully giving his shoulder a shove.

He pulled her tightly against him, kissing her soundly. "Well, you're mine now. No big day with Davis, got it?" he teased.

She shrugged. "I wasn't a big fan of the stuff in the book anyway."

"So reassuring, you are."

Evie laughed, and when she caught Grant's gaze, she melted. She understood the meaning behind starry-eyed now. Between that and continually floating on clouds, everything seemed far too good to be true. He captured her lips and pulled her close. Her eyes closed and she wrapped her arms around him, her fingers running through his hair at the nape of his neck. She sighed softly, lost in his kisses as she pulled him closer.

Grant pulled away from her so quickly she almost bumped her head on his retreating elbow as he moved to the other end of the sofa.

"W-wh-at in the . . ." she stammered, straightening.

"Evie, I respect you and your vow and things were getting way too intense," he explained.

She nodded slowly. "Grant, you make me feel like I want to toss that vow out the window, and at the same time so thankful I've never shared myself with anyone else."

He took her hand and held it between both of his. "And that's why I can't let you break it. I'd never forgive myself. I care about you way too much."

Evie's feelings were all over the place—a mix of love, disappointment, admiration and frustration. She yawned. "I guess I'd better get home then. It's really late."

She moved to rise, but he stopped her.

"Look, it's really late and it isn't like you haven't slept over before. I just don't trust myself half asleep and in the same bed with you right now. You can sleep in my bed, and I'll take the couch. I don't want you driving home this late alone."

"Grant, I don't want to toss you out of your own bed."

He rolled his eyes at her. "Evie, I offered it. I wouldn't dare make you sleep on the couch. But it is getting late, so we'd better get some sleep. We've got a busy day tomorrow."

She stretched and rose from her cozy spot. "What else is new?"

Hours later, Grant nudged her shoulder.

"Hmm?" she asked, more asleep than awake.

"Your phone has been ringing for at least five minutes. How have you not heard it?" His voice was low and intimate in the predawn of the day. She smiled up at him. "This bed is so comfortable, I must've been dead to the world," she said with a yawn. The cozy moment was interrupted by the buzzing and beeping of her phone again.

Grabbing the phone from the nightstand, she tried to focus her eyes on the bright screen to see who was calling ridiculously too early. As soon as her eyes could focus and her mind could process the gibberish on the screen into actual words and numbers, sure enough, her parent's number shone across the screen. Her mother tended to forget that Evie was two hours behind in LA.

She answered the call—something must be pretty darn important to warrant so many calls. "Mom, it's barely five in the morning," she croaked when she answered the call.

"What have you done?" her mother sobbed.

Alarmed, Evie sat straight up in the bed. "What's wrong?"

"Does Davis know?"

A dreadful knot formed in the pit of her stomach. Grant took a seat beside her on the bed, eyes full of worry. "Know what?" she asked.

"That you and that dancer are secretly dating! There's a whole article about it on that website. You know, the one that your agent is always saying don't read. Lorraine called me first thing this morning and sent me the link. We're real upset, Evie. Real upset. There's pictures and everything."

"Pictures? What pictures?" she asked, sharing a wide-eyed look with Grant. As loud as her mom wailed, he could hear everything she was saying. He picked up his phone and started searching the internet.

"A bunch of them are of you two at a fancy looking restaurant. Another holding hands. Another of y'all kissing at what looks like the studio. Evie! I'm telling you, this is not good. He seems too smooth and," she lowered her voice, "I bet he seduces all of his partners." Evie rolled her eyes, despite the dreadful nausea overtaking her.

"Mom, I guess now is as good a time as any to tell you that Davis and I broke up over three weeks ago. I did not cheat on him, I promise. I would never do that to him."

"Are you really dating your dance partner?" her mother asked over the line. Evie sighed. What was the point in denying the truth? It was going to come out sooner or later. This was just a whole lot sooner than she'd anticipated.

"Yes, Mom, we are dating and you know that his name is Grant."

"I think I need to come to LA. You seem confused, like you're having a hard time out there," her mother rambled, refusing to accept Evie's confession.

"NO, no! I am not confused at all. I know what I want, and that happens to be Grant, who I care about a lot, Mom. I know it seems sudden, but we immediately connected and started growing close. We just get each other. It's like nothing I've ever experienced before. But I swear, nothing happened romantically between us until about a week ago."

"How can you just throw everything away with Davis like that? I bet he is heartbroken," her mother sighed glumly.

"Mom, last time I checked, Davis is not your child. I am. And I know that he is not right for me anymore. I think I've known that for a while."

"And this Grant guy is?"

"Yes, he's very right."

"I guess we'll have to see, won't we? I love you, Evie, but I think you're making a big mistake." She sighed unhappily.

"It's my decision, Mom, and I have a great feeling about this decision and my future, too," she smiled as the words escaped her lips. Grant took her hand in his, rubbing his thumb across the inside of her wrist before lifting it to his lips, kissing it softly.

"Well, I guess I'll talk to you later then, honey." Her mother's voice dripped with disappointment.

Evie stared at the phone after she'd hung up. "That was awful, much worse than I expected."

"Houston, we have a much bigger problem." Grant showed her the images he'd pulled up on his phone. Photo after photo of the two of them—including a couple of kisses.

She laid back down and pulled the covers over her head. "I don't think I'm going to get out of bed today," she groaned, burrowing into her cocoon of warmth. Grant yanked the covers back.

Yes, you are. We have rehearsals with the troupe, an interview with a radio station later this afternoon, and a song session."

"Do you really think an interview is a good idea today?"

"Actually, yes. It gives us an opportunity to answer the speculation and really get on top of the situation before it snowballs out of control."

"This sucks, Grant. I was enjoying our little bubble, and I thought we were being careful, but clearly, there are cameras everywhere. Now, we have to come up with a spiel for the press, and for the networks, and blah, blah, blah a whole bunch of other stuff, too." She hopped out of the bed. "I need coffee if you expect me to really think this early in the morning."

"Evie, once we get through this interview and all of the blah, blah, blah as you like to call it, things will be so much better for everyone involved—most of all us."

"I know, I know. It just makes me wonder who leaked the story."

"It could've been any number of people. Paparazzi are everywhere. It could've been a crew member, another competitor—really anyone."

Evie scrunched her nose. "My money is on Kacie or Nell."

Grant leaned in conspiratorially. "Mine is too."

* * * *

Later that day, they sat in a radio station, waiting to give their carefully prepared answers to the questions they both knew were coming.

"Hello and thanks for listening to 102.7 The Burn's drive home with me, Jamie K. Today, we have some very special guests in the studio. *Song & Dance* finalists, Evie Michaelson and Grant Merritt, are here to have a chat with us and to answer some questions, so call us up," the deejay began.

Grant squeezed Evie's hand.

"Hello," Grant said into the mic.

"Hi, guys," Evie added.

"So, Grant, Evie, let's get straight to the question everyone is dying for you two to answer. Are the dating rumors true?"

"Rumors? What rumors?" Grant teased. Evie laughed nervously, hardly believing the deejay jumped right in like that.

"Come on, guys. Shoot straight with me. And for all of you listening out there, just wanted you to know that they're holding hands in the studio right now. Just saying."

"Okay, okay. Evie, do you want to answer this or should I?"

"To answer your question, Jamie, yes, it's true. Grant and I are dating."

"I knew it! Really, the whole world knew it!" Jamie shouted in excitement, probably at having the first exclusive on their dating status.

"It's not really breaking news," Grant said into the mic.

"In Hollywood, it most certainly is. Give us details!" Jamie exclaimed.

"We would very much like to keep our relationship between the two of us," Evie replied diplomatically.

"But, we can tell you that we do care greatly for one another and are very thankful for the show providing us the opportunity to meet," Grant added.

"Wow. I like your honesty. Not something we get all that much of these days. Unfortunately, you know I have to bring this up—weren't you both dating other people when the season first started?"

Evie and Grant shared a knowing glance.

"Yes, we were. But both relationships had already ended prior to anything happening between the two of us," Grant said.

"Did they end because you had feelings for someone else?"

"I think we're getting a little too personal, Jamie," Evie admonished, keeping her voice light.

Jamie laughed. "Alright, ha ha. You got me. I'll back off."

The interview continued and they moved away from romance and onto show questions. Evie shifted in her seat, aware that a huge burden had just lifted from her shoulders. The truth had set her free.

* * * *

Hands intertwined, Evie struggled to keep up with Grant's brisk pace, but the crowd outside the studio had substantially grown since their radio announcement the day before. Everyone seemed to want to snap a picture of the two of them. Bustling into the private studio, Kim, Steve and Harper were all waiting for them in the break room.

"Hey guys," Evie started, smiling tentatively.

"We already knew," Kim said frankly. "And you two are great together. Personally, I'm really happy for you guys, but professionally . . ." She sighed. "This is a real mess to clean up."

"What's there to clean up? We were honest, we didn't cheat, and they're throwing us the showmance angle anyway," Grant offered, reaching into the fridge for a bottle of water.

"Grant, Grant, Grant," Kim said, shaking her head. "A 'showmance' and a romance are two very different things. You of all people should know that. Think back, has there ever been a successful affair between partners on the show?"

"Evie and I are different. This is not an 'affair.' What we have is real."

Kim rolled her eyes. "Like I haven't heard that before." She eyed the two of them critically. "Look, I have a meeting with the PR department in an hour. They're analyzing the reaction to the story and your little announcement on the radio earlier. Please guys, keep a low profile until you hear back from me. Then, we'll go from there."

"Go where?" Evie asked in confusion.

"We'll decide jointly what are next steps should be in your relationship's presentation. It may be best to remain radio silent or stage a breakup, or it may go over favorably with our key demographics. Just stay incognito for now, okay?"

"We have dance practice for the next couple of hours, then we're working on our music in Studio C. We can stay low-key."

"We won't be filming today. We may stage a few scenes regarding this situation, but we have to see what PR has to say first," Steve piped in, his camera nowhere to be seen.

Grant and Evie both nodded simultaneously. "Well, we'll get to work then," Grant offered stiffly, leaving the room with Evie.

"What was that?" Evie hissed under her breath after they'd rounded the corner.

"The entertainment industry at its best," Grant remarked, the cynicism thick.

"I don't like how they're telling us what to do and when. Like we have no say over our own relationship," Evie's hushed tones were close to his ear.

"Me either, but with the leak and our contractual obligations to this show, we kind of have to go along with what they want," he shrugged.

"I don't want to fake a breakup," she pouted.

"Do you think that I do?"

"No, but if we have to go through all of this, we better work our rear-ends off and win this thing."

"I couldn't agree with you more, Evie."

Kim caught up with them in the music room a few hours later. When she entered the studio, both of their heads shot up, waiting expectantly to find out what the deal was.

"Alright. PR has been monitoring the situation, and everything actually seems to be working out in our favor. There was only a trace of backlash, we're thinking mainly Kacie fans and a handful of Auburn football fanatics, but overall, initial reactions are positive. I had a phone conversation with Dan Dean, and though he wants to throttle you Grant, he said there was no going back now. You two are too popular to chastise, and a breakup would be even worse for publicity. So, we're spinning it as a natural thing that just sort of happened over the past couple of weeks. I'm sure we have some footage to work with, and we'll tape tomorrow with you guys just acting like you normally would around each other now."

They both sighed in relief at exactly the same time and laughed at the synchronicity of it. "That's good to hear," Grant said nodding. "I was really worried there for a minute."

"We're not out of the woods yet, Grant. You two need to make sure to mind your p's and q's for the rest of this competition. We have to handle this situation with kid gloves," Kim said hurriedly before leaving them to finish practicing so she could continue on with her damage control.

"It sounded like she was talking about a bomb, not us. This is so surreal," Evie murmured after Kim had left.

"I feel like we're actors in a play, or at least, that's how they view us," Grant added.

"Only a few more weeks, though, right?" Evie said, beginning to play the piano again.

"Yeah, but what happens after that?" Grant asked, turning to her.

"We haven't really talked about it . . ." she trailed off, her hands resting in her lap.

"Maybe we should talk about it?" Grant suggested, coming and taking a seat next to her on the piano bench.

"I leave on tour a week after the show wraps," Evie reminded him, unsure how he would handle it, memories of multiple arguments with Davis flooding her thoughts. However, Grant didn't miss a beat.

"I know, and I'm really happy for you," he said earnestly, "But what does that mean for us?"

Evie stared at the piano keys. "This whole thing is so new—we haven't really talked about what will happen next."

"Would you ever consider moving to LA?" he asked.

Her eyes widened at the abrupt question, but it wasn't a new idea to her. "I'd actually been thinking about a move before anything ever even happened between us—even before the show. It's time for me to find my first place, and I'm not going to buy a house in Thompson, Alabama. I love it there, and it will always have a special place in my heart, but it makes no sense, as a musician and artist, for me to live there."

"You make a valid point. But just so you know, if you were planning on settling in Thompson, I'd still figure out a way to make us work."

"I don't think that would be feasible, but that's neither here nor there. I really want to be in LA. I love it here, my agent is here, and most importantly, you are here," she smiled at him. He put his forehead against hers, their lips inches apart.

"Evie, I know we've only been 'officially' dating for a few days, and it sounds crazy, but I don't take this or you lightly. I didn't tell you I love you just to be saying it. This is a forever kind of love for me."

"I'm with you on that, Grant," she beamed at him, "we should sing 'Sunday Kind of Love.' That sums it up, doesn't it?" She played the song's opening chords.

"You're amazing," he said, pressing a kiss against her temple. She started singing, but a few lines in, didn't know any more of the words. He took the opportunity to pull her to him.

"We'll definitely sing it, but right now, why don't we just call it a day and go on a date? I'd like to take you out and show you off since I have permission now."

Evie laughed. "I'd be just as happy with ice cream and Netflix, for the record."

"While I'd be good with that, too, I want to take you dancing for the fun of it, if you're up for it."

"Dancing with you? I'm always up for it, Grant," she said, standing and taking his hand as they left the music room.

CHAPTER TWENTY-THREE

The following morning, after his four-mile run, Grant called his mom. The two of them didn't talk all that often, but given recent and unexpected circumstances, he wanted to run a few things over with her.

"Hello, son," she greeted. He heard the ever-present smile on her face resonating through her sweet voice and missed her instantly. He needed to visit more.

"Hi, Mom. How have you been?"

"Lovely, just lovely. Are you coming home for Easter, dear?" She'd wasted no time getting right to her agenda, even though he was the one that had actually called her.

He froze—he'd forgotten the upcoming holiday altogether. "I'll have to check my schedule and see what I can do, Mom. I hope I can make it, but we're in the thick of the competition right now."

"I hope you'll be able to be here, too, Grant. Your father is getting one of those hams from the local butcher, and Jane and her family will be here. It just won't be the same without you," she told him.

"I promise, I'll try to get there."

"Will you be bringing Evie?" She blindsided him, which she had a habit of doing. No one would ever suspect the capabilities of Claudia Merritt with her chambray shirts and kind eyes when they met her, but the woman said whatever was on her mind and cut right to the quick of a situation. No nonsense or beating around the bush.

"Uh . . . wow. I didn't expect you to ask that, but if I'm able to come, I would like to bring her if that is alright with you," he responded.

"Of course! Please bring her—I'd love to meet her. You know, I've been watching the show and reading the news, Grant. It's a shame a mother has to find out about his son's new love interest from an online news article."

Grant cleared his throat. "That's actually why I was calling, Mom. Would you be interested in coming to the show this Tuesday so that I can officially introduce you and Dad to Evie?"

"I'd love to, Grant!" she exclaimed before adding, "And I'm sure I speak for your father, as well. Besides, we haven't been to one of the shows in quite some time."

Grant smiled. "I really want you and Dad to meet her . . . the rest of the family, too. Hopefully everything will work out for Easter. It's next week, right?"

"Yes, work it out with your schedule and I'll see you Tuesday night, all right, dear?"

"Great, Mom. Thanks so much. I've got to run— I'm supposed to be at the studio soon."

"Okay, Grant. See you, Tuesday."

Grant hung up the phone. Tossing it on the counter, he rushed to shower so he wouldn't be late meeting Evie at the studio. He'd never cared about his parents meeting one of his girlfriends before, but he couldn't wait for them to meet Evie—especially since their relationship was already headlining certain news outlets.

As he threw on a black shirt and workout pants, he wondered if he should mention to Evie that his parents would be attending the show Tuesday night.

Nah. No need to make her nervous.

* * * *

Evie slipped through his arms, her form tight and clipped, just like they'd practiced, before he ran to her full force, swooping her up and tossing her across the dance floor. She leapt, a graceful glide, before sticking her landing and whipping back around to face him once more.

Her skirt, the shade of moonlight, reflected the ballroom's strategic lights as she danced towards him once more—swinging the shimmering fabric high in the air as expected in a traditional Paso Doble. Not that their dance could be categorized as traditional. The choreography was creative and out-of-the-box, even though it still adhered to the rules of the Spanish dance.

With a fierce expression, Evie marched towards Grant before he caught her in his arms again, leading her through the precise movements. This song was like a new personal anthem—the producers couldn't have made a more appropriate choice. She was a bird set free, flying high with a new love she hadn't planned.

Grant tossed her again and she soared through the air, hands and feet pointed and still before Grant caught her with ease and swung them into the next step. Strong and confident, their Paso showcased his raw masculinity.

Focus, Evie, she reminded herself. She had to play her part in this dance and not melt at his touch and give into the temptation to sneak a kiss. Despite knowing the intense dance like the back of her hand, she still fought that urge. After all, Grant was *shirtless* for this number.

She still couldn't believe it. The man leading her across the dance floor was *her* man. Lord, but she loved him and playing the part of fierce, angry and intense proved nigh to impossible as she tried not to laugh with giddy happiness in his arms. She furrowed her brow and glared at him as he spun her out. She hid a smile, her stomach full of butterflies as he pulled her close again. She felt all warm and fuzzy, not fierce and needing to be set free like the song proclaimed. She *was* free.

They danced through the rest of the number, and he dipped her low as the song came to an end before swinging her back upright with force, and she grabbed his arms tightly to keep in hold. Her breath came out quivering and uncertain as the crowd erupted into wild applause at their dramatic ending.

"Good job, babe," Grant told her, smiling broadly, breaking the intensity still lingering from the dance. She beamed back at him, wanting to kiss him then and there, but kept herself in check.

Later backstage, after they'd received their perfect dance score and cooled down a bit, Grant checked his phone and looked up at her strangely.

"Don't get mad, okay?" he asked her.

"What is that supposed to mean? How could I be mad at you?" she replied.

"Just keep that in mind for the next five minutes or so."

Taking her hand, he pulled her up from the director's chair where she sat and led her back to his trailer. When they entered, she was surprised to see an older couple seated on the tiny sofa. The petite woman with jet black hair, smile lines and a lavender pantsuit had the kindest brown eyes she'd ever seen, and the man seated next to her and holding her hand was a 60-year-old replica of Grant wearing a blazer.
Evie shot Grant a quizzical look as she fidgeted with the folds of her skirt.

"Evie, I'd like you to meet my parents, Scott and Claudia Merritt. Mom, Dad, this is my dance partner and my wonderful girlfriend, Evie Michaelson," Grant announced, about to burst with pride.

Evie swallowed her nerves as his parents rose to greet her. She hugged his mother and kissed his father's cheek, still in shock that she was meeting his parents for the first time wearing a Wild West saloon girl getup. At least Grant could've waited to introduce her until after she'd changed into the pale pink tulle midi-length skirt, white top and classy heels for their song set—not looking like a sweaty bar floozy from the 1800s.

"I'm thrilled to meet you both," she told them with a genuine smile. Grant had blindsided her with the parental introductions, but that didn't mean she wasn't pleased with the gesture. It was a big step for them.

"The pleasure is ours, Evie," Grant's mother replied as they took their seats back on the sofa again. Evie perched nervously against the counter a respectable distance from Grant. He took her hand in his and scooted closer to her. She tugged at the costume. Sure, it covered everything that needed covering, but it was in no way "meet the parents" appropriate and she wanted to give off a good first impression. She snuck a glance at Grant beside her, still shirtless, but completely at ease. She took a deep breath and willed the worrisome concerns from her mind. So, it wasn't brunch at a classy restaurant or dinner with crystal and china—she was meeting Grant's parents for the first time in a lot trailer dressed like a saloon girl. It was what it was.

"Did you guys fly in for the show?" Evie asked, squeezing Grant's hand.

"Yes, Grant asked us to come, which he never does, so of course we wanted to oblige him," his mother explained. "Your dancing is exquisite, Evie—hands down the best I've seen on this show in a long time," she added.

"Thank you, Mrs. Merritt," Evie blushed. Now she knew where Grant had gotten his complimentary nature.

"Please call me Claudia," she replied warmly, a twinkle in her soft brown eyes.

"Grant has told us you hail from Alabama, Evie. How's LA treating you?" Grant's dad asked politely.

"I love it here . . . I'm actually considering purchasing an apartment here," she told them, her eyes darting briefly to Grant, hoping she hadn't said too much. It's not like her moving plans were the sole effect of her relationship with their son, but proximity to him would certainly be a plus.

His parents shared a knowing glance. "That's wonderful, dear. Now, I'm sure Grant has mentioned the invitation we extended to have Easter dinner with us," Claudia prompted.

She swallowed. It was the first she'd heard of the invitation. Evie turned to Grant for guidance.

He squeezed her hand looking sheepish. "She doesn't know and that's my bad. In the midst of preparing for the show this week it slipped my mind," he told his parents before turning to her and adding, "we can talk about it later."

"It would mean so much if you both could make it for Easter, Grant," Claudia implored her son.

With their jam-packed, relentless schedule, Evie hadn't even realized that the holiday was right around the corner. She usually attended her home church in Thompson wearing some sort of pastel concoction she let her mother pick out that coordinated with her parents' Easter Sunday clothes. After church, her entire extended family headed over to Granny June's for a spread that featured baked ham with pineapple slices, chicken and dressing, and deviled eggs. Not to mention the best caramel cake in the South. She'd never missed Easter with her family before.

"Mom, we haven't discussed it yet, but we will and I'll get back to you about it, okay?" she heard Grant say.

"Alright," Claudia surrendered, dropping the subject.

Grant checked his watch and announced, "It's time for us to head back and get ready for our song set. We'll see you two after the show." He tugged Evie out of the trailer as she tossed a smile and wave over her shoulder at his parents.

"Way to surprise me there," Evie murmured as he escorted her to her trailer to change.

Grant's face fell. "You didn't want to meet my parents?"

"Of course, I wanted to meet your parents! However, it would've been nice to not be dressed like a barmaid and had time to mentally prepare for the introduction. First impressions are important."

"Gotcha. So, as far as Easter goes . . ."

"Will we even be able to take the time off?" she questioned as they approached her trailer.

"Yes, we can work our scheduling around it. Would you want to fly to Palo Alto with me and spend the weekend with my parents and my sister and her family?"

She stopped walking and faced him. "I would love to go, Grant, but what about my family? I've never missed spending Easter with them."

His eyes widened. "I'm so sorry, Evie! I didn't even think about that. Mom asked me about it a few days ago, and then you saw how she was pressing me for an answer in there. I never told her we would officially be there. I just said we would try. We can go to Alabama and spend the weekend there instead."

This time she was the one in shock. "You would go to Alabama with me?"

"Of course, I would."

"I don't want you to disappoint your mother."

"I don't want to disappoint you."

She took the last few steps to her trailer. They would be pressed for time now. "No, don't worry about that. You aren't disappointing me at all. You need to spend Easter with your family—it will mean so much to your mom. I think the best way to handle the holiday is for you to head to Palo Alto and I'll go to Alabama— we should divide and conquer," she told him firmly.

"You don't want me to go with you?"

"I'd love for you to go with me and meet my extended family . . . but things are kind of rocky with my parents right now and I need to smooth it over. Besides, I don't want to take you away from your family either."

He sighed. "For the first time in over two months, we're going to be spending two days apart."

She shrugged. "I guess so. Are you going to make it?" She winked at him.

"I'll manage to survive somehow," he laughed. She could still hear the echo of his laughter as she hurried inside her trailer to change and he headed back inside the studio.

CHAPTER TWENTY-FOUR

At Granny June's house for Easter Sunday lunch, a card table had been pushed up against Granny's farmhouse kitchen table and mismatched vinyl tablecloths covered them and the other folding tables out on the sunporch. Evie sat amidst a dozen family members at the combined table, while the children and young teens sat at the folding tables or anywhere they could find a seat, perching paper plates and red Solo cups on any surface that would hold them. Her parents had insisted that she sit at the "adult table" and eat with them rather than outside on the steps with her cousins around her age, seeing as they never saw her anymore.

"That slick dancer friend of yours didn't come to Alabama with you? I thought y'all was as thick as thieves," her Aunt Bev called out from the other end of the table. Aunt Bev was a spitfire and the queen of gossip in Thompson. Evie fought the urge to roll her eyes before answering Aunt Bev's barbed question. Seated among a sea of blatant Davis supporters, the only pro-Grant ally she knew of was Granny June.

"Grant is spending Easter with his family. I insisted—even though he wanted to come with me and meet y'all. I knew how much it meant to his mother for him to be with her for the holiday," she replied with an even tone.

"You two have something real special," Granny June piped in as she spooned hot banana peppers over the pile of butter beans on her Chinette plate.

Evie ducked her head, smiling shyly as she took a bite of baked macaroni and cheese. "Thanks, Granny. I think so, too."

"Did you see Davis and that new girl he brought to church this morning?" Aunt Bev asked.

The macaroni noodles stuck to the back of her throat. She swallowed hard, no longer hungry. "I saw that," Evie admitted and added, "They make a cute couple." She'd recognized the girl he'd brought from the cheerleading team at Auburn but couldn't recall her name.

"You're not going to be able to smooth things over with him if you wait too much longer," Evie's mother warned, taking a sip of her sweet tea as she eyed Evie.

"I've told you that I don't want to get back together with Davis, Mom," Evie replied evenly. "I'm honestly happy for him if he has found someone else."

"But Evie . . . he was just drafted to the NFL!" Her father exclaimed, piping into the conversation for the first time with the argument he personally believed to be strongest as to why his only daughter needed to reunite with her ex-boyfriend.

"That's great, Dad. But . . . I'm in love with someone else—not Davis," she told him and the table at large. She pushed the ham and dressing around on her plate with no appetite as the entire family stared at her. What she wouldn't give to be in Palo Alto right about now.

"Love, Evie? What y'all have is not love," her mother squeaked. "Love is knowing one another's strengths and weaknesses. Love is seasons of both good and bad. Love is eight years of commitment. Love is not getting swept up in a fantasy dance competition with a Don Juan dance partner too handsome for his own good!" By the end of her diatribe, her mother's face flushed bright red and she exuded indignation.

"It's not a fantasy, Mom. It is the real thing. Davis meant—and still means—a lot to me. But what we had wasn't right. It was comfortable and safe, but we both knew we were over. Our breakup wasn't one-sided."

"Let the girl make her own decisions, Sue Anne. She's a grown woman with a good head on those pretty shoulders," Granny June encouraged, tossing Evie a wink. Thank the Lord Granny June was on her side in this.

"How's the peanut crop?" Evie turned and asked her uncle, refusing to participate in the conversation about her personal life any further.

* * * *

That afternoon in Palo Alto thousands of miles away, Grant took a seat at the elegant table his mother had set in the dining room. The crisp linen and fine china was, as usual, so perfectly set it felt wrong to mess it all up with food. His sister, Jane, her husband, Rich, their two kids, six-year-old Tess and four-year-old Brody, along with his parents each took their places, marked by printed place cards atop the full china settings. As they all settled into their seats, he wished Evie had been able to make the trip with him. She would've completed the whole scene for him.

"So, Grant, Mom tells me you've met the one," Jane started in on him as soon as Mrs. Katt, his parents' housekeeper since he was in elementary school, served the first course.

Grant nearly choked on a sip of wine. He glanced over at his mother, who only shrugged, waiting herself to see how he would answer his meddlesome older sister. He weighed his options. Honesty would be the best policy.

"Yep, sure have," he said with a concise nod.

Jane's eyes widened in surprise, but a smile quickly spread across her face. "Grant, I'm so happy to hear that."

"I told you so," his mother leaned over and murmured to Jane, though all at the table could hear her. "I knew something was special about Evie the first time I saw the two of you on television together. I've never seen you look at someone the way you look at her, Grant."

Grant laughed. "That seems to be the popular opinion."

"Why isn't she here then?" Jane asked.

"Because she had her own Easter family gathering to attend," Grant replied, grabbing a dinner roll.

"What happens when you two get married? I'm personally assuming that's where you guys are headed, so in the future will you go to her family get-togethers for the holidays, or will she come here to ours?" Jane pried, spearing at her goat cheese and pear salad.

"Way to put the cart before the horse, Jane. We'll cross that bridge when we get to it," Grant said.

"Evie really is a lovely girl," his father added to the conversation with a nod in Grant's direction. "I'm sure you two will figure something out when you reach that point in your relationship."

"Thanks, Dad."

Later, after dinner had been cleared and he and his sister and mother were hiding Easter eggs in the backyard while his dad and Rich entertained Tess and Brody, Grant pulled his mom aside.

"Mom, I need to talk to you about something," he said as they tucked pastel eggs into the flower gardens close to the house.

"Sure. What's on your mind?"

"I'm ready for the ring I inherited from Nana. I'd like to take it back to LA."

His mother's eyes illuminated, but also held a hint of reservation within their depths. "Are you sure, Grant? Don't you think it's a bit soon for that?"

Grant thought on how best to answer her. He understood her concerns—he and Evie had only been "official" for a couple of weeks. But, for the entire two months leading up to him confessing his feelings for her, they'd spent every single day together. They knew what each other's bad moods looked like and their love was rooted in a friendship that had grown fast, strong, and deep. The saying rang true for him—when you know, you know. And he knew.

"I'm not sure exactly when I'll ask her, but I will ask her. I figure it's best to prepared in case the perfect moment strikes," Grant finally said.

Tears glistened in his mother's eyes. "I am so happy for you, Grant. She's the one, she really is. I feel it in here," she told him, patting her heart. She pulled him in for a big hug.

"Thanks, Mom. I feel it, too. I've never been more certain of anything."

* * * *

Early the next morning with coffee cup in hand, he waited for Evie's flight to arrive at LAX. He saw her before she saw him as she rolled her bag out of the gate, yawning widely. He watched her draw closer before she spotted him. Something in the tense set of her jaw made him uneasy.

"Hey there, stranger," he called out, opening his arms as he made his way toward her. Finally seeing him approach, her eyes brightened and she rushed toward him, dropping her bags as she wrapped her arms around him, squeezing him tight.

"I missed you," she breathed against his neck.

"I missed you, too," he said softly, pulling back just enough to give her a gentle kiss in greeting. "I brought you coffee," he added, extending the cup. She took it with excitement.

"Aw, thanks! I definitely need it," she smiled in gratitude before taking a long sip.

"How was sweet home Alabama?" He asked her as he gathered up her bags from the floor.

"I don't want to talk about it," she sighed. "Let's just say next Easter, I'll be in Palo Alto with you."

"It was that bad?" He asked, eyebrows raised.

"I wish I could say it wasn't, but it was much, much worse than I thought it would be. Davis brought a new girl to church and since he's just been drafted, which by the way makes him the best thing since sliced bread in Thompson, I'm ranked below Nick Saban with my family members.

"Nick Saban?" Grant questioned.

"Alabama's head coach. My family is die-hard Auburn fans—they bleed blue and orange. They refer to The Tide's coach as Nick Satan."

Grant laughed—he couldn't help it. As he led them to his car he asked her, "So, what you're telling me is that your family is none too pleased with your current choice of boyfriend?"

"I don't want to tell you that because their reasons are biased and stupid."

"Evie, you were with the guy forever and he sounds like football royalty. I mean, it makes sense that the star quarterback, family friend would be ranked higher than the stranger that's a ballroom dancer from television that you've known for barely three months. Naturally, they probably think that I broke you guys up and they aren't happy about it."

"But that's not what happened!" Evie exclaimed.

"Davis and I needed to break up like a year ago. We weren't right for each other. I wish I could smooth everything over, but I didn't even talk to him—I didn't have a chance. It would've been too weird at Sunday service while Sorority Barbie was on his arm."

"Sorority Barbie?"

"If you would've seen her, you would know exactly why I call her that."

"If you say so."

They drove to Evie's apartment and Grant helped her up with her bags. "If we make it through on Tuesday, we're in the semi-finals," he reminded her.

"I know, it's crazy to me. Time has flown. I guess we need to head to the studio, don't we?" she asked, stretching and yawning.

Grant nodded, pulling her close. "Yes, unfortunately we do. We can't waste any time—we have to make up for the weekend."

"At least we'll be together," she said with a wink and he kissed her.

"Yes," he said against her lips. "Always."

* * * *

They'd missed two days of practice and had to make up for it big time. From the moment they'd arrived at the studio on Monday they didn't stop. By the time Grant dropped her off late Monday night, she felt comatose. She'd barely made it into bed before conking out.

When Tuesday morning dawned bright and early, the inside of Evie's throat felt scratchy. Peeling her head from the pillow was no easy feat. She worried how the scratchiness would affect her vocals. The song they were singing for the show that evening was already a stretch for her range.

She grabbed her phone off of the bedside table and typed out a quick text to Grant: *My throat hurts this morning. I'm going to try to sleep for a bit longer but shouldn't be too late to the studio. Praying that it feels better before tonight!*

His response was immediate: *I'll be there in fifteen minutes to check on you. Just rest. I'll let myself in.*

She smiled. It was so sweet of him to go out of his way and stop everything on a live show day to come see about her. He didn't have to do that, but there wasn't a point in arguing with him.

She dozed back off, but roused a bit when she heard Grant at the door using the key code she'd given him. She heard him moving around in the kitchen. A few minutes later, he came into the bedroom carrying a white mug.

"Hey babe. How are you feeling? I made you a cup of tea with honey and lemon," he told her as he walked over to her bed. She sat up and he handed her the cup of tea, perching on the side.

"I'm okay, I guess," she croaked. He smoothed a wayward lock of hair out of her face. She must look awful if how she felt held any sway with her looks. Her eyes were bleary with exhaustion.

"Just a couple more weeks and it's all over," Grant told her. "It would probably help to take a spoonful of honey and cinnamon, too."

"Thanks for coming and checking on me," she said, sipping from the steaming cup. "But, you know it's not over for me in two weeks. I get a week off after the finale, but then the *America Sings* tour starts. No rest for the weary." She tried to smile. All she could think about was how good it would feel to lay in bed all day and rest, rather than work out, practice the Argentine tango for two hours, their song for another hour, then spend the rest of the time up until pre-show interviews in hair and makeup.

"I feel like craaaaaap," she whined. "I wonder if I'm getting a cold?"

Grant put his hand on her forehead. "You feel a tiny bit warm. We've been going at a break neck speed for weeks, and even though we had time off this weekend, we both spent it traveling. Tomorrow, we'll start late—not until after lunch. So, if we can just get through today, you can have all of tomorrow morning to sleep or watch Netflix or whatever," he promised.

"Ohh, that sounds amazing," she replied, closing her eyes. "Are you sure you can't give me a pass on the gym this morning?"

"As your boyfriend, I would love to do that. I hate that you don't feel well. But as your coach and dance partner, I can't."

"Boo," she sighed. She sat the mug on the table and flopped the covers off, swinging her legs out of the bed. She had to start getting ready. "You really suck, Grant," she complained, exhaustion making her grouchy.

"I love you, too, sweetie," Grant told her, rising to leave so she could dress and they could head to the gym.

Hours later, in a black lace dress dripping with fringe and her hair pulled into a low bun complete with pin curls, she stretched out as best she could on her trailer's infinitesimal couch. She had forty-five minutes until they were due for the press line, and a power nap seemed to be the best free-time filler. Grant was at the final dress rehearsal for the pros' opening number. She'd seen it twice already and would see it later during the live show, too, so it wasn't like she was missing anything. Besides, fighting this cold was really taking it out of her and she'd need all the energy she had to get through their performances later. Over the course of the day, her symptoms had only grown worse.

A light knock at the trailer door stirred her from her nap twenty minutes later. She rose, her head pounding.

"Who is it?" she called out, hurrying to answer the door.

"It's just me," Grant's deep voice rang through the door. She pulled it open.

"You woke me up," she told him, laying back down.

"Don't lay back down," he told her. "The press interviews were moved up half an hour and we're already late. We have to get going." He reached for her hands to help her up. "How are you feeling?"

"I promise, I'm not normally such a baby. I really feel bad, Grant."

"I know," he said, kissing her forehead. "I'm sorry that you don't feel up to all of this."

"It's not like there's an option. I want to win. I've just got to get my head in the game," she said more to herself than to him.

"I believe in your capabilities, Evs. Now let's get going or we'll be late," Grant said, placing a hand on the small of her back, guiding her out the door.

Somehow, she made it through the press line and the live show, despite a massive headache and a seriously sore throat. She even managed to sing their song—using the raspiness of her voice to her advantage. But as soon as they found out they weren't eliminated and the credits rolled, Grant whisked her backstage.

"We're skipping post-show interviews tonight. You feel warm, and you look terrible," he told her as he guided her toward the exit, his hand pressing her forehead to check her temp. "Let's get you to your trailer."

She let him lead her, too tired and sick to argue or give him a hard time for saying she looked terrible. Not looking to the right or left, Grant zoomed through the flood of contestants, press, and crew members, reaching her trailer in record time.

"Why don't you get changed into something more comfortable?" he asked her.

"Could you grab my jeans and sweatshirt out of that bag?" she asked him, holding onto the wall for support. She watched him walk over and dig through her duffel, pulling out the ripped jeans and studded sweatshirt she'd worn to set. He placed them on the sofa.

"Grant, I need your help getting out of this," she said, tugging at the clingy scarlet gown she'd worn for the second half of the show. The snug mermaid fit made walking difficult—in her sickly state she couldn't get out of it by herself.

With no hesitation, Grant jumped into action. He walked over, stood behind her and unzipped the dress, slipping it off her shoulders and tugging it past her hips. She balanced with a hand on his shoulder as she stepped out of the pool of fabric.

As she hurried to throw on the jeans and sweatshirt, Grant looked elsewhere. Collapsing on the sofa, she watched as he carefully collected the couture gown from the floor, hung it up and slipped it into a garment bag.

"I'll take this back to wardrobe and change myself then meet you back here in twenty minutes to drive you home. You just rest here until I get back," he said, helping her get situated and tossing her black fluffy robe over her as she shivered. He kissed her forehead and dashed out of the trailer.

She closed her eyes, feeling terrible but strangely thankful. She'd just seen the most tender side of Grant.

He'd commandeered the situation, got her out of the fray, helped her undress, took care of her gown and would take her home and see to it that she had everything she needed to get better. She was blessed, indeed—even if she was sick with a cold.

CHAPTER TWENTY-FIVE

"Okay, this is exhausting," Evie commented a week and a half later as she flopped onto Grant's sofa following a particularly grueling practice.

"We're gearing up for the finale. It's a big deal and we've got to work harder than we ever have before," Grant said in his coach voice. She threw her empty water bottle at him.

"We are working our tails off. We eat, sleep and breathe performance. But two dances and three songs?? It's a bit much, don't you think?"

"Well, one of our dances is a repeat and the other is a freestyle, so we aren't having to work on anything too new or difficult, and singing is your area of strength anyway. I think you're going a little overkill on the complaining," Grant said, taking his shirt off and tossing it in the vicinity of his laundry basket. Distracted, she swallowed the sarcastic comment on the tip of her tongue.

"I'm going to take a quick shower. I'll be out in a second," he told her, headed into his room.

Evie nodded, too tired to say anything or move. She felt completely at home at Grant's. Not so much because it was a well-decorated loft outfitted in masculine, but cozy, leather and wood finishes. No, it was homey because that's what she associated Grant with now. Grant felt like home. Her lips curved into a smile, and she smiled blissfully. Would she ever get enough of him? She thought of dancing with him, kissing him, the way he held her so tight against him. No, she wouldn't.

After Grant showered, she did, too, changing into a flowy top and yoga pants. They curled up on the sofa and turned on a movie. She dozed lazily, tucked against Grant's side with his arm firm and secure around her.

"I could stay like this forever," he murmured close to her ear. She closed her eyes, reveling in the feel of his lips so close to her ear as much as the endearing words themselves.

"Me, too," she replied sleepily. Just then, her stomach growled loudly, causing them both to laugh. "But I guess we do have to eat," she added.

Grant stood up and stretched. "Chinese takeout?" He suggested.

"Mmm. Perfect," she smiled at him.

He leaned down and kissed her. "I'll be back in ten minutes."

"I miss you already," she replied sappily, then rolled her eyes at herself. "Forget I said that—it was way too cheesy."

He walked towards the door, shrugging. "I love you—cheese factor and all."

She tossed a throw pillow at him. "Now who's the cheesy one?" She laughed.

After Grant left, she jumped up and walked in her bare feet to the kitchen for a glass of water. As she reached into the fridge for the pitcher, her phone buzzed in her bag on the counter. Figuring it was Grant double-checking that she wanted her usual, she hurried to grab it.

Looking down at the name on the screen, she frowned. It wasn't Grant. With a sigh, she pressed "answer."

"Hello?" she asked pensively.

"Hey, Evie."

"What do you want, Davis?" she asked, unsure why he was calling her, but already ready for the conversation to be over.

"I was just calling to see how you were. We didn't end things on such a great note, and I feel really bad about that."

"That's true. We didn't, but it's water under the bridge now. I'm not mad anymore."

"I figured that—seeing as you moved on so fast."

"Davis, I don't want to do this."

"I think you can at least give me a minute of your time, seeing as we've known each other basically since birth."

"You got me there."

"Are you sure this is what you want, Evie? Your parents are really worried about you."

Evie sighed, perching on a barstool. "I'm 100 percent sure this is what I want. I care about Grant— and when Mom and Dad get to know him, they will, too. I'm really sorry if I hurt you, Davis, but everything ended up working out for the best. I wish you only happiness," she told him.

A long sigh was Davis' only response. "I'm sorry if I hurt you, too—I really am."

Evie nodded, though he couldn't see her, relieved to have closure with Davis. It meant more to her than she'd realized.

"Take care, Davis," she said softly.

"You too, Evergreen," he replied, using the dorky nickname he used to call her when they were kids. It never even made sense, but it had driven her crazy and he knew it, using it mercilessly in their elementary days.

She laughed at the memories. "Goodbye, Davis."

CHAPTER TWENTY-SIX

"I can't believe I'm wearing cowboy boots for this dance," Evie said one week later, admiring her rhinestone and leather-clad feet as they stood backstage. Her hand in Grant's, she rubbed her thumb idly back and forth across the top of his hand.

"It's the finale and it's all about you, babe. We're going out there to have fun and be happy. You're wearing boots for a dance, a request you made months ago, and my mission is accomplished," he said, tugging at his collar and fidgeting.

She snuggled up next to Grant and raised an eyebrow at him. "I was half-kidding when I made that request, and to what mission are you referring?"

"Teaching you how to dance."

Her face fell. "Oh."

He laughed and kissed her cheek. "Did you want me to say meeting you, the love of my life?"

"That doesn't sound all that bad," she shrugged playfully.

"Well that happened, but it wasn't intentional," he digressed. He tapped at the earpiece in his right ear, listening as someone on the other end gave him instructions.

"We're on in five," he relayed the message to her. She put a hand on his arm, stopping him from hurrying away.

"Before we do this, are you okay, Grant? You seem really nervous."

"I'm fine—perfectly fine. There's always a lot of pressure here at the end—that's all." He shrugged.

Evie nodded, satisfied enough with his answer. They made their way from the green room to the darkened edge of the ballroom floor, getting ready to take their places for their number.

"You ready? Mic's on and secure?" he checked, squeezing her hand.

"Yes and yes, sure am. I still can't believe the song choice for us though," she said, rolling her eyes.

"They wanted to bookend everything. Especially since the cat's out of the bag about our relationship. It makes for good TV." He shrugged.

"Well, it's not like I'm seriously complaining. I love this song and dance combination. It reminds me of my high school show choir days all over again, but like a million times cooler."

"I'd say so. I'm glad you love it." He smiled to himself.

They got into their positions—Evie stationed with two of the troupe members, Hallie and Lydia, ready to run onto the dance floor as soon as the music started, and Grant waiting further back, as he didn't join the performance until the song reached the chorus.

When Evie heard her cue, she dashed to the center of the floor and did the quick dance steps in sync with Hallie and Lydia, all while singing the first verse. The moves were similar to the flash mob video featuring the iconic song, so most people in the audience were already familiar with the premise of the performance. Even though singing and dancing at the same time wasn't ever easy for her, she kept her smile bright and her feet felt like feathers as her off-white dress twirled around her as she kicked and jumped in time to the beat. Grant came in on the first chorus and then he sang the second verse while simultaneously dancing a routine with the male troupe members, while Evie, Hallie and Lydia stood to the side and watched.

I'll go get a ring, let the choir bells sing like ooh, what you wanna do? Let's run girl!

After the verse, they joined up altogether and danced again before separating once more. When the dance came to the part where Grant started to croon, *"Just say I do . . ."* instead of continuing into their next practiced steps, the four troupe dancers got into a formation behind Grant and danced an intricate group number as Evie watched dumbfounded on live national television with no clue what was happening. The dance had just totally switched gears. When Grant got down on one knee, her hands flew to her mouth in utter shock. And when he produced a black velvet box from his back pocket, opening it to reveal an antique diamond ring, her eyes grew to the size of saucers.

The crowd started going crazy, chanting "Say yes! Say yes! Say yes!" Evie just stood there, completely floored. Was this really happening?

"Marry me," Grant said, as the music ebbed away. "There's no one for me but you. You're it, Evie and from our first moments together, there's not been a single doubt in my mind. Marry me, please. I don't want to do life without you."

She didn't have to hesitate—even though it seemed crazy and exhilarating to accept a proposal on live television from a man she'd only known for three months. This was the easiest question she'd ever answer. Not a single iota of doubt found harbor in her heart.

As the word left her mouth, everything inside of her screamed along, "YES! YES! YES!"

Evie took his hands and he stood up, slipping the ring on her finger before sealing their promise with a forever kiss.

"Now, we've got a dance to finish," he told her, spinning her out as the music picked back up again.

She floated in his arms as white rose petals rained down from the ceiling and he twirled her around once more, dipping her back as the song ended on a triumphant note. She and Grant locked gazes as they stayed in hold, both grinning at each other.

"I can't imagine there ever being a moment more amazing than this one is right now," she said, still catching her breath.

"I know what you mean—because I feel that way every moment I get to spend with you," he whispered before leaning down and kissing her softly once more.

"Do you even care if we win anymore?" She asked, as he lifted her upright.

"Heck yes, I still care," Grant replied with a wink.

She laughed. "Me, too."

They rushed off the stage as the crowd continued to applaud and nearly collided with her parents.

"Mom! Dad!" She cried, overwhelmed with emotion and surprise. "Y'all are here! I'm so happy that you're here. Did you guys know about this?"

Her Dad hugged her tightly. "Yes, Grant called and let us in on what he planned to do. To tell the truth, we were a little shocked—it is pretty soon—but there's no way we could've missed this big moment in our baby girl's life and ever forgive ourselves. You're a grown woman, Evie. We can't make decisions for you. If you're happy, we're going to be happy."

"Dad, Grant is a good man, and he makes me so happy. I know it's fast, I do. But we have only been engaged about five minutes. We're not going to be in a rush to plan a wedding."

"Evie, we want you to be happy, baby. That's all we've ever wanted, and I've never seen your eyes sparkle the way they have the past couple of months," her mom added, rubbing her back. "I'm real sorry I gave you such a hard time."

"I know it's been hard to see me make decisions that differed from what y'all expected for me. I'm just so thankful you're here. I love you both so much," she pulled them both in again for another hug.

"Now, girl, watch out. You're going to smear your makeup and wrinkle my blouse," her mother cautioned.

Evie laughed. "Some things never change," she said with a wink in Grant's direction. His own parents were there—giving hugs and offering their congratulations, waiting to meet Evie's parents. Evie glanced over her mother's shoulder and caught a familiar glint of silver hair set in quintessential, elderly Southern woman style.

"Granny June!" she cried, rushing over and hugging her grandmother's neck. "Are you really here right now?!? You actually got on a plane and flew to Los Angeles?"

Granny June laughed heartily, crushing Evie against her floral polyester dress. "This is a night that will go down in the books. I couldn't miss watching a real-life fairytale play out for my Evie-girl!"

"A fairytale—that is exactly what this feels like, Granny," she whispered, tears of joy pooling in her eyes again as she hugged her grandmother tight.

* * * *

Grant's fingers laced with hers as she clutched his hand. The spotlights glared, bouncing off the diamond ring that now graced her left hand, those same lights keeping her from making out her parents' and grandmother's faces where they sat in the audience. The final moment of the season—announcing a winner—had arrived at last. Three months prior, she couldn't have imagined this particular outcome in her wildest, most outlandish, of dreams.

They stood on the erected stage, Nell and Adam to their left with Corey in the front situated between the two remaining couples. A hush fell over the audience as they waited to find out the season six champions. Cameras panned from every angle, and on this stage with Grant by her side she was warm and happy and content, whether they won or not.

Of course, she wanted to win, but tonight nothing could steal her joy. Could people see how knees-shaking, earth-shattering, desperately in love she was with Grant? How incredibly happy she was?

She'd give up everything and follow the man beside her to the ends of the earth, and they sure had a lot of stuff to figure out—tour schedules, appearances, where they would live, but she had faith that they would sort everything out together. Everything would work out. They'd already proven how much they supported each other. Touring would be hard, but they would get through it.

"Earth to Evie, Earth to Evie." Grant's voice pulled her out of her reverie.

"Hmm?" she asked, distracted.

"We're coming back from commercial break. Are you ready?" He searched her face.

"I'm as ready as I'll ever be," she said, nervous, but with the happiest of smiles adorning her face. Here she was again, before a live television audience, waiting to find out if she'd won a reality talent competition. The only difference this time was the hand that held hers so securely. She wasn't alone, and she never would be again. This was a team effort, and she hoped with all that was within her that they had won. She wanted it more for Grant than for herself. He'd worked so hard, pushed her, helped her, and been there for her every moment of the way—as the best coach in the world, he deserved this win. The fact that they'd fallen in love and decided to spend their lives together was the ultimate prize, but this win still meant something, and spoke to their ability to work as a team.

"The votes from you, our viewers, along with the judges' scores for tonight's performance, have been tallied and we will announce our Season 6 *Song & Dance* champions . . . Evie, from the very beginning, your talent and connection with your partner has wowed the audience and the judges alike. You've won Grant's heart, but did you win the hearts of the viewers, as well?" Corey paused for effect. "Nell, you've steadily climbed to the top of the scoreboard with your tenacity and overall appeal. Was it enough to take home the trophy?" He paused in his monologue once more. "We'll find out right after the break," Corey dramatically informed everyone.

As the show went to commercial break, Evie let out a breath she hadn't realized she'd been holding.

"Talk about playing with our emotions!" she half-joked as Corey turned to face them. Her nerves were raw and her hands slightly shook from too much coffee and adrenaline.

"Hey, I have to drag it out to the very end. It's my job." He shrugged. "Congratulations, by the way, you two," Corey replied with a wink.

"I know you do, and thanks," Evie replied. Still holding Grant's hand, she brought it to her lips and kissed it while she shifted her weight from side to side. The rose gold heels she'd donned may have been breathtaking, but they pinched her toes something fierce.

"Just so you know, honestly, whether we win or not, I've enjoyed every second of our time competing together, and I've already won in my book because I got to meet and fall completely in love with you," Grant leaned over and whispered in her ear. The hushed, hurried words meant for her ears only sent a thrill down her spine as his five o'clock shadow brushed against her earlobe. They had cause to celebrate that night no matter what happened.

"Right back at you, my love," she whispered, straightening as Corey welcomed back the viewing audience.

Here we go . . .

"Now, for the moment you've all been waiting. The winners of the sixth season of *Song & Dance* by the biggest percentage of votes in the show's history is . . ." Of course, Corey had to pause for several more ridiculously agonizing seconds.

"EVIE MICHAELSON AND GRANT MERRITT!" Corey finally shouted as the ballroom erupted into frenzied cheering and music played in celebration.

"We did it, baby!" Grant shouted, scooping her up and twirling her around as he kissed her and swarms of cast and crew surrounded them while sparkly confetti and balloons fell from the studio's ceiling. Tears of happiness trickled down her cheeks as he hugged her tight and planted kisses on her cheeks as their song from earlier played through the studio. They'd won. Together. This was, hands down, the best night of her life.

Shocked, she couldn't register everything as it happened. Sure, she was beyond ecstatic, but so many people were patting her on the back, pulling her this way and that, and before she knew it, a huge crowd managed to steadily make their way between her and Grant. She'd hardly had a chance to celebrate with him before being pulled into a massive press line, but almost immediately, he found her again and slipped his arm securely around her waist.

"We're in this together, and nothing will ever get between us," he said matter-of-factly, lightly kissing her cheek before they continued down the press line as one. From that moment forward, they would always be one.

The End

60454468R00198

Made in the USA
Columbia, SC
16 June 2019